THE TANGLE

Justin Robertson

WHITE
RABBIT

First published in Great Britain in 2021 by White Rabbit
This paperback edition published in Great Britain in 2023 by White Rabbit,
an imprint of The Orion Publishing Group Ltd
Carmelite House, 50 Victoria Embankment
London EC4Y 0DZ

An Hachette UK Company

1 3 5 7 9 10 8 6 4 2

ISBN (MMP) 978 1 4746 2283 7
ISBN (eBook) 978 1 4746 2284 4
ISBN (Audio) 978 1 4746 2285 1

Typeset by seagulls.net
Printed and bound in Great Britain by Clays Ltd, Elcograf S.p.A.

MIX
Paper from
responsible sources
FSC® C104740

www.whiterabbitbooks.co.uk
www.orionbooks.co.uk

For Andrew

Foreword

What happens in The Tangle stays in The Tangle. It is a self-generating organism, a Word Horde.

The poet Jack Spicer claimed that the moment of inspiration in writing is akin to a visitation from a Martian – an entity – that must attempt to communicate using twenty-six building blocks. The Tangle is alphabet as entity.

Caxton Wood holds time. Each Tangle functions as a point of ingress, and as exit, too. Time too, in The Tangle, is palimpsest. What has happened keeps on happening.

In the time of apocalypse, which is all-time, animals speak. Trees speak, insects word. The grotesque is atavistic, the return of animal souls, as language, from the underworld. Our first language, our first art, our first attempts at communal speech, took place underground, on the walls of the caves – the hybrid animals, rising up, in speech. In the sepulchres too, the early Christian burial sites, we see art, and language, begin their ascent from the underworld, and evoke The Tangle.

William S. Burroughs made the terrifying assertion that language is something that we have been infected with and that we can never be cured of, this constant low-level babbling of words in thought – but Burroughs got it wrong. Push further, to the very precipice of language, out into the air, and there stands the thing itself, revealed and un-worded. Through The Tangle to the clearing, Justin Robertson points to the end of language with words, to the silence at the heart of the wood with sounds, to The Tangle with twenty-six building blocks.

The stories are like tarot cards, The Tangle itself a constantly morphing spread. There is uncanny life in these pages. Every time I reread it, I feel like the scenes have shifted slightly, that there is something newly out of place, that behind the scenes the book has been creepy-crawled, an item misplaced, a character you hadn't really noticed before, a movement, there in the trees, the snap of a branch, in the dark.

The Tangle is a classic of New Weird fiction, a rewilding of the terrain of M.R. James, Denton Welch, Ballard and Burroughs, Catling and Grant, and a spell – via those twenty-six blocks – set on assassinating modernism with modernism.

David Keenan

When I am in that darkness, I do not remember anything about anything human, or the God-man, or anything which has form. Nevertheless, I see all and I see nothing.

Angela of Foligno, *The Memorial*

Everything is blooming most recklessly; if it were voices instead of colours, there would be an unbelievable shrieking into the heart of the night.

Rainer Maria Rilke, *Letters*

Come walk with me to lilac glade, through woodland, stream and knot.
Come stand beneath the gallows' shade till all weeping is forgot.
Leave the tears and terrors to the mischief of the town.
Come walk with me to lilac glade, to the oak tree's shady crown.

In darkness now from darkness born, circumference, length and span.
In lilac glade the wreath and thorn, wove mockeries of man.
In lilac glade beneath the earth, in death's ecstatic bond.
Come walk with me in lilac shade, to the emptiness beyond.

Unknown, *The Ballad of the Tangle*

The Maker's Mark

The fleece dangled from the branch like so much morbid laundry left out in the rain. As the water fell in persistent rods, blood and gore dripped down severed sinews onto the mud. On every branch hung animal skins. Freshly cut from village herds. Weeping fluid into the bark. Erwan, head shaved. Woad running down his cheeks. Waved a ceremonial sickle. The holy man called on the gods to bless the trees of the wood. For their gift of shelter. For their branches to be bent into bows. For the timber of their trunks to be cut into planks and honed into oars. Erwan called on the gods. Here under the holy ash, ruler of the third lunar month. Come spring, its berries would be plucked from its twigs and placed into the cribs of children to keep the spirits of the Tangle at bay. Through the winter rains Erwan brought the sacrifice. Blood and skin to buy the favour of the woods. He rubbed his bloody hands into the trunk until it was slick. Red darkening the grey into black. But the ash tree had no need for blood. No need for skin or sinew. Its roots sucked deep from the soil. Its leaves bathed in the sunlight. It had no need for the charnel gifts of men.

Every year, for centuries, in the last days of winter before the sun grew strong enough to break the grip of frost and snow, they traipsed through the Tangle. Every year they brought their sacrifice. Death paying for life. Yet the ash remained unmoved. Their children died and their crops failed.

Their oars still broke in the swell and their boats foundered on the rocks. Still they came in joyful procession. Then, as times changed in the world of men, the sacrifice was made by God instead. No longer did they call on the spirits of the wood. Though their presence lingered. They renamed the day for a saint and brought trinkets and toys, carved to represent the animals. They hung them in the trees and sang hymns. Still the ash remained unmoved.

The village began to grow. Spreading out like an unctuous wave. It became a town. The Tangle shrank back from the settlement as it was hacked and cleared. Trunks were cut and hewn, bent and carved to make pews for the faithful and roofs for the righteous. The ash became curious. These troublesome creatures had once lived in the Tangle. But they had changed. They would pass away in time and the forest would reclaim the land. That was how it always went. Memories were measured in millennia in the woods; these inconvenient animals had occupied only a micro-moment of it, an insignificant blur, like a fly buzzing by. The ash stirred. Some intangible part of the forest had once been human. Young wraiths that had only recently joined the web. They were struggling to shed their former concerns. But they were instructive on a number of points. Humans yearned for transcendence. But lacked the skills to achieve it. Humans liked to make things. But lacked the finesse to make them truly beautiful. They killed, cut, broke and smashed living things and made them into dead parodies of their former forms. Furniture. There were buildings too, like nests but more rigid and prone to decay. They made vehicles, like wings or feet, but too numerous to function as efficiently as either. All these things made them unhappy, yet they kept on making them. The ash consulted the other entities of the forest. Scouts were sent to the world of men.

*

Detective Inspector Sarah Ward of Caxton CID slipped under the police cordon that had been set up around a crime scene tent. The tent flapped in the winter wind. Under the canvas was a body. She pulled back the hood of her cagoule as she trudged across the muddy grass to where the victim had been discovered by a late-night dog walker. She felt older than her years. The force was sucking the life out of her. The rain hissed in her face, insolent and rude. Her superiors were public school misogynists or talentless hacks. The wind drove the drops into her eyes, blurring her vision. The younger officers were a mixture of bored hotheads and those who just never got around to leaving. Just like her, they had joined the force because there was fuck all else to do. The rain rasped and punched. In Caxton there was the meat processing plant, the sawmill or the call centre. You moved on, did acid or joined the force. The crime rate was lively though. Public drunkenness, urinating and affray every weekend. Domestic violence was popular, as was cannabis cultivation. There was a scattering of amphetamine laboratories, a thriving heroin trade and a range of sexual crimes to deal with. But murder was rare. Especially murders like this one. She nodded, attempting a smile for the young PC who was emerging from the forensic tent. One of the better ones. Anthony Barrowman was his name. Her smile stalled as PC Barrowman pushed past a colleague and threw up through his fingers.

'Fuck me. Are you alright, Barrow boy?'

Barrowman's concerned co-worker saluted awkwardly when he caught sight of DI Ward approaching through the rain.

'Sorry, ma'am, didn't see you there.'

She shot him a resigned look.

'Language on duty, what have I told you, Franklin? Barrowman, are you alright? Take the contents of your stomach away from the crime scene, if you please.'

She placed a reassuring hand on the young PC's shoulder as she passed. But he didn't look up or acknowledge her. His eyes stared fixedly into black drizzle.

She pushed the flaps of the tent open and stepped inside. The only sound was the buzzing of the spotlights and the occasional supressed wretch. She looked around at the gathered group. Caxton's finest, and even a couple of forensic scientists from the city. Hardened professionals. They were all staring in silence at the grizzly pile that stained the floor like offal in an abattoir. At first, she thought it was a carcass that had dropped from the back of Sullivan's butcher's van. It was gleaming and glossy. Freshly slaughtered. Maybe it was the poachers? They'd been at the deer again. Caught lugging it across the park, no doubt. They must have decided to dump it here rather than risk getting nicked. She looked at her colleagues. Why the silence? Why those wide-eyed stares? She looked again at the mound of flesh. Gradually her eyes began to decode the muddle of blood and tissue. A form began to take shape. It was a man. She knew it was a man because she could just about make out his testicles. They looked like two plum tomatoes dangling from white fibrous stalks. The penis had been removed. The scrotal skin too. In fact, all the skin had been removed from the entire body. As had the legs below the knee, the arms below the elbow, the eyes, the hair and the nose. All that remained was a bloody stump. She wanted to run out of the tent, but she was too fascinated to move. There was no reason why anyone should have to witness this kind of carnage. It just wasn't reasonable. One of the forensic team finally broke the grim stillness.

'Time of death was somewhere between eight and ten post meridiem, though I'd have to run some more tests back at the lab to be certain. Cause of death was . . .'

Her voice was shaking, and you could hear her gag reflex triggering as she tried to hold her professional tone.

'Judging by the pattern of the arterial spray and the pooling of blood, also the angle of the cut here on the legs, it suggests the victim was still alive while the amputations took place. Again, I'll need to run some more . . .'

The forensics expert jumped up and ran out of the tent. Vomit had begun to escape from the sides of her face mask. Sarah Ward followed her out as the reluctant clicking of cameras began inside. She tried to arrange the picture. The murderer was stealthy, quick and skilled. A doctor? A butcher? A vet? Or perhaps a keen amateur. She paced around the perimeter of the crime scene, projecting theories that might account for the atrocity inside the tent. The rain blackened her shoes and began to work its way inside. Mud sucked at her soles. She cursed and started to make her way back to the certainties of concrete. But something on the grass between the path and the edge of the woods caught her eye. She turned and lifted the tape. She squelched through the gloom, her curiosity momentarily eclipsing her discomfort. Pulling her torch from her pocket, she scanned the ground. The beam settled on an object. It looked like a makeshift mausoleum. She shone the torch over the surface. It was a pyramid of leaves; actually, it was more like a cone. The leaves had been neatly twisted to form the structure. About 7 inches tall, it gleamed through the downpour. It was glistening with fresh blood.

*

Mike Stains turned off the lights and tutted as the cold winter rain spat at his window. It would be a miserable walk home from Mike's Militaria. He decided to wait a while until the rain had died down. He'd have a couple of cans, maybe flick through a few of the specialist magazines he kept out the back for his more discreet customers. He shuffled behind the counter and slid through the curtain to his back office. There was a door on the right, sealed with a padlock. He fumbled for his keychain and unlocked the door. This was Mike's inner sanctum. A space where he could commune with the past. It contained a desk, a small kitchen, a fridge and the memorabilia from several unsavoury regimes, their insignia, uniforms and propaganda. Mike casually donned the cap of a dead field marshal. He imagined himself as a powerful man. He coughed and cleared his nose into the sink, before opening the fridge and helping himself to a can of lager. He sat down, pulled a magazine from the pile on the table and absentmindedly flicked through the pages. He belched and turned the magazine around for an alternative view. A knock on the door disturbed his recreation. Not the police again? Nah, they wouldn't be bothering him since the sergeant's last parcel arrived. Maybe it was one of his special customers? They sometimes came late. Fucking degenerates, no respect for opening hours. He retraced his steps back into the shop, leaving his shrine open. He turned on the lights and peered out. There was no one there. A branch from the tree that was planted on the pavement outside clattered against the window. Rattling the pain. It made him jump. That must have been it. The wind was fierce tonight. It was the tree, nothing else. He turned off the light and returned to the back of the shop. The weather was getting worse; it looked like he might be here for a while. Mike Stains paused at the entrance to his secret room. Something was wrong. There wasn't a tree outside the shop this morning.

*

Rik Storm clinked the ice against the edges of his cut glass tumbler, admiring the reflection of the open fire in its multifaceted surface. He clicked the stop button on the remote control. His VCR clonked to a halt. He'd seen this one before. It failed to raise even the faintest stirring in him. He let out a sigh. Things had been so much better when he'd been on tour. He'd had the finest then, no questions asked. But things had changed. That fourth album. The reviews were bad; the record was bad. People stopped coming to the shows and the favours dried up. Then people started asking awkward questions. Worried parents wrote to radio stations. That's why he was holed up here in Caxton. He knew most of the cops out here couldn't give a shit about a washed-up pomp rocker. He could just about manage on his royalties. He had enough to pay a few people off. He would ignore the rest. He could call up Mike Stains for the necessaries. The guy was a prick, but he delivered. He even liked the fourth album. Fuck me, he must be a prick. Rik Storm put down his tumbler and reached for his cordless phone. He dialled Mike's Militaria. No reply. Prick must have gone home. He opened a draw and pulled out a spliff. Lighting it, he got up and went to his record shelf. He reached up and pulled out the first Rik Storm album, admiring the svelte figure of his former self as he placed it on the deck. Rik began to nod his head in time to

the beat, eyes closed, smoke sucking in and out. He was on
a stage gyrating and pointing at the crowd. A smile began to
break out on his face. Outside, the sound of the storm was like
the roar of the Storm's faithful fans. Rik Storm, Rik Storm,
Rik Storm! The rain pelted against his French windows.
Rik Storm, Rik Storm! He air guitared as the solo came in.
All of those hands reaching to touch him. The trees in the
garden swayed violently in the gathering gale. Rik Storm,
Rik Storm, Rik Storm! He cranked the stereo to maximum.
No neighbours, no bother. His fingers ran over the invisible
fretboard. Rik Storm! Rik Storm! Rik Storm! The French
windows buckled. At first the glass bulged like a membrane.
Leaves and stems spinning in the cavity, drilling through the
soft boarder between life and afterlife. The Tangle was here.
The Tangle was here to harvest. The window could not resist
any longer and came crashing in. Branches, like the arms of
roadies, pushed the frame aside and streamed into the room.
Creepers and vines crawled across the walls, dislodging silver
discs and the arrogant gallery of a lifetime. Arms around
politicians. Arms around actors. Arms around royalty. Arms
around the blossoming waist of an uncomprehending rock
star. Rik Storm! Rik Storm! Rik Storm! With a scream that
was once loud enough to fill the Odeon, he was dragged into
the darkness.

*

Brigitte Molin was a sadist. A reluctant teacher with no time
for children. Always wanting, grasping, needing. She hated
their optimism most. She adopted punitive measures to drive
such thoughts from their young minds. These indolent dolts
in her care, fat through indulgence and slack parenting, chips
and fizzy drinks. These punk rock and rollers with their

ripped trousers and blasphemous haircuts. No discipline, no future. She sought to belittle and harry them at every opportunity, to crush their confidence with her relentless, barbed commentary. At least then a new generation might yet rise, one that would be nearly as miserable as her. The Reverend Molin wore his resentment for all to see. In the creases of his anachronistic suits. In the pomade that held firm his dictator's wedge hair. He gave sermons of monstrous length with dispiriting content. Long, rambling diatribes about sinners and hell that, in an earlier age, would have been characterised as 'fire and brimstone' had they not been so tortuously dull. He was pissed off. Promises of a respectable position in a respectable town had vanished as his prejudices emerged in the seminary. But his father still had enough clout with the bishops to allow his son to find a quiet parish in which to ferment his bitterness. Caxton was deadly dull, but monochrome enough for his tastes. Besides, hardly anyone attended these days, so he had plenty of time to indulge in his other pursuits.

'Pass me the knife, would you?'

Brigitte passed the reverend the special curled blade used to cut the precious pods. He skilfully sliced into the flesh, biting down on his tongue in concentration.

'There she goes.'

Dark, thick sap oozed from the cut, brown and gummy. The reverend scooped it up and let it drip into the brick moulds his wife was holding out for him. It was warm in the greenhouse; he wiped a bead of sweat from his brow before attending to another pod. Such hard work, much harder than marijuana, but he did so prefer the outcome.

'Just one more row, then dinner. I have a lot of marking to do.'

'You'll need a little bit of relaxation to help you through that pile of bollocks!'

The reverend waved his knife and mock injected himself, making a comical show of 'nodding out'. Stupid, talentless bastard, she thought. His smile died on his lips. Dried up hag, he thought.

'Right you are.'

He turned his attention back to the poppies. He stuck his knife into the flesh of the next plant in the row. But the knife refused to cut. He tried again, applying more pressure this time. Still the knife seemed to skim off the surface.

'Bloody thing's gone blunt.'

He drew the blade across his finger to test it. A bright red line burst from his skin as the knife sliced a gully through it.

'Fuck it.'

He sucked the cut and returned to the pod as the metallic tang dribbled down his throat. The bulb was like thick leather, impervious to his cuts. Brigitte sighed and leaned in.

> *Unseen backs bent to the purpose carried the parts for the art of the woods.*
> *Unseen hands silently weaving the flax and the thread for the throne of the gods.*

'Here, let me try.'

She snatched the blade testily from her husband's bleeding hand. Blood dripped into the soil. Its lively signal generating a pulse. These were the subjects of interest. The material, the matter.

> *Unseen eyes measured the cuts.*

Take only what you need. The filament probed beneath the surface. The harvest was here. Brigitte harrumphed and curled her spine. She moved closer, raising her arm to cut the bulb. The filament passed the command and the poppy shot from the soil. Its stem lengthening like an electrical flex. Green fibres wove across the space between teacher and plant, grasping her hand, directing it in an alternative arc.

Unseen arms directed the cuts.

The blade in Brigitte's hand swept down. It sliced the reverend across the eyes, splitting his corneas like ripe tomatoes. At first he was too stunned to scream. By the time he had found his voice, the poppy-primed hand of his wife had slashed his throat, reducing the scream to a gurgle. All she could do was stare.

Unseen shoulders would carry the load.

To the maker in the woods. On quiet stems. On quiet stems. The other poppies in the greenhouse rose. Their fronds spread across the bed at speed, shooting towards the reluctant teacher. The stems whirled around her like a tornado, binding her tight. The filaments began to crawl up her cheeks, until they reached her mouth. An incoherent moan was emanating from her like the sound of a failing foghorn. The filaments entered her mouth, pulling her lips apart. She stared, wide eyed, the tuneless tone continuing to rattle around the greenhouse. Her hand groped towards her own gaping mouth. The knife, like a bloody harpoon lashed to her fist, plunged into her. Her knuckles, moist with sap and gore, were pulled across her teeth as the knife took her tongue.

The moan was drowned as bright arcs of blood-spray hit the panes of the greenhouse.

> *Unseen backs bent to the purpose carried the parts for the*
> *   art of the woods.*
> *Unseen hands silently weaving the flax and the thread for*
> *   the throne of the gods.*

Then there was silence. Caxton was a quiet parish.

*

DI Ward stared at the hastily assembled incident board. Photos had been pinned to the cork. Barely believable images of broken bodies and severed limbs. She was late in this morning. Her phone unanswered all night. She thought of the whiskey bottle on her kitchen table. Empty. She'd woken up face down on the Formica surface, still dressed in the clothes she'd come home in. There was blood on her shoes and trousers from the grass in the park. The glistening stalks. The phone had been bleeping out an irritating Morse code. She remembered replacing the receiver, bleary eyed and hungover. Fuck.

'Get me a car, I want to visit all three sites immediately! And get hold of whoever's in charge at each crime scene and tell them to secure them properly. I don't want any press snooping about or kids looking for souvenirs. And tell the duty sergeant . . . tell him to . . . just tell him to check my number in future and send a fucking squad car if he can't get me on the phone!'

Fuck. She remembered the tone pulsing through the receiver. The boss had talked about getting those new mobile phones for the DIs, but they looked like house bricks and weighed nearly as much. She didn't fancy lugging that about. It's what all the dealers were using though, that's how you could spot them. Leisure wear and fucking massive phones. She mustn't screw this one up. They were watching her, all those nicotine-stained lads, five pints at lunch, cosy with the gangsters at the golf club. Blind eyes turned, backhanders paid. They didn't much like women cops. 'You call that progress?' She'd put up with it for years, the leering and sniggering. But she was better than them and they knew it. Because she cared just enough not to be a monster like them. Not that she liked people. Most of the ones she came across were awful, it went with the territory. The body in the park, now that was something else, no one could process that. Only the monsters could, only the monsters. An eager-faced policeman poked his head around the door of the incident room.

'Your car's ready, ma'am. Oh, and we had a call from that dog walker from last night, reckons he remembers seeing Tam knocking about near the woods about twenty minutes before he found the body. I've sent a couple of officers to see if they can pick him up. They're checking the usual haunts, but nothing yet. You don't reckon it's Tam do you, ma'am? The body, I mean.'

Not Tam Stamp? The happy hippy? She liked him. He was a local character, more eccentric than insane. The kids taunted him, but he always took it well. She had no idea where he lived, if indeed he had a place to call his own. Some said he lived in the woods; some said they had found his shelters hidden in the dark nooks of the forest. Others thought he lived with his mother. He kept her body in her bedroom like Norman Bates, they said. The nonsense these gossips came out with. He was adrift, in another world.

A smiling traveller. No trouble, no killer, but perhaps a victim? He used to make little figures from sticks. He would hang them in the trees for children to find. She thought of the glistening cone of bloody leaves and shuddered. She knocked back her coffee and pushed through the swing doors.

She sat in silence on the way to the crime scene. The driver was a junior detective, cocky, thick as mince, with the beginnings of a beer belly troubling the buttons of his Burton shirt. It was doubtful he could offer any insight. It was true that all the victims had skeletons in their closets, barely concealed sins that could well warrant a degree of retribution from outraged family members or criminal gangs. But that wasn't unusual round here. There were so many secrets behind Caxton's twitching curtains that she wouldn't be surprised if a thunderbolt didn't smite the whole fucking place one day. The victims were known to each other to a greater or lesser extent. Rik Storm bought gear and dodgy videos off Mike Stains. Stains got the gear from the Reverend Molin, or at least that was the working hypothesis. Once they had discovered the reverend's laboratory, it looked likely that he was serving up in some capacity. The officers that were called to the rectory had found his head and feet in the blood-spattered greenhouse. They'd been crudely squashed into the torso of his wife, who's own head was missing, along with her legs and arms. They also found rows and rows of empty flower beds, with neat holes where the plants had once been. From the residue found in containers, the presumption was they were opium poppies. But all the poppies were gone. There was a strange neatness to the carnage. No upturned pots or loose soil littering the floor. It was as if the plants had upped and left of their own accord. So, there was a connection between them. All except Tam. Tam was a strictly magic mushrooms type of guy. Acid maybe. But morphine and smut? It wasn't his style. If the body in the park turned out to be him. Who'd want to kill a hippy?

They started at the rectory. It was the closest to the station. When she arrived, everything was in order, cordons up and protective clothing issued. The outrage was obvious, but the clues were less apparent.

'No prints? With all this blood? Not a shoe print? No fibres?'

'Not a thing, ma'am. It looks like they did it to themselves?'

'What? Why? When? Cut their own fucking heads off and scurried away?'

Sarah Ward left the question hanging in the horror. She walked out of the blood-spattered greenhouse and into the large rectory garden. She greedily gulped in the fresh air. Only the monsters. Only the monsters. She started to walk towards the back of the garden, where it dipped down to a tall privet hedge. Beyond the hedge was the Tangle. A vague sense of foreboding rose in her veins; her nerves began to tingle. Only the monsters. Only the monsters. She reached the hedge and paused. She looked back at the crime scene. She could smell death in the air. Turning back to the solid wall of green, she began to push through the hedge. The spindly density of branches scratched and stabbed at her face, causing small lesions to swell on her cheeks. The hedge was too thick to pass through. But then, quite gradually at first, the hedge seemed to give way, as if it was begrudgingly letting her pass. She felt like Lucy in the wardrobe, pushing coats out of her way en route to some inverted Narnia. Sarah stepped through the other side. There was silence. No birdsong or the expected distant thrum of traffic from the new bypass. Only the static buzz of emptiness. Across a thin strip of scrub lay the edge of the wood. She stepped into the spiteful stalks, their roughness scratching her calves as she walked. She knew it was there before she saw it. The knotty stalks lay flat, arranged in a circle as if they had been scythed down. In the centre of the circle was a green, glistening cone of blood and leaves.

*

The backyard of Mike's Militaria was a jumble of rust. Old bikes, exhaust pipes and discarded panels from a host of stolen vehicles were decaying in untidy piles. Loosely secured plastic sheets hovered over the mountains of debris like ghosts. Driven by the wind, they fluttered violently, making a cracking sound like the volley of a firing squad. DI Ward pushed past them, looking for bloodied leaves amongst the rotting carcasses of machines. Her colleagues looked on, detached and uninterested. She knew it was here somewhere, that grim trademark. The assailant considered themselves an artist, or at least a keen apprentice. A collector of parts and materials for some great work, a sculptor or craftsman. That's what she thought now. Not a medic, the parts had been chosen for aesthetic reasons. The killer was making something. But here, so far, she had drawn a blank. She rooted about in the rubbish that was piled up against the back fence. That strange tingle again. She shouted up the yard to where two young PCs were loafing about.

'Get this lot shifted away from the fence, will you?'
'Yes, ma'am.'

The two constables raised their eyebrows and looked at each other in a quiet conspiracy of misplaced superiority. Sarah pretended not to notice. The young coppers clumsily shifted the rubbish, cursing as pools of water that had gathered on the plastic sheets overflowed onto their shoes.

She was reminded of her father putting up furniture without reading the instructions. Armed with bluster and a toolbox he would fire into every task in the same way: as if the world would bend to his will if he swore at it enough. Eventually the fence was clear of debris. She began to explore along its perimeter. The tingle was growing into a pulse. A loose slat tipped and opened. She squeezed through. Mike Stains's yard backed onto the railway, where freight trains rattled down from the town to the docks. The embankment plunged and rose, forming a drab valley of ragged grass and weeds. On the far side, the trees of Caxton Wood stood on the edge of the embankment like a squadron of cavalry tensed to charge. She inhaled sharply. She held onto her breath. She slowly exhaled as the vague outline of a theory took shape. The woods, always the woods. Was he hiding out in there? In the trees. Watching, planning, waiting for his materials to ripen. Checking on the sturdiness of his victims. Waiting to carve them open. Was he there now watching her? The sides of the cutting were dotted with cans and plastic bags, looking like ugly flowers blooming out of season. She began to tack her way down, scanning as she went. She reached the track without finding anything. On the other side, the cutting rose up in the same untidy fashion. The pulse was now throbbing like a kick drum. She began to climb, less diligent in her search this time; she knew she wouldn't find it here. Breathless, she reached the top. The fence at the summit provided only the vaguest suggestion of a barrier. She climbed over the fence. She was drawn to a shape where the thick, ugly scrub had been scythed down. Circles. Circles. The pulsing stopped. The static hissed. On the edge of the Tangle the green cone glistened red.

*

The siren's strangled whine was jarring. Out of time with the rhythmical metronome of the squad car's windscreen wipers, it sounded like a nursery school music lesson. Inside the car, the atonal anti-rhythm was not helping DI Ward's concentration.

'Do you need to have that thing on?'

PC Barrowman had collected her from Mike's Militaria in his squad car. He had volunteered for the job. Sarah offered him a weak smile. *He's got potential this one, so let's hope the lads at the station don't get to him any time soon.* She tapped impatiently on the dashboard, trying to get a clear picture of what happened that night. *The more information she got, the less sense it all made.*

'I don't understand the preliminary pathology reports, Barrowman.'

She was talking *at* him, not *to* him.

'They put the time of death between eight and ten for all the murders. How can that be right? It would mean the assailant had to kill and dismember all the victims within half an hour of each other. They'd have to get across town, kill the next victim, butcher them immediately, and then move on to the next one. All the while leaving no trace, either at the crime scene or between locations. Something isn't right, even the most skilled surgeon couldn't do that. So, there's got to be a team of them, highly organised, well co-ordinated. But why is there no trace of them, no witnesses, no prints, nothing? You would have thought someone would have noticed groups of people dismembering bodies in four locations at exactly the same time.'

But she knew there was a single intelligence behind all of this. Those blood-drenched cones were identical in every respect, dimensions the same down to the last millimetre.

They could have been made before the murders. Taken by each team and left as some kind of warning? No, that wasn't it, they were too obscurely placed to be warnings. They were the trademarks of a craftsman.

'Did the lab have any luck with those cones?'

'Ash, Barrowman. They were leaves from an ash tree, freshly cut and twisted, by fuck knows who.'

They were approaching the country pile of Rik Storm. Tasteless columns and faux grandeur. The squad car scrunched to a halt on the gravel. DI Ward nodded to PC Barrowman to follow her round the back of the house. He looked confused, but she was insistent. They pushed through the side gate and entered the back garden. She wasn't interested in picking through pop memorabilia, old LPs and gold discs. She wasn't into Rik Storm's bombastic nonsense. Nor did she want to spend her time pulling up floorboards looking for elicit magazines and dirty photos. She knew they were there, they all did. She was there for the tiny tower of blood and leaves that she knew was nestling in the scrub. That was death, alive in all its terrible ingenuity. She wanted to know its secrets.

She drifted across the garden, pulled by imperceptible ropes. She was only dimly aware of Barrowman and the other officers. They were milling about, analysing the crime scene, doing police work, wasting their time. Again, the tingling sensation began to rise. An impossible itch making her twitch as she walked across the lawn. The same glances were exchanged, the same old tuts and shaking heads. Sarah was floating above it all, drifting through trailing stems, covered in soft weeping leaves. She smelled the strong aroma of honeysuckle and witch hazel. Her head began to swim. She was caught in a tangle of flowers, each bloom's perfume more pungent than the next. Her nostrils flared. There was a sour note lurking in the perfume. It tried to hide, but she could smell it. The note of decay. The metallic hum of blood. What are you hiding in that beautiful coil? She started to run. Rik Storm's garden was long, blending from well-kept lawn to rough brush before colliding with a wall at the forest's edge. The reek of death asserted itself above the sweetness of the garden. Sarah pushed the stems aside. Still floating above the ground. In another world. In another dimension. The tingle of the Tangle. The raw buzzing screech of silence. She could see it now. There on the edge. A blood-black cone. Barrowman's breathless voice dragged her back through the stems until she found herself staring at Rik Storm's garden wall.

'Sorry, ma'am, we just had a call from control . . .'

Barrowman was panting hard, steaming in the drizzle. He was struggling to get the words out. She looked at him through strobing eyes. She was still hovering between the dimensions, unable to settle. Everything seemed to be out of focus and flat like a medieval painting. The constable's words extended into protracted tones, as if his voice was playing on a broken tape recorder.

'There's been another. Up at the playground on Wentford Hill, a couple out for a stroll . . .'

'There's a witness too. Says he saw them being dragged into the woods. They were still alive.'

'Wentford Hill? That's not far from here.'

Her words had a dreamlike quality to them, almost as if pronouncing them was alien to her. Barrowman looked concerned and confused.

'Is everything OK, ma'am?'

She didn't answer. Her movements were entirely without urgency. Slow and languid. She pressed her palms against

the wet bricks of the wall. Beyond it, the Tangle rippled. A
shock passed up her arm, causing her to spasm suddenly.
She spun around.

'We must go. Radio control. Tell them to set up a
perimeter. No one in. No one out. Tell the others to bring
weapons.'

'Yes, ma'am.'

The squad car tore down the country lanes, its blue
light flashing across the fields like a hyperactive lighthouse.
Windscreen wipers beat out a doleful rhythm as the fine
rain fell. DI Ward was glued to the radio, gathering every
bit of information she could. They had a witness. To find a
witness was a stroke of luck. But the testimony being relayed
to the detective was nonsensical and garbled. Barrowman
kept glancing over at her as she spoke to control. His face
was blending from a perplexed frown into the wide-eyed
incredulity of an officer who was used to hearing bullshit
stories every day.

'They thought it might be kids?' The detective rolled
her eyes and banged the dashboard. 'Because? What? Why?
Where? Yeah, yep, yes.'

She clicked off the radio and stared out of the window
in silence. Barrowman started to say something but
thought better of it. The road looked like a river of
mist on which they floated, the car a faint outline like a
fading pencil drawing. Thin arms bent at knobbly joints.
Deformed limbs with tiny hands at their end. Dragging
bodies through the undergrowth. Barely visible above the
grass. She saw razors cutting, and cruel blades skinning.
Two humans lost in the woods. Two humans offered as a
sacrifice to the artisan of the forest.

*Unseen backs bent to the purpose carried the parts for the
art of the woods.*
*Unseen hands silently weaving the flax and the thread for
the throne of the gods.*

'Hurry, Barrowman, we haven't much time . . . Time, time,
time, time to run, time to run.'

The car had reached Wentford Hill car park, a popular spot
for doggers and lovers alike. This morning it was empty except
for the single patrol car that had responded to the 999 call.
A bored-looking, plump PC was leaning on the bonnet with his
arms folded as his wiry colleague paced around the car kicking
the loose stones and scratching his scalp under his peaked
cap. They looked up with only mild interest as the squad car
screeched into the car park with sirens blaring. Barrowman
remembered this place from his school days. A path bisected
a picnic area on one side, dotted with rickety wooden tables
covered in tediously obscene graffiti, whittled by bored
youths. On the other side, a playground of rusty swings and a
roundabout so dangerous it should have been condemned long
ago. No children came up here anymore. The youths would
progress from the tables to the swings as the Thunderbird
wine took hold. It was great for sex and drugs; the cops never
bothered them. Barrowman wondered if the couple who had
been snatched had really been 'out for a stroll'. The detective
just kept staring out of the window, her eyes flickering this
way and that, as if she was experiencing an entirely different
view from him. Her gaze settled on a spot beyond the
playground. Somewhere beyond the dark fringe of the Tangle.

'We're here, ma'am. Shall we wait for backup?'

She looked at him as if he had asked the most ridiculous
question in the world.

'Oh, no, there's no time for that.'

In this world, she jumped out of the squad car, ignoring the two officers already at the scene. She offered them no direction. PC Barrowman, though it was above his pay grade, tried to give them some instructions of his own.

'Get a perimeter set up, will you, lads? No one's to go up to the woods. The DI will be back to direct the team when they get here. Alright?'

But he couldn't help looking somewhat unsure about that statement. DI Ward was already quite some way up the path. The two policemen glared at him. They looked like a washed-up comedy duo on receiving a less than favourable review in the Caxton Gazette. The plump one unfurled his crossed arms and gave Barrowman a mock salute.

'Right you are, guv'nor.'

'Wanker.'

The wiry one muttered under his breath. Barrowman smiled to himself and followed his boss up the path. He'd get a couple more stripes, maybe a pip or two on his collar. He quite enjoyed the feeling of command.

'Ma'am, shouldn't we wait for the firearms team at least? Won't we be just adding to the casualty list if we charge in there?'

He was confident now. Powerful. In charge. He was striding towards the detective. Here to save the day with his instinct for detection. Sarah Ward had stopped at the end of the path, where the cinder track changed to worn earth as it entered the woods. She didn't react to the constable's voice. His confidence began to dissipate in the fine drizzle. His voice softened to a shy schoolboy murmur.

'I was thinking it might be better if we wait for backup, ma'am. The perimeter will be set up soon, so they won't be able to get out without being spotted. We can push in from all sides that way.'

Sarah turned around slowly. Her eyes were expressionless. Her pupils, like black pools, reflected back his dripping, uncertain face. She reached out her hand and grasped him firmly by the arm. Her mouth began to arch up haltingly as if her lips were being winched into place. A smile was suspended on her face.

'Bless you, Barrowman, bless you. Don't you see? There's no time. We have to go now. They are waiting.'

She took his hand and led him into the Tangle.

*

Inside the wood the air was dense. The hiss of white noise underpinned a faint throb, like the pulse of a heartbeat. It was warm. She had played in these woods as a little girl, and so had he, but things were different now. The path had been swallowed by the undergrowth, so they picked their own passage through the stems. Directions and distance became impossible to judge as the world outside the wood vanished from view. There was no sound of traffic. No car horn chatter, no sirens or shouts of command. All the usual points of reference were absent. This was a new, alien landscape. Here they were strangers, interlopers, invaders.

Sarah Ward let go of his hand. The two officers wandered steadily through the boughs, brushing against the soft leaves with their faulty skin. The womb-like cadence of the woods reduced any feeling of urgency. Time had no meaning here. Had they been searching for days, hours or years? It was impossible to tell. Neither seemed to care. The abducted couple. The murderous artist. The severed limbs and broken corpses, all parts of the pitiless necropolis they lived in.

The constant flow of construction and destruction, death, birth and the stagnant torpor in between. The snap of a twig broke the reverie like a needle skidding off a record. Sarah froze and signalled for Barrowman to follow her example.

'Over there,'

She whispered as the dimensions of the forest settled into recognisable shapes. Up, down, left, right. Barrowman nodded silently. They crept through the undergrowth. Another crack. This time a faint cry too. Human wailing. They picked their way with increased urgency. The sounds became clearer. A woman and a man. They were close enough to separate the tones of their cries. But the wood was still too thick to see them clearly. Snap. A desiccated branch broke as something was dragged over the ground. More cries. This time the sound seemed to come from behind them. They wheeled around and stopped, momentarily disorientated. Thumps and scrapes and a hideous scuttling sound. They froze. A sound rose through the hiss. The crackle of thin limbs scampering over dead leaves. Pincer-tipped tarsus tapping. Barrowman instinctively reached for a stick to use as a weapon. DI Ward scanned the trees. Another scream, this time long and continuous. Both sexes harmonizing in a terrible anguished howl. The scuttling sound grew more intense.

DI Ward signalled a manoeuvre with her eyes. They split up and approached the source of the cries from different directions. The undergrowth began to thin. Sarah was drifting through the mist again. She was a little girl in a procession of village girls and boys, skipping towards the great ash. Erwan with the scythe, the vicar with his hymn book. Come to sing for the spirits of the winter and all the saints. All the saints. All the saints are here. The branches melted away as she glided through the woods. The chanting rose. The animals lowed in mournful tones anticipating their demise. The scythe swept, and the blood flowed. The hymns rang out as the villagers danced around the ash. God is here. God is here. DI Ward stood on the edge of the clearing, her eyes as black as Dante's well.

Barrowman tried his radio, more out of habit than hope. The wood had done things to him since the DI had dragged him in. His perspective had shifted onto a new, unfamiliar axis. His duty was still his duty, he guessed. But in some strange way it felt like someone else's concern. He crept closer to the sound. He could make out a glade up ahead where the trees had formed into a natural amphitheatre. The soft hum of the forest began to blend with the unsettling cries that were growing in intensity as he got closer. He was a boy again. A boy scout within a troop of boy scouts. They had whittled figures to hang in the branches of the great ash. He was proud of his. A man with no arms or legs, grinning through a mouth with no lips. They hung them on the boughs and sang songs. PC Barrowman stood on the edge of the clearing, his eyes as black as Dante's well.

Two bodies hung from the branches of the great ash. Ruler of the third lunar month. Queen of the glade. The bodies kicked and swung. Cut and bruised but alive. Around them busy artists were at work. DI Ward stepped into the clearing. Her mouth wanted to form a scream of her own, but she drove it back down. She was face to face with the craftsman of the forest. Behold her work. The ash seemed to spread its branches, like arms, proudly displaying the fruits of its labour. Down its trunk, spider entities scuttled on spindly twig legs that jutted from a brain-like core. The brain looked like a furry walnut oozing with sap. They were perfect facsimiles of arachnids, born from the bark of the ash tree. Outriders of itself, sent into the world of men to hunt and gather. They reminded her of huge huntsman spiders. Sightless and fast, they filled the glade with their hideous industry. A fresh scream pierced the momentary silence. A spider creature was using its pincers to pull a strip of skin from the leg of the flailing man. It gathered up the skin and ran down the branch to join the flow of its comrades who were scuttling down the trunk. Sarah followed its progress, unable to turn her gaze from the fascinating tableau. The spider thing crossed the forest floor where it joined a further group of creatures hard at work. The skin was passed carefully between mute mandibles before being skilfully stitched onto an evolving patchwork using fine strands of silk woven from their abdomen. They were upholstering furniture.

Barrowman staggered into the glade waving his stick impotently in front of him. The wood spiders ignored him. They were too busy to kill. Besides they had all the materials they needed for now. Take only what you need. That was the first law of the Tangle. He glanced across the clearing to DI Ward, looking for guidance. But they had not been trained for anything like this. The two dangling captives. Hostages, victims, prisoners. He recognized those designations. It was in the handbook. What to do in a hostage situation. But this . . .

'Help us, please, for pity's sake.'

'I don't want to die. Oh, God.'

The spider things cut another strip. Barrowman looked desperately over to the DI. Sarah Ward shook her head. Don't do it. It's no good. Barrowman struggled. Duty, training, instinct, all rendered irrelevant by the artistry of the Tangle. The black blood and stitch, the weaver's bobbin of sinew and skin. Barrowman broke from his mooring and ran towards the hanging couple. A line of ash spiders formed a palisade with their stick legs. Sharp points menaced the constable as he tried to get closer.

Sarah Ward turned to admire their work. Her eyes as black as Dante's well. She was a little girl in her best Sunday robes, holding a doll made from the stalks, sat on a cushion, patiently embroidered. She stepped to the altar and placed the cushion on the simple wooden table. In the centre of the cushion, she placed the doll. She sat it upright. Like a monarch.

'Oh, that is wonderful Sarah. You are so talented at weaving the stems, and such delicate needle work. Would you like to make beautiful things when you grow up?'

The ash continued its craft. She smiled.

'Thank you, reverend. I wanted to make something special for the festival. She's the queen, the queen of the woods.'

Across the bloody workshop, Barrowman watched his commanding officer's face in horror. She was smiling. At this? Yet even he had to admit it was beautiful. Bones, bent and carved to form a delicate frame, were being carefully engraved by the sharp tips of the spiders' legs. Over the frame they then carefully fitted the upholstery of skin and sinew. Faces cut from skulls poked out from the folds of the fabric, like curious children behind their mothers' skirts as the parade passed by. The beautiful furniture of humanity. A throne of blood. The legs were legs, the arms were arms. Eyes inlaid, tongues tied and stitched in an exquisite tapestry. The ash had mastered its craft. Just a few more details and the work would be complete.

'Take me.'

Sarah's voice was barely discernible over the busy clicking of the creatures. The ash swayed as it caught her words.

She wanted to make beautiful things. She wanted to make a difference.

'Let them go. Take me instead.'

Louder this time, more insistent. The ash swayed. The voice. The voice of God. The spider creatures paused, lowering the palisade of pincers. Barrowman seized his chance and ran towards the dangling couple. Jumping over the ranks of spiders, he managed to clear their menacing spikes as they attempted to impale him. He hurriedly untied the twine of stems that held the dangling couple. They dropped screaming to the floor. As they rose, they found themselves surrounded by agitated creatures. They began to swarm around the captives, waving their pincers menacingly. The humans were trapped. Barrowman looked anxiously at his DI. Too impetuous, that's what his scout master said.

'Don't do anything, Anthony, just stay there.'

Sarah Ward held out her arm, palm facing the constable and the shivering couple. She was ready to go now. She saw it all. The master maker. The final detail. She edged towards the tree. The spider creatures clicked and prickled. Barrowman looked uncertain. Paralyzed. Initial spontaneity marred by a lack of caution. That was his fateful flaw. It had always been that way. Too quick to make bold choices without considering the consequences. He'd joined the force on a whim, just to piss his Dad off. He shouldn't be here. He should have left Caxton years ago. Got a trade like his old man, travelled a bit, gone to the city, made a life for himself with the talents he squandered.

'Your father won't be happy.'

He could hear his dead mother's voice.

'You'd better not mess this up.'

Barrowman swept his stick like a sword, trying to cut a path out of the glade. The ranks of spikey stick legs broke momentarily as he smashed at them with his desiccated weapon. But they soon surged again.

The spider creatures cut his legs at the ankles and he toppled to the forest floor. His cries were soon drowned in the frantic click-clack of creaking pincers as they swarmed all over him. Stabbing and cutting with precision. Blood began to pour over the woodland floor. Dark reeking rags from his torn uniform were chucked out of the seething pile to be collected by yet more scurrying things. Sarah saw Barrowman's severed head being carried along through the mesh of tangled legs. It was passed along the swarm until it reached the macabre monument they were constructing. His face joined the gallery in the upholstery of the furniture. Tears welled and overflowed, staining her cheeks. They never listen, these foolish boys, they never listen. She looked over at the helpless couple, bleeding and useless on the blood-soaked ground. Pincers click-clacked. Sarah ran to the tree. Pressing her filthy hands against the trunk she spoke into the bark.

'Take me, for God's sake, take me.'

The ash swayed. The spider creatures stopped. God? Yes, God. The ash had heard of God. The offerings. The dangling effigies of dead men and women. The hymns and chants. The blood. This was not God. The ash knew God. The ash swayed. The spider creatures began to reverse away from the cowering couple. A path formed from the tree to the edge of the clearing. In the far distance DI Ward could hear the sound of sirens. She pressed her palms against the bark with increased intensity.

'Take me. Take me. I am ready. *I wanted to make something special for the festival.*'

She wasn't sure if she had spoken. Her words were a whisper, uttered in a language that was not her own.

Erwan's scythe. The bloody skins hanging in the branches, the hymns and the corn dolls.

'Oh, that is wonderful Sarah. You are so talented at weaving the stems.'

The offerings piled high on the altar. Tins and toys, dolls and games. Skulls and blood. Erwan's scythe and the woad on his face running in the rain. The spider things scuttled backwards up the trunk until they were re-absorbed into the bark.

'Run!'

Her last words, imperious, like a decree. The woman nodded mutely. Standing on shaking legs she dragged her bleeding partner up and ran out of the clearing. Sarah watched them until they had been swallowed up by the Tangle. The sirens. Run to the sirens. Silence returned to the glade. Slowly a branch curled down from the canopy and gently slipped around her waist, like a partner at the start of a waltz. She felt herself float through the air. She was a windblown leaf. The glistening cone was forming silently below her. The branch deposited her tenderly on a cushion of human furniture. She noted absentmindedly that it had been fashioned from the bloated stomach of Mike Stains, she remembered his distinctive birthmark from the photographs in his special room. Her hands spread over the soft skin. Such exemplary work. Faultless. She was a monarch on a throne. A queen of the forest. But there were no monarchs here. No subjects either. She felt a stillness that she had never felt before. The tears ran in steady streams. But she was not sad, nor even frightened. She could no longer hear the sirens or the sounds of her world. Perspectives began to shift. New vectors opened and revealed themselves. The warmth of the womb enveloped her as she sat on the throne of skin and blood. Through a crack in the membrane that separated the dimensions, she saw herself dancing around the throne, the blossoms of spring in her hair. The delicate scent of the Tangle flooded her senses like the perfume of a cathedral. A prelate stood in the chancel waving a ball of incense on a silver chain as DI Ward was adorned with the baubles of her office. Orb, sceptre and Crown. Another branch unfurled from the knot. It straightened its length and pierced her stomach. Its twigs spread out across her, pulling her apart. She was sucked into the structure of the throne until her spine splintered and her features fused with the fabric. The prelate waved the ball of incense as the officers of state came up to the throne one by one to pay homage to their new queen. A faint gurgle escaped the remains of her mouth. The ash welcomed her into the roots, and with the last tiny spark of her former human self, she complimented it on its fine craftsmanship. So very comfortable. She smiled.

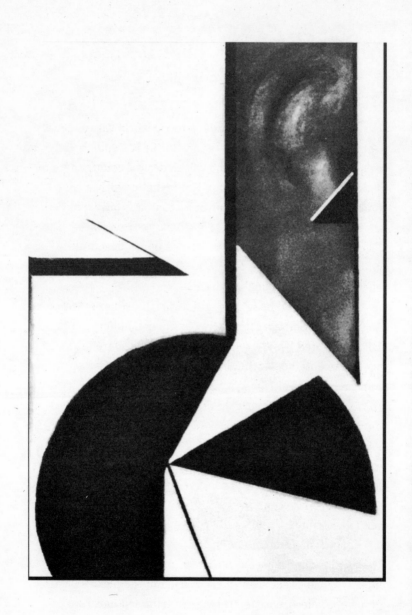

Notification from the A.B.A.C.U.S.

No one went out any more. The outside world was difficult, uncertain and probably best avoided. But Kavendish Jeremiah was one of those rare Citizens whose desires could not be satisfied by fresh air generators or daylight synthesisers. He knew some would mock his strange customs, but he did enjoy the simple communion of foot on concrete from time to time. People may call him a 'Walker' with a faint sneer, but it didn't matter. He was content with his carefully constructed oddity; it kept his quotient healthy.

Kavendish had been delivered from the annexed womb of an unknown Service Citizen in the Inner London Hatcheries. His designated 'How Are You?' device had declared him fit within acceptable parameters. His appearance, 'strikingly handsome', was only a few points short of 'gorgeous'. Although he enjoyed surgery as much as the next person, he did at least bear some resemblance to his hatchery graduation picture. Kavendish was a member of the most privileged cadre, selected and designated according to an ancient line of inheritance that stretched back into the distant past. Tall and lean for an Aristoian, he was something of an athlete. At least sexually. Today he was wearing his hair long.

Kavendish Jeremiah adjusted the position of his Sensory Nexus Mask and selected the odour of a freshly mown meadow. The sweet scent flowed through the plexi-holes of his nose piece, exciting the neatly trimmed hairs of his nostrils. He shook his velvet fedora and placed it on his head at a rakish angle, enjoying the feel of its stout brim on his fingertips. He smoothed the mask over his features, relishing its sleek, shiny texture. The mask covered his face with a translucent film that offered excellent clarity of view whilst maintaining his connection to the Nexus. The mask was his second skin. Every Aristoian wore one. It was the only tolerable way to deal with the outside world, after all.

Kavendish harmonised the tint of his mask to compensate for the bright blue tones of the sky. The huge, open sky. Untroubled by aircraft or pylons. Free of pollutants and urban gas. A perfect azure dome. A sudden breath of wind raised the brim of his hat. Kavendish secured it and pulled his jacket closer to him as phantom gusts swept between the buildings, playing a haunting melody like an orchestra tuning up before the conductor's arrival. He let his eyes play across the panorama of his home. This was London. A former capital of nowhere. A bewildering conurbation on a small island. A city where all your desires were met with a blink of an eye. A place of carefully controlled disorder. A temple to indulgence, whim and fancy. Outside the dome lay the Tangle.

He turned his attention to his screen. He blinked rapidly, registering his reaction to the posts and images that were flowing steadily across it. Faces stared out at him. Faces in rooms. Rooms revealed by cameras and open access feeds. The pornography of everyday life. The constant exhibition. Kavendish was on near-permanent display. His outer life was completely transparent most of the time. Only his inner life remained hidden, even from himself. It was rare for him to log off. Others would become suspicious if you were absent for too long, and anyway, the A.B.A.C.U.S.

didn't like it. There was a risk of melancholy creeping in with the silence.

Kavendish began to walk along the riverbank, heading towards the park. He consulted his Personal Advisory Terminal, looking for inspiration. When it came to suggestions for pleasurable diversion, it had never let him down. Kavendish winked open an icon. The Terminal scrolled into life.

- The Oil Pit
- The Mystery Coupling Cubicle
- Jelly Man
- The Willing Torturer
- Dream Capsule
- The Gentle Pastures of Pleasure

Kavendish digested the list. Most of the suggestions seemed a little stale to him. He had fucked, dined and swallowed in most of these establishments. That was the problem with going outside. The architects never really kept pace with desire. Kavendish was impatient for satisfaction. He had left the pleasure café early. He found that particular establishment boring and had especially deplored the décor. But narcotics and nature were something that never failed to please him. The chance to dream amongst the blooms. It was always changing in unpredictable ways. That was its attraction. The chaos. The park was a reliable solution. It would be the perfect start to another perfect day.

In a glade of lilac shadows, a ripple turned to a wave. The child race was at a crossroads. Or at an end, who could tell?

*Erwan cut the bough for me, let the sap drip down. Send a
sign to the child of the magus. For the reckoning is now.*

The outside world was conspiring against him. Disruption
of the normal was its mode. Dark clouds contaminated the
sky. It began to rain. Unscheduled, uninvited rain. This
was strange in itself, as one was used to the accuracy of the
A.B.A.C.U.S. weather reports; every day was dissected and
predicted in a generally efficient manner. The unexpected was
rarely unexpected. Dark clouds were not welcome here. Only
the perfection of perpetual daylight. Twenty-four hours of
sunshine, every day, every year, for as long as anyone could
remember. Though 'day' was not an idea anyone entertained.
There was something like the passing of time, marked in
hours and minutes and so forth, but it bore no relation to any
changes in the apparent movement of the sun. It was simply
an ancient affectation inherited from some previous mode of
being that had long since been abandoned. If the light faded,
then the powerful daylight bulbs of the city would spring into
life. Pushing back the darkness, banishing the night. Night-
time was a waste of time. Once a week he would sleep. If he
needed it or not. But otherwise, he would fill his time with
amusing diversions. Stimulants kept him awake and alert.
Pleasure could not rest, there was no time for it.

As the unexpected rain began to splatter on the pavement,
Kavendish looked around for shelter. He was keen not to
ruin the new suit his auto-tailor had recently created and
was, in any case, too far from a terminal to get a new one.
The riverside was exposed. There was little need for havens
or hiding places, as so few people ever went out. But now
Kavendish needed shelter as splatter turned to torrent.
Gazing down the riverside path, his attention was drawn to a

wild oak that looked like it had burst through the pavement. That was not the way of things. It was an ugly looking object. Twisted and gnarled. Not at all like the beautiful oaks found in the city's parks. Was this something new? The latest fashion in arboreal decoration? He had not seen it mentioned on the Nexus. He stared at the bizarre carbuncle. It was without structure or symmetry. Its very presence violated his sensibilities. He watched its ugliness pulse. In out. In out. Like a lung. Like a heart. Like a valve. As he stared, its canopy began to swell and expand. Kavendish was fascinated and repulsed. As he watched the tree suck and blow, the dizzying confusion of London dissolved around him. The roots split the pavement. Concrete buckled, then shattered. Branches streamed into the cracks, occupying every crevice. Soon he was under the spreading leaves, his palms pressed on the contorted trunk. Time and location momentarily forgotten. Under the dense structure of branches, a strange atmosphere began to smother him. Kavendish was alone, and for the first time in as long as he could remember, he was separated and detached from the city. His mind began to wander. A rare and unwelcome feeling. A strange darkness grew. Shapes emerged, then splintered. The branches began to twist, creating the walls of an endless tunnel. The unruly stems began to knot into a thick weave. The roots began to writhe. The whole strange clump then began to spin, as if dancing a frenetic reel. Faster and faster it spun, until a vortex formed that threatened to suck him into its core. He was sweating uncontrollably. This was not the way of things. Waves of nausea travelled around his body. The dislocation was horrifying. This was not the way of things.

Who will carry the weight of the golden seed to the door?
Who will turn the key to the vault under the floor?

Who will find the prize hidden deep within the tomb?
Who will see the lights glinting in the gloom?

The vortex slowed and stopped. The wave changed back to pulse. The Tangle retreated. Reversing into the trunk. Back down through the cracks in the pavement. The message had been delivered. Kavendish sat on an empty walkway in an empty city. His mask regained its connection to the Nexus and chimed back into life with a melodious tone. Most blessed notifications!

- The A.B.A.C.U.S. benevolent resource.
- The A.B.A.C.U.S. locus of all desire.
- The A.B.A.C.U.S. omni-competent living device.

The icons had returned one by one, but now they seemed distant and strangely shrunken. A new suggestion occupied the centre of the screen: a map. But not the map he was used to. A single dot that looked like an acorn blinked on a crude street plan. Above it the words:

The Museum of Ignorance.

The script had an almost hieroglyphic quality. Letters elongated. Words twisting about the page like vipers. Crude words. Primitive words. Words that were unfamiliar, their meaning obscure.

The Museum of Ignorance.

Kavendish blinked to raise an enquiry with his Sensory Nexus Mask. But there was no response. Was this a mystery?

He wasn't sure he had ever experienced a mystery before. He was certainly not a seeker of wisdom. No one went in for that kind of thing. Many years ago, before the time of the Complete Theorem, before the Great Equilibrium, people had had awkward 'opinions': they argued about everything, from economics to physics, philosophy to politics. No one knew the best way to do anything. There was discord, disagreement and unhappiness. But now, thank the A.B.A.C.U.S., that dark time was hundreds of years in the past. Now all was known. All was in balance. It was the way of things. Scientists had become historians, before themselves becoming history, and, as we all know, history finished years ago.

The dot winked on the map. The acorn fading in and out.

The Museum of Ignorance.

These obsolete hieroglyphics. This primitive map. What were these awkward anomalies? Why hadn't they been dissolved like all the other useless things? The dot pulsed on the map. The dot like a seed. The dot like a kernel ready to sprout.

Who will carry the weight of the golden seed to the door?
Who will turn the key to the vault under the floor?
Who will find the prize hidden deep within the tomb?
Who will see the lights glinting in the gloom?

His Environment Wall was near, reliable, fun, easy. He had devices to try, positions to adopt, cocktails to taste. The dot winked. Kavendish followed the path.

He stepped onto the pneumatic pavement and made for one of the riverside's many elegant crossings. As he glided along, he felt as if he was flowing through the city like the ancient river. When he reached the crossing, he engaged the interchange and stepped onto the bridge's moving pathway. The glass bridge sang as the wind caught its delicate fronds. The river magnificent in perpetual sunshine. Now the unexpected squall had passed, London was all shiny, a sumptuous paradise of architectural excess: glass-fronted apartments, baroque towers and mock Tudor maisonettes nestled next to brutalist concrete cubes and quasi-medieval artisan huts. The A.B.A.C.U.S. indulged and the cyborg tradesmen built. The dull cramp of overindulgence settled on the city. The surfeit of desire. Dulling the appetites of the perpetually bored occupants. Pleasure cafés, arousal points, the love theatre; a schizophrenic vista of decadent brilliance. All flamboyantly constructed. All mainly empty.

As he sped along, a flock of green sea parrots darted over the water. They had been bred to compliment the azure tones of the purified river. As they swooped over the surface they appeared as polished emeralds cast by some unseen hand. Perhaps one last throw in an intangible game of chance. Making their elegant progress up the river's marble embankment they joined a host of other colourful birds that were darting to and fro amongst the exotic plants that covered the riverbanks. Here and there one could spot curious creatures who had been designed to frolic amongst the boughs for the amusement of the dissolute citizenry. Monkeys with brightly coloured backsides, sloths of unfathomable charm, fangless snakes, Antipodean marsupials stoned on eucalyptus, lobotomised bears, toothless big cats bred to be small cats, here a warm-weather penguin, there a polar camel. The parrots added their call to the chaos. The plants shared the same unfettered exoticism as the animals. They had been selected in accordance to the contradictory whims of the city's inhabitants. A ghastly explosion of conflicting colours and overpowering odours emanated from the foliage as it erupted along the embankment. This riotous garden was tended to by Service Citizens dressed in the plain green smocks of their class. Their dreary costumes rendered them virtually invisible amongst the exuberant shrubs. These were the hidden drones of the city, resigned to a life of comfortable drabness. Pruning the arbours of the detached populace.

Under the thin city soil the filaments creep and crawl.
Through stone and filth 'neath battlements, palisade
*   and wall.*
The acorn and the dandelion, the bird's foot and the dock.
They come to break the fetters and the master's bitter lock.

They come to free the captives, the tortured and the lost.
They come to slay the gaolers, mad with tyranny and lust.
Through cracks and jagged injuries, in stems, in roots,
*   in flowers.*
They come to bear grim witness in the gaoler's final hours.

Kavendish left the bridge and headed along the edge of the park. Silently gliding. Following the path of the blinking seed. The map flattened the landscape, deadening the psychic geography of the city. It exulted only the destination. The single relevant terminus. Diversions popped up along the way. The 'Bulging Man' ecstasy café; a superb venue. Kavendish had a very enjoyable encounter there recently. The Service Citizen had received a great boost to their Utility Quotient. He glanced in as he passed. No time to stop. Buildings of every shape and size drifted by. They cast bizarre dark shapes on the spotless pavements, like figures in a shadow play.

As his journey continued, so his Kudos Quotient grew. Like the spreading roots under the pavement. Kudos. The only thing of value in a world where everything was free. It was the contentment index, an equation for a successful world. It was the language of performance, the language of efficiency. It stood for the maintenance of the Great Equilibrium, a public affirmation of a perfect society. Anything that resisted quantification simply ceased to be. For in the time of the A.B.A.C.U.S. there was but one crime: the crime of unhappiness, the only possible act of sedition.

Happiness is everything.

The park was behind him now. Great stone monoliths from a less-amusing time dominated the riverside. There was none of the random jumble of architecture that was to be found elsewhere. Kavendish had now entered the ancient heart of the city; it had been frozen in time. A mummified nostalgia platz. Kavendish passed an old statue, green with age, its head permanently caked with the shit of the city's birds. No amount of scrubbing by droid or man could keep it clean. There were many similar statues dotted around this part of the metropolis. Some were carved from stone, others forged from bronze. All frozen in time in the midst of some dramatic action: pointing towards an imagined future or waving swords on the backs of horses. Their deeds were long forgotten. Kavendish glided by the Gothic frontage of a particularly ancient pile. Something to do with politics or some such decrepit notion. His friend Quintella had a dildo that was shaped to resemble the imposing clock tower; its tiny bell would ring as she climaxed. So important to preserve the past.

Kavendish continued to glide through the city, turning away from the river now and into yet another lattice of mismatched buildings. He followed the blinking seed. Though in truth, he simply let it pull him through the streets. Like a leaf looking for light in a crowded bed, he wriggled through the byways of the city of Ra. The quiet buildings towered above him, reflecting the permanent daylight off their pristine shells. Behind the glass the Citizens fucked. They drank and ate. They puked and shat.

Happiness is everything.

Kavendish raised his eyes to the summit of a great stone monolith carved in the perfect likeness of a great cock and balls. Veins full and ripe. He laughed as the seed pulled him on. His Kudos Quotient surged. The Nexus was happy.

Happiness is everything.

He paused at the Brompton Road to allow a noisy pack of hunters to pass. He was pleased to see that the rain had not put them off either. He knew them all, of course. He knew most of the people in the city. But those who stepped outside tended to be drawn to one another, like peculiar magnets. Kavendish admired their attire: they were clad in the traditional scarlet. Hard hats, knee-length boots, rubber shorts. They hallooed as they galloped by. Kavendish touched the brim of his fedora in reply, beaming and shouting his greetings. As the tooting of the huntsmen's horns faded into the distance, he found his eyes losing focus. The acorn sigil now swelled and began to sprout. The screen of his mask faded into the distance. For a few brief seconds, the confusing skyline of the city was replaced. The pneumatic pavement was the track of an ancient railway. Kavendish was a passenger clunking along its rusty girders. He pulled into a station. It was familiar to him. It was home. Caxton Wood. He was inside the calm interior of a library. The ground on which he stood was no longer the pavement of London, but instead, the herringboned lattice of a parquet floor. He had the impression of being inside a country cottage. He could see a pleasant meadow from out of its lead-lined window. An old clock tick-tocked in the corner. His eyes were drawn to some well-appointed shelves. They were full of leather-bound volumes. These must be books. He reached out and took one from the shelf. The clock struck. The whiplash of a switch stung his cheek. Kavendish spun around to confront his assailant. He was under the tree. Palms pressed against its gnarled trunk. The black vortex of roots spun. Whispering, broken network chatter, moans and pillow talk from a variety of sex parties. A Discipline Drone hovering. His barber's pre-programmed synthetic gossip module. A gathering of hooded figures chanting incantations in the night. A gallows. A girl. A courtroom. A mob. Drug talk, fuck talk. A.B.A.C.U.S. talk. Kavendish's head clattered and rang like an old telephone. The clock struck again. He was back on the pavement, looking through the prism of his Sensory Nexus Mask. The whole episode lasted no more than a few seconds, so fast in fact that he doubted it had even occurred. The map flickered back into focus. The acorn flashed.

On his screen the seedling was now a sapling. The roots began to travel along the streets of the map. Kavendish followed. Train track. Clunking over points. Click. Clack. Stations flashing past. The hanging baskets of Caxton Wood. Alight here. The sapling swelled. Its juvenile branches swayed like foals on untested hooves. They clattered at the surface of his screen, trying to break through the translucent skin. To pierce his eyes with their woody fingers, or perhaps to point the way? Soon the branches were so thick he couldn't see beyond them. He became lost in a forest that was wrapped around his face. The London that he knew seemed to dissolve to nothing. Images from a forgotten past. Images from an uncertain future.

> *Under the thin city soil the filaments creep and crawl.*
> *Through stone and filth 'neath battlements, palisade*
> *   and wall.*
> *The acorn and the dandelion, the bird's foot and the dock.*
> *They come to break the fetters and the master's bitter lock.*
>
> *They come to free the captives, the tortured and the lost.*
> *They come to slay the gaolers mad with tyranny and lust.*
> *Through cracks and jagged injuries, in stems, in roots,*
> *   in flowers.*
> *They come to bear grim witness in the gaoler's final hours.*

Hallucinations occupied his mind and spun him up into the air. He was far above the forest. He could see the city, but it was not his city. It was a grimy, busy place, full of conflict and fumes. Kavendish was repulsed, but he couldn't break free. These bleak visions offended him. He was floating above a vile version of his beloved London. Millions of Citizens teeming on its litter-strewn pavements. There was no space, no grace; it was an unhappy place. The sight made Kavendish sick. He fought to keep his stomach in its place. Now he was diving down out of the sky towards the tangled web of a forest. Kavendish tried to slow his fall. He flapped his useless arms, trying to stay aloft. The ground was coming up fast. Kavendish shut his eyes tight. Braced for impact. The impact never came. Instead, he found himself in front of a single structure, standing all alone at the end of a broad tree-lined boulevard. He recognised it immediately.

The Museum of Ignorance.

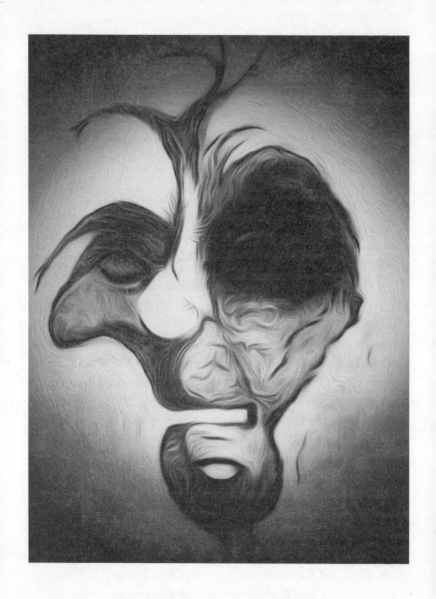

The Queen Anne Chair

In the folds where all worlds touch. At the intersection of
tessellating planes. The jagged edge of a wound is exposed.
In this wound a dark magic broods. Born from the discharge
and the dislocation of joints. It seeks for reasons for its
painful cuts. The bleeding weal where the cruel rope eats
into its back, reminds it of its doom. It asks why it alone
carries the burden. That terrible knowledge. Ripped from the
heart of the Tangle. As a weapon. As a gift. As a right. As a
curse. Once the dark magic was without form. It seduced and
occupied the child creatures of the forest. It lent them armour
for their war on creation. Confidence. Ignorance. Blindness.
Will. The children flourished and died. Alone. Their souls fed
the wound, and its dark magic grew. But it needed names.
It longed for shape and purpose. It needed blood and skin.
It needed sacrifice. Erwan's scythe swept in those first
moments. When the first number was counted. When the first
second ticked. Carry the weight of the curse. Until there are
no seconds left to count.

The Bull was busy for a Wednesday. Tobias Lean had put
a few quid behind the bar for his sister-in-law's wake. Cut
sandwiches. Modest spread. There had been a reasonable
turnout for the funeral; she was a popular woman. Her
brother-in-law was less popular. But he was paying, so why
not. It's what she would have wanted. The lounge bar was
buzzing with gossip, shaking heads and impromptu eulogies.

They were two deep at the bar already. The landlady had called in help. Caxton youth. Hilda Wilton. Last days of school. Don't touch the taps, I'll lose my licence. Hilda picked up plates. Hilda picked up pots. Hilda sidestepped drunken hands. She deposited a tray of empty tankards at the end of the bar. Foam scum and lip spit. The landlady pushed a frothing pint towards her, pointing at the old high-backed Queen Anne chair that lived in permanent residence in front of the fire. Hilda raised an eyebrow and exhaled. Erwan's pint. Never leave him with an empty glass. It was unlucky. That was the lore around these parts. Like the ravens at the Tower. Hilda found his presence unnerving, and she always deposited his drink and left as quickly and politely as she could. 'Here you go.' Never catch his eye. He'll have your soul. That's what they said.

Erwan was a fixture, like a beam or a door. The landlady had inherited him, just as the owner before her had done. Before the Bull there was the Packhorse. Before the Packhorse, the Cup. Before the Cup, Ad Cucu. Then the hut, the fire, the cave. Erwan stared into the flames, sipping his ale. Waiting. Waiting. No one ever saw him come in, no one ever saw him leave. Occasionally he would speak. He told stories. Long, rambling, barely comprehensible tales. Sometimes in a recognisable dialect. More often not. The Caxton youth liked to try and take the piss out of him when they were drunk. It was a 'rite of passage' type of arrangement. But few found it funny when he turned his eye on you.

Eyes without sight, vision or focus. No lens or pupil,
motion or locus.

By the evening the sandwiches had curled and the quiche
was but a distant memory. Beer flowed and tears were shed.
Many returned to their homes. Dedicated drinkers stayed.
The wisdom of the saloon bar philosopher began to be heard
above the clack of billiard balls. Debates about politics. Rights
and wrongs. What does it all mean, eh? Young woman like
that, taken so young. That poor boy. How can there be a
God that allows such things to happen? A group of scholars
searching for enlightenment picked up their pints and bags of
scratchings and moved instinctively towards the fire. Erwan
stared at the flames as the hungry fire ate through the logs.
He sat at the junction of many interlocking planes. Waiting.
Waiting. The sound of a glass placed on a table drew him to
a particular place, a particular time. A young woman was
retreating having just placed a foaming mug of beer by his
hand. He knew her. Or would know her. Or had at one time
known her. For a split second she caught his eye. 'Here you
go, Erwan.' He saw the blood yet to come. The pincers and the
thread. She saw it too. Their paths intersected as the vision
was shared. She shuddered, unable to escape, held by his
gaze. But it was not yet time. There were trials still to pass.
He nodded his thanks, as was customary in this world. Hilda
hurried away carrying his empty glass.

'Erwan will know, won't he? I reckon he's cleverer than
he looks. Has us all at it with his mad tales. Gets free fucking
drinks all day so he's certainly not daft. Here, Erwan, Barry
wants to know . . .'

Beer fumes and shots. The miasma of public house
summits. Erwan was only dimly aware of their ridiculous
chatter. They often came seeking his council. For the harvest.
For the pox. For wealth, health and good fortune. He told
them stories they didn't understand, for they had long

ceased to speak the language of the Tangle. These dolts
were not different. They served an entity they could not
name. Who dwelt in their doubts? Who dwelt in their fears?
A Mesmeriser. One of the clodhoppers stumbled. Beer was
spilled. The amber stream flowed slowly across the floor until
it reached Erwan's swaddled feet. The ale soaked into the
cloth. For a moment there was silence in the Bull. Hilda put
down her tray of empty glasses. The landlady froze at the
optics. The drunken men stared at the tragic pool. Erwan
turned his black eyes on them and spoke.

At the summit of a dais made of broken glass and razor
blades sits a rough metal throne, on the throne a twisted
figure shifts its skeletal frame. In its hands it holds a dark
globe. The entity is known by many names, in many places
and times, and yet you do not know him. It is the deceiver,
the sower of confusion, the pitiless will, the father of
desire, the mother of longing. In your world it is known
by a name of human tongue. The Mesmeriser. The magic
in the cut. The spell woven from blood. The Mesmeriser
waves a taloned hand over the globe. An image emerges
from the mist, revealing a lonely speck floating in the
void. You call this speck the sun. It is the only sun in
this universe. The solitary source of light in the blank
emptiness of space. You are alone. Now the cut grows
wider. The sebum and the sap. The sacrifice is called. The
Mesmeriser will tap the surface of the globe with its metal
claw. Can you see it? Another speck, smaller than before.
Hugging the sun like a new-born chick huddled up to an

incubator's lightbulb. Do you see it now? This was your home before the war in heaven.

The Bull public house is frozen. Its occupants still. Unblinking. Static. Only Hilda moves. Only Hilda hears. She will forget all that has been said. For now. The amber stream reverses into the glass. Erwan raises his wrinkled hand. His words cascade from his mouth.

Now the dark black pellet is near. See the ancient sarcophagus. This is the weapon you requested. You have paid well for it. The Mesmeriser utters an incantation that sounds like a thousand penitent souls crying at once. The sarcophagus opens and a bright rainbow of smoke drifts out. Can you see? Can you see the smoke?

The fire in the grate is held by his stare. It does not move. It does not burn.

Look at the smoke. Look as it fills the darkness of the globe. The speck comes alive, its dull surface transformed into a swirl of colour. Can you see? Can you see? Faces bulge from the surface, melting and morphing before being sucked back inside. Flames flicker in its obsidian heart. It begins to spin at a terrifying speed, colours shooting around the interior before blending together to form an intense anti-colour of infinite darkness. The Mesmeriser waves its talon over the globe again. The spinning stops in an instant. A smile forms in the blank cavity of its mouth. The Mesmeriser is pleased. The tiny speck has changed. Millions of years of slow, unfolding evolution condensed into a single moment. Can you see? Can you see? This is you. This is your home. You are alone. This is what you asked for, is it not? This palace of infinite happiness. Where the sun never sets, and the darkness never comes. Look into the fire. Now can you see the name of your lord?

Hilda threw down a paper towel on the bitter lake of beer. It darkened the weave like the blood from a gunshot wound. She placed a fresh mug of ale on the table by Erwan's wizened hand. Never leave him with an empty glass. It was unlucky. That's what they said. His black eyes stared into the fire as the flames began to lick over the logs again.

The Museum of Ignorance

Grey slabs of stone buttressed dirty grey windows. Grime
seemed to cling to it all like a dust cloth. Huge pillars led up
to a roof made from some undefinable amalgam, tarnished
and pitted by age and the elements. Under the roof was
a carved frieze. Effigies had been hacked into the stone.
Signifiers of a grubby era. A time when an ignorant populace
had attempted to grasp its place in a lifeless universe.
Kavendish approached with caution. As he drew nearer, he
made out the figures of human beings. Not Aristoians, but
human nonetheless. Around the entrance to the museum
a small team of low-grade Service Citizens were sweeping
the paths, clearing the way for the crowds that would never
come. They were nestling somewhere near the bottom of the
alphabet, maybe R or S. Bowed and silent they continued
their routine. He thought their Utility Quotient must be
quite low. Surely these Service Citizens would soon be re-
designated, or simply dissolved? This kind of difficult problem
was for the A.B.A.C.U.S. to decide. He passed by the Service
Citizens. He ignored them, they ignored him. A Discipline
Drone hovered above, quietly policing the balance.

Inside, no one laughed, no one fucked. The dank foyer
of the museum was illuminated by an unenthusiastic, dull
orange glow that was struggling out of some ancient light
fittings. A few faded portraits of long-forgotten pioneers hung
on the walls. An engine of uncertain purpose occupied a plinth

at its centre. Kavendish shrugged. It all looked cumbersome and useless. The air was musty and unused. More like a tomb than an attraction. His feet disturbed deposits of dust that sprang up from the floor as he walked. The sound of his heels clicking echoed around the room. Everything was grey. The vaulted ceiling was high, with elaborate cornices and panels, the images painted on them now faded beyond recognition. Gothic pillars held the ceiling in place. It felt like the interior of a cathedral. There was an air of sturdy permanence in the carved stonework, confidence in its sweeping arches. Just like the edifices of the A.B.A.C.U.S., it spoke of certainty. The foyer swept under an impressive arch into a large hall that was accessed via some worn-out stone steps. The hall was filled with a variety of dusty exhibits.

Kavendish made his way down the steps and entered the exhibition hall. His eyes were drawn to a tall, tubular, metal vehicle. It had a living unit crudely bolted to the top. It seemed to be a significant exhibit judging by its prominent position in the hall. Kavendish approached with only the faintest hint of interest. A series of ladders provided access to the summit. Kavendish climbed. At the summit he found a dull, grey gantry. He stepped around the living unit until he found a grimy porthole. He wiped the glass and peered into the dark interior of the capsule. Inside there were bodies. Inert and static. Cracked plastic dummies. They were sat mutely at the controls, with great bulbous helmets on their heads like filthy fishbowls. Kavendish was puzzled, but bored. These dead things.

In the seams of the cut as the sutures dissolve
The filament weaves as the tempest revolves
Under the thin city soil the filaments creep

Through concrete and stone while the prisoner sleeps
The acorn and oak, the dandelion seed
The trunk and the bark, the stem of the weed
They come to free captives lousy with lust
They come to find secrets hidden in dust.

He descended the steps. He located the relevant sign. He
wiped away a thick layer of grime to reveal the information
underneath.

Space Capsule

His face creased into perplexed folds. Space was a dead useless
place, a vast ocean of nothing. The Museum of Ignorance
appeared to house hundreds of similarly pointless artefacts,
the relics of a more unfortunate time. There were trinkets
pillaged at the point of a bayonet. Ugly, brutal, barbaric things
that made Kavendish wince. A primitive motorised vehicle.
Why would anyone want to go anywhere? A pre-A.B.A.C.U.S.
computer. Inefficient. Incorrect. Why were they here, these
dull instruments? Kavendish wondered why they hadn't been
dissolved long ago. That was the way of things.

The Great Equilibrium

The sound of his footsteps ricocheted around the shrine
of futile things. All around him, shadows hid spores that
settled on the barren materials. Hoping to gain the slightest
purchase in the gloom. Further down the hall he came across
more cracked dummies. They were bent over an open wound
filled with plastic gore. They held knives and saws. They
wore masks and gowns. One of the cracked dummies had

lost an eye to decay. She was consulting some type of medical
appliance. A plastic patient was lying on the surgeon's table.
The patient would always lie there. No hope of recovery.
No chance to walk again or spend quiet hours in the arms
of its loving plastic family. He thanked the A.B.A.C.U.S. for
his 'How Are You?' device. All these cabinets full of archaic
contraptions. The fetishes of ignorance.

The Great Equilibrium

The hall narrowed into a passageway that was lined with
noticeboards full of informative nonsense. Kavendish
wandered past, barely registering. He began to move down
lanes, paths, byways, snickets. The fusty interior of the
museum came apart as he stepped. He was in the park. He
was heavily stoned. He was slumped against the trunk of a
gnarled tree, the same unruly tree he had encountered earlier.
The tree loomed over him. From out of the branches a figure
muttered, a conclave of hooded acolytes chanted, a Discipline
Drone hovered. Everything was out of focus. He caught
sight of something from the corner of his eye. There was an
unmistakable shadow of a figure sat at the end of the echoing
corridor. Kavendish was drawn towards it like a hapless
insect sucked into a whirlpool. The figure sat at the end of
the vortex. Beckoning him. Kavendish spiralled out of the
building and into the sky. The dark empty sky. He travelled
towards a dimly flickering light that hovered on the edge of
space. As he drew nearer the light, it became brighter. Too
bright to look at. Like a thousand suns focused to a point of
unbearable intensity. Kavendish raised his hands to shield his
eyes, fearing he would go blind.

Eyes without sight, vision or focus. No lens or pupil,
motion or locus.

He was back in the corridor. The dust of the museum dancing
in the weak shafts thrown by the pendulous light fittings.
A wizened administrator sat dozing at a tired-looking
information kiosk. An old man. Kavendish had never seen an
old Service Citizen before. In fact, he wasn't sure he had ever
met anyone old. Service Citizens were young and vigorous.
Useful. Useless things must be dissolved. It was the way of
things. Demand must be managed if desires are to be satisfied.

The old man seemed completely unaware of Kavendish.
He remained motionless. Still. Static. For a few moments
Kavendish thought he might be an exhibit. Another cracked
dummy enacting another pointless task. Closer. Closer. He
was so close now he could smell his musty odour. The scent of
soil and decay. Closer. Closer. Inches from his back. His breath
ruffled the hairs on the old man's neck. The fine follicles
waved in the breeze of breath and then settled back gently
into the folds of his ancient skin. The old man turned around
slowly, rising like an uncoiling snake. As the old man settled
on his feet, he enacted a mocking bow. He adjusted his cap on
his balding pate. Two plumes of curly orange hair stuck out
from the sides of his head. He looked like an old-fashioned
clown. His uniform was tatty, held together with mismatched
patches. His shoes were not a pair; they didn't even seem to
be the same size. He fixed Kavendish with a look that was
both amused and dismissive.

'Are you lost?'

A smile seeped out of the old man's skin, settling into a
grotesque crescent. He drew closer to Kavendish. Walking
around him, sizing him up, as if he was examining a newly

found artefact. The old man produced a monocle from his pocket, placing it over his left eye, then his right. He looked Kavendish up and down. The monocle had no lens in it.

'Are you a scholar? You have the look of a scholar, if you don't mind me saying so. A wise face. Is it your own?'

The old man drew his face up to Kavendish's. His eyes were black. Bottomless pits. Kavendish could smell his breath. It smelled of honey. The old man tapped a gnarled finger on the translucent screen of Kavendish's Sensory Nexus Mask.

'Do I know you? I feel we have met before. Or will meet soon. I forget.'

The old man tapped his forehead with a bent finger. His head moved from side to side as if his face was being slapped by an invisible hand. His tongue dangling out like a strangled man. Eyes crossed. A resident of Bedlam. His face snapped back, suddenly serious. Riddled with reflection. He looked younger. Closer to Kavendish's age than the wizened, bent creature he had first met. His black eyes sparkled.

'Are the artefacts not to your taste? You look disappointed. Is this not what you were expecting?'

Kavendish tried to form words but his mouth was a jumble of roots. His tongue was a trunk, pitted and bent. The old man. Now a young man. Tilted his head in curiosity. The clown entity thrust out its arm. Like a tentacle covered in suckers. The arm wrapped around the roots. The arm tugged and pulled. The roots began to separate from the soil. Blood filled his mouth. Kavendish spat out gore and teeth. The clown entity's eyes bored into him. You shall not pass. You shall not pass. The clown spun him around. The clown spun too.

'I'm a scholar and a dancer, once a famous romancer! Quite the twinkletoes in days gone by. All the people said so.'

A medieval jester. A fool. A joker. You shall not pass. You shall not pass. The A.B.A.C.U.S., the gossip module, the Sensory Nexus mask. The Discipline Drone. You shall not pass. The roots resurged. The roots began to twine around the entity's tentacle. Suffocating and cutting. The roots wrapped the suckers tight. The arm was cut, falling to the dusty floor of the museum. The old man merely looked puzzled as his body evaporated into the murky air. As he dissolved, he tipped his hat theatrically, leaving a vague outline of a final bow hanging in the gloom.

The corridor was empty. The information kiosk was empty too. A Cleaning Drone hovered past.

> *In the seams of the cut as the sutures dissolve*
> *The filament weaves as the tempest revolves*
> *Under the thin city soil the filaments creep*
> *Through concrete and stone while the prisoner sleeps*
> *The acorn and oak, the dandelion seed*
> *The trunk and the bark, the stem of the weed*
> *They come to free captives lousy with lust*
> *They come to find secrets hidden in dust.*

Kavendish stood in a glum trance. He was facing a drab room filled with dusty shelves. They were stuffed with endless rows of files and folios. The acorn had led him here. Into this pleasureless palace of ignorance. It was no fun, no fun at all. Difficult situations call for reliable solutions. Kavendish felt inside his pockets. His fingers lighted on the smooth surface of a stimulant vial. Perfect. He needed something speedy to focus his mind. He pulled the vial free of his pocket. But it was slippery, and it slid through his fingers. The capsule rolled across the old wooden floor and disappeared under one of the shelves.

He sank to his knees in the manner of a supplicant, pressing his cheek to the floor. He could see it glinting in the gloom. Kavendish attempted to reach under the shelf to pull it free. It remained out of reach. He activated the torch on his mask. The light lit up the shadows. The vial was wedged in the crack of a door. A door. Hidden behind a shelf. There was a gap between the shelves and the wall that was just wide enough for Kavendish's modest frame to squeeze through. He shuffled through the crack until he reached the door. He manged to free his hands. He located the door handle. He pushed and grunted. The door creaked open. The vial, now free of the door, clinked down the stairs and disappeared into the dark. Kavendish instinctively recoiled. Darkness. As unfamiliar as the wastes of space. As rare as a rainstorm in summer. Darkness. It was ugly and repulsive. But the need for speed was too great. He stepped inside. The cold stone stairwell stank of ancient damp and was decorated with a complex latticework of cobwebs that the spiders had abandoned years ago.

His torch lit up the stairwell as he revolved like a lighthouse lamp. He took in the Stygian surroundings. He brushed away the cobwebs, blowing and spitting as they collided with his mouth. The torch played across the drab steps. He spotted the vial in the middle of an old, grey flagstone. Kavendish headed down the steps, keeping his torch fixed on the vial, trying to blot out the darkness that pressed all around him. He stooped to collect it. He examined the delicate white powder, it's clear crystalline shine standing testament to its potency. Kavendish smiled. His torch lit up the room beyond the vial. As above, so below. This room was also full of shelves packed with grimy boxes. Kavendish had no desire to investigate these dull containers. He turned around and began to climb the stairs, eager for daylight and drugs. But his feet were fixed to the flagstones. As he tried to lift his feet from their imperceptible bonds, the staircase flattened out into an endless tunnel. The floor changed from cold stone to a viscous bitumen that began to suck his feet under the surface. Branches, like the arms of barbaric wrestlers, burst out of the walls, entwining their sinewy limbs around his torso. Tiny tendrils sprouted from the bark and began to crawl across his face. They insinuated themselves into his eyes. He could feel them, inching through his nerves. Entering his brain. Altering the pathways. Kavendish saw himself as a child in the hatcheries. As an old man. He saw his friends from the Nexus. Fucking, sucking, pointing. They were surging around him like phantoms, swirling up into the black void. The eddies from their frantic reel spun Kavendish around. His feet made a sickening sound in the glutinous river as he turned. The nightmarish figures swirled. Pointing, pointing, pointing. Then they were gone. Kavendish was facing the vault once again.

He located a panel of old brass switches. Tarnished and filthy. He flicked them on. The bulbs sputtered into life, emitting the same dull glow as the museum above. Now he could see the entire room. It had an arched ceiling like a wine cellar constructed from brick. It was full of metal shelves identical to the ones in the room above. There were no tables, no chairs; this was clearly a forgotten storeroom.

Kavendish explored the shelves. Digging in dirt and dust. Small tornados of crumbling fragments mushroomed as he removed each box from its shelf. He produced an elaborately monogrammed handkerchief to wipe away the layer of grime that had gathered on his mask. Why he searched he could not say. Curiosity was not a feature of modern life. But something lurked in the archive. Something hidden.

SCIENCE MINISTRY CAT NO – 0006754

CONTENTS – photographs, graphite pencil sketches, field
notes, biographical ephemera
LOCATION – Caxton Wood. Sector 9
A.B.A.C.U.S. CONCLUSION – irrelevant/dangerous . . .
destruction recommended

Kavendish lifted the box off the shelf, leaving a dark rectangle
in the dust. It was tightly sealed with bright yellow and black
tape. DESTRUCTION RECOMMENDED. The faintest feeling
of recognition flickered. The knot. The root. He clasped the
box close to his chest, cradling it like a new-born child. He left
the vault and headed for the surface.

Kavendish walked around the table like a wary animal
circling a waterhole. He had placed his find at its centre. The
box was present. The box was now. A faint hum hovered in
the room. He moved closer to the box. Pulled in like a fish
caught on a line. Filthy nails on wizened fingers. Gnarled
digits jutting from decaying hands. The clown entity's face.
Lift the lid. Look inside. Voices whispered. Lift the lid. Look
inside. His hands felt for edges. His fingers bent round the
crease. The lid began to rise.

The box was deep. Deeper than a well. It was empty. Not
simply an absence of objects but a pure anti-object. A void.
Kavendish was disappointed. The pleasure café. The narc
parlour. These were the places where useful work could be
done, and where true discoveries could be made. He picked up
the battered lid and went to replace it.

Who will carry the weight of the golden seed to the door?
Who will turn the key to the vault under the floor?

Who will find the prize hidden deep within the tomb?
Who will see the lights glinting in the gloom?

The hum changed pitch, up and down the scale like a child let loose on a synthesiser. The light in the museum grew darker and darker. Night was approaching. Dread night. Dread darkness. Kavendish needed light to live. Like an orchid in a hothouse, he could only flourish when the sun shone. Night was a curse. Sleep was a curse. His eyes swizzled to catch a beam. The box was glowing. Holy sun. Holy light. He looked into the box. Patterns were forming, slowly becoming solid. Objects. Things. Artefacts. He looked down into the box. The light in the room reverted to the dull glow of ancient lamps. The hum settled into silence. The box was still a box. But now it was full.

Inside there was an assortment of papers and documents. Some printed with official stamps and letterheads, others handwritten in an almost childlike scrawl. There were graphs and tables, assorted lists and annotations. There were photographs too. A face stared out from the stack. A woman's face. His face. Aquiline and handsome. Dark hair cut into a rough bob. Clothing functional but worn with flare. Kavendish picked it up and studied it. Something in the curve of her mouth, the tone of her eyes, the shape of her limbs. It was an undefinable reflection. A feeling of connection across time. Her figure again, this time standing with a ragged-looking man. Long beard. Unkempt. A hint of wild eyes behind thick spectacles. They appeared to be on an expedition. They were stood around a makeshift bivouac. Canvas carelessly hung from trees, a pile of scientific gadgets at their feet. They were smiling. In the foreground was the handsome woman. She was holding the camera at arm's length, attempting to capture the moment for posterity. The picture disturbed him. It was the sky. The sky was dark. Dark. But not black. There was light. The blankness of the vault was alive with tiny luminous pinpricks, dotting the inky darkness like sequins on velvet. A thousand glimmering particles cast into the sky by the hand of some careless god. Kavendish had never seen the stars before. No one had. The dark was where useless things dwelt. Where time was wasted and pleasure forgotten. The dark must be dissolved like all the other useless things. Her face. His face. This woman. She occupied a very different dimension to him. A dimension of darkness. A dimension of contrast and change. Her face. His face.

Who will carry the weight of the golden seed to the door?
Who will turn the key to the vault under the floor?
Who will find the prize hidden deep within the tomb?
Who will see the lights glinting in the gloom?

He pulled out more documents from the box, spreading them out on the table. They were meaningless. Scribbles and charts. Another picture. Scrolls and accolades. Gowns. Awards. Professor Helen Cavendish, chair of Psychic Ecology, Caxton University. His face. Her face. She was a scholar. Someone with something to learn. Doubts rose like a spring tide. Inside the Great Equilibrium, a fault line grew. He looked into the box. Unfamiliar feelings of curiosity spread inside his nodes. He removed more documents. Scribbles and charts. Ignorant signs and markers. At the bottom of the stack was an obsidian shape. Kavendish recoiled. The clown entity's face. You shall not pass. You shall not pass. The hum in the room gathered its volume again. He would have run if he could, but there was nowhere to run to. There was only

the box. The box and Kavendish. He placed his arms
reluctantly into the cauldron and pulled out the final artefact.

It was a book. Reeking of soil and decay. The cover was
thick and unyielding. Constructed from tree bark. On the
front was a knot of thorny branches cut into the wood. Above
the carving were words. Barbaric, unruly, useless words.
Drawn by a faltering hand.

The Tangle.

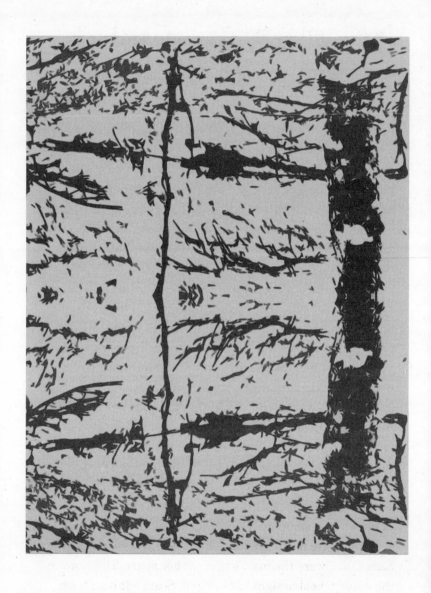

In Caxton Wood

In Caxton Wood the branches rattled together in warning
as the swarm approached. Their torches flickered through
the thicket. Muffled cries and angry shouts. A grim echo
of their impotent fury. In their hands they carried cudgels,
pitchforks, shovels, broken chair legs and a variety of other
ersatz armaments. Objects repurposed from everyday use to
bludgeon and beat the enemy. They were seeking scapegoats
and sacrifices to appease their vengeful god. In a forest of
obstinate indifference.

As the rain poured through the crown of trees, Elizabeth
Duncan trembled under the spreading oak. There was
nowhere left to run. She had been selected as an offering
to the flames. A solemn oblation to insure against another
poor harvest and the return of the pox. The villagers did not
care for her kind, or any other outsider. She lived alone in
the woods; it wasn't right. So as the first sores of the plague
began to weep and the stock market crashed, the villagers
looked for reasons for their bad luck. Some pointed towards
the woods and the humble cottage of Elizabeth Duncan.
She must be a witch. A concubine of the devil. Sent to bring
down ill fortune on the people. Her appearance counted
against her: a stooping frame that was bent from a lifetime
of misuse. She had a random cluster of blood vessels on her
face. These were the marks that set her apart. These were
the unmistakeable signs of the devil. Scars left over from

their unholy congress. The blemished must carry the weight
of their sin.

Jeremiah Cavendish urged the mob on. His sombre
clothing matched his puritan beliefs and rendered him
virtually invisible in the darkness of the wood. Only the dull
glow of his torch lit his righteous grimace. He was the law.
County magistrate, managing director, diligent administrator,
temporal and spiritual. He abhorred the criminal, the sinful
and the blasphemous. He sought out the pickpockets, the
thieves, the traitors, the rogue traders, the witches. He
applied techniques of persuasion, learned in the trenches
where the rules of engagement were forgotten. He never
failed to get the confessions he sought and would apply the
maximum penalty on every occasion. Death. The purifying
flames, the snap of the noose, the salvation of the axe and
sword. Hell would soon overflow with the worthless. Only
then could the elect flourish.

'Come, my brothers and sisters! Forward my brethren,
we have work to do.'

There was always work to do. Out here where no train
ever stopped. A dot on the map on the way to somewhere else.
A cry echoed around the density of the wood.

'Here, here, here!'

They came upon Elizabeth Duncan under the spreading
oak. They snarled and slavered. Surrounding her with a ring
of righteous hate.

'Seize her! Hold her fast!'

Jeremiah Cavendish pushed his way through the company
to where two farmhands were holding the weeping figure
of Elizabeth Duncan. They grasped her thin arms with
unkindness, causing bruises to rise on her broken skin. There
was no need for such force. She was defeated and without the

resources to resist. But the men feared the power of demons. They may yet rise and surge through her bedraggled frame, lifting her into the endless mystery of night, away from the pyre or the hungry noose. Jeremiah Cavendish feared it too. He slapped the captive hard. The power of the spirit fortifying his palms. The sting of flesh on flesh aroused the magistrate. The fire of punishment tingled on his palm like stigmata. The work was good. He slapped her face again. Her head turned violently. Her thin neck unable to offer any resistance. Blood bloomed from her cuts and stained the forest floor.

'Now we have you, whore of Satan! Prepare the fire! Build the pyre! Quickly now, quickly!'

The burly men tied Elizabeth to the trunk of the oak. The rope bit. Rough twine binding her with an excessive thickness. Three members of the local constabulary stood guard, shotguns held menacingly at her face. Elizabeth's fingers pressed against the bark of the tree. The bark seemed to yield to her touch as if it was trying to offer her some comfort. Her fingers sank into its ridges. She longed to sink into those ridges too. To hide in the cracks until the ignorant tide had ebbed. She was not of the Tangle, though she was sympathetic to its pulse. The roots felt the embryo of awareness growing in this unremarkable being. These were the allies it sought. Those it could send to the world of men. To find things. To act where it could not. She was not a stranger to the forest. Its fruits had sustained her, and its herbs had healed her. At night she had danced amongst the trees to the impalpable melody of silence. But for now, she must face the flood. Some industrious villagers had gathered up a pile of brush wood. While others, hoping to impress the magistrate with demonstrations of zeal, had begun to snap the branches from the oak tree to add to the pyre. The tree groaned and thrashed in the wind as the steady deluge of rain fell. Elizabeth could feel the tree's complaining pulse through her fingers. Sympathy flowed between them.

The ridges of bark were scars on her arms. Branches were arms covered in scars. Torn from her sockets as the villagers snapped. Her fingers were twigs, bent as they fell. The sticks were the fingers pointing to hell.

The mob worked hard as the cold rain mocked them. Like one great excited organism they built their altar. Ties were loosened. Jackets discarded. Sleeves rolled up. Saws and axes chewed and bit. The sap dripped into the soil.

Under the loam the fluids combined, joined by the flow and the surge of the flood, into the roots the blood and the muscle, torn from the witches born in the mud.

Elizabeth closed her eyes and drifted into the trunk. Her blood seeped into the pith, into the veins of the leaves, and down. Down into the roots. The intimacy of fluids combining. Deep in the wooden heart of the forest. In the clearing the villagers lit their brands. Sparks leapt from flints. The lessons the lightning taught, made deadly by human hands. Tied to the trunk, the husk of Elizabeth Duncan waited to wither in the flames.

The villagers took her body, punching, slapping and poking at it with lustful fists. They dragged her across the ground and tied her to the stake. The rain spat contempt through the leaves, forming into black pools around the place of execution. Jeremiah Cavendish walked to the pyre with his sputtering torch raised high.

'In the name of all that is holy, I cast Satan out of this village. With fire I cast you out! With fire I send you to hell! With flame I cast you out! With flame I cast you out! With flame! With flame!'

His sodden suit weighed heavily on his shoulders. His black city brogues were claggy and sucked in the muck as he strode. His hair hung like miserable curtains over his temples, the pomade too diluted to stick. But the fire in his belly could not be so easily quenched. He thrust the torch into the kindling. It would not burn.

'Bring me the oil, quickly now, quickly.'

An eager lieutenant carried a pitcher. Jeremiah Cavendish sprinkled the oil over the sticks. Every fibre of the broken forest resisted the flame. Here and there the fire would catch hold. The flame struggling to a peak before collapsing into a blue pool, then finally vanishing. Jeremiah Cavendish cursed and threw on more oil. But the sap dowsed the flame again. Around the glade, the wood groaned as the tempest grew. The rain hammered the people of the village. In the damp their blood frenzy was subsiding. Rumbles of discontent broke out. Fears of the demon's revenge. The beast has sent the rain to drown God's flame. Some began to cower from the woods as it pressed in around them.

'Hang the witch!'

An enterprising bank clerk spoke up. Murmurs of approval amongst the villagers. Nods, shrugs, hideous grins.

'Hang her! hang her!'

'Take her down, if you please, Mr Wheeler.'

A stern-faced sergeant stepped over the steaming faggots and cut the ropes. Elizabeth's battered body was dragged from the pyre and taken back to the tree again. A rope and noose were flung over one of the oak's high branches. Inside the

tree, the hybrid soul of wood and woman watched. They began
to hoist her broken body up. Her legs kicked in feeble protest.
Awful spasms jolted through her empty frame, making her
body twist in unnatural directions. One last dance in the thick
darkness of night. Then she was gone. The face of Jeremiah
Cavendish was caught in the guttering torch light. He looked
like a gargoyle melting in the rain. In the grain, the cells of
a woman became cells of the wood. Senses dissolved to be
replaced by nameless perceptions. These undefinable faculties
studied the magistrate. They read the grim satisfaction in
the subtle upturn of his lips. The crack of a branch as the
lightning struck. Jeremiah Cavendish froze. He was in the
Tangle now, not the boardroom. His pious cruelty had no
meaning here. The tree creaked and swayed, shaking the
useless shell from its bough. The body of Elizabeth Duncan
crashed to the floor at his feet. The villagers scattered.
Leaving cudgels and kitchen knives behind. The constables,
no more than criminals with badges, waved their shotguns
at phantoms. The sergeant drew his service revolver from its
holster. Jeremiah Cavendish closed his eyes and prayed. He
stood before the Kaiser's demon cavalry in Flanders Fields. He
nursed his father, rotten with pox. He watched his dead son
eaten by rats. He watched as the graves filled with the flood.
He saw the rain and the lightning flash.

The Tangle sensed their passing. Through leaf and root, it
marked them.

Ten summers passed in Caxton Wood. Flames burned
bright in its dark interior. Gallows swayed and heads rolled.
The ranks of the dead swelled under the spreading leaves. On
the oak tree, the green shoots of repair hardened into sturdy
boughs. Elizabeth was not yet nothing. She was a wraith,
a phantom, still residually connected to the human frame.

Bit by bit, all that had once been her would be liquidated and transformed. She drifted through the soil like a vapour. Curling through stems, visiting the stamen of flowers as she merged with the bright corolla of summer petals. Not yet nothing. Waiting. Waiting. Waiting to perform her final human obligation. In the Tangle, time was already a concept to which she was no longer shackled. Patience was its own reward. She had almost forgotten the creaking rigidity of her former human existence. But still she carried the burden. The reminders were never too far away; the clearing, the chopping, the hacking and burning, all steadily diminished the forest. The hands of the villagers were always ready with the axe and rope. She would never forget the rope.

In the village, things had settled into the familiar pattern of semi-feudal life. Regimes changed with regularity in the far-off parliament. But out here, nothing had changed. In Caxton, tithes were paid, their children got sick, and livings were scratched from the land. The facades of modernity were evident: electric lights, motor cars for those who could afford them, tractors, banks, a hospital, and even a telephone or two. But for most it was still the scythe or the quarry. The local flint was prized in the city and a minor aristocracy had grown up around its exploitation. Gold pocket watches and Savile Row blazers. The river would carry the flint down to the docks. The boatsmen never tarried in Caxton's zombie port, where vessels were loaded by silent men with suspicious faces. The land remained in the hands of a few wealthy landowners, whose disdain for the lower orders was worn with pride. Breeding and the divine rights of birth held sway. Suffrage was not suffered here. Around the village, the tides of atheism broke on the rocks of their faith. Long ago church and state had gone their separate ways, but in

Caxton, the Lord's word was still the law. They praised him as they always had, with blood. With sacrifice. But the great depression had bitten hard in the world beyond the village, and now rumours of war began to percolate through the populace. Still, those brewing storms were of little concern out here. Here the conflict took on a different dimension. Some heretics who'd placed their faith in stocks and shares had been inconvenienced. Some had chosen the fall from Ardlington viaduct or deliverance by shot and gunfire. Some had perished in the flames. The pyre in Caxton Wood. The pyre and the rope. Others would burn soon.

As the world prepared to be torn apart, there was a great feeling of unity in the village. They had all played their part, and now they worked together to build a new church. For the elect. For Caxton. The old church had recently burned down, victim of an unfortunate lightning strike on another fateful night. The vengeance of demons was the rumour. The Tangle's languid timetable of retribution had been set in motion.

Eyes without sight, vision or focus. No lens or pupil, motion or locus.

What was once Elizabeth had felt the church burn from the crown of a sycamore tree. Patience was its own reward. The villagers worked tirelessly to restore the temple to its former glory. They sang hymns to fortify themselves against the elements as they placed stone upon stone. It would rise again greater than ever, that was their solemn vow.

The spectral residue flowed through the trees, down through their trunks and out into the bushes that formed the limit of the wood. The last fragment of Elizabeth settled into the budding fruit of a bramble bush. Aware of the villagers

going about their work. By scent, by vibration, by senses with
no name. The remaining pillars of the burned-out church
had been torn down and building work on the new structure
was well underway. The frame of the building was rising,
the outline of its form beginning to take shape. It was to be
a modest church, in keeping with the austerity of the times.
A simple church for righteous people. The church would be
made by sweat and sacrifice. By hand and muscle. No lathe or
machine would spoil its beams.

*Eyes without sight, vision or focus. No lens or pupil,
    motion or locus.*

The residue sensed the carpenters gathering with their
long logging saws and double-handed axes. The magistrate
pulled into the site in his Hillman saloon. He consulted
with the architect and the foreman. They bent over plans
and diagrams. The needs of the structure were debated.
Instructions were given. The carpenters gathered their tools.
They stepped on the path to the heart of the forest. They
came to cut. They came to claim a trunk. The last fragment
of Elizabeth. The last sliver of the absurd entity she once was
flowed back through the forest. Sensing her chance had come.

The phantom seeped back into the trunk of the old
oak, settling deep inside the grain of the wood. She waited.
Absorbing the movements of the men through the filaments.
The carpenters had marched in ragged procession from the
village and were now entering the clearing. One of their
number slapped the trunk of the oak tree, as if he could divine
its provenance by touch alone.

'This will do the job, Gilbert. Let's get her down.'

'Right you are, gaffer.'

The carpenters chopped a wedge into the trunk to direct its fall. Each notch sent a spasm of sorrow through the forest. The last fragment of Elizabeth felt the disruption as she clung to the cells of the wood. Then came the agony of the crosscut saw as it bit into the trunk. Like an amputation without anaesthetic. She screamed inside. The horses they had brought to carry the severed trunk whinnied nervously and scratched the floor with their hooves. The woodland birds took flight. Only the disconnected and oblivious carpenters continued their rhythmic hacking. Soon the oak was down. It crashed into the surrounding forest, the branches of the neighbouring trees brushing against its rough bark as it fell. The carpenters loaded the trunk onto the cart and headed back to the village. The last fragment of Elizabeth waited patiently inside.

Within a few weeks the carpenters had skilfully honed beams from the trunk of the oak. The beams were then hoisted into place for the roofers to add their slates. The remaining planks were carved into benches, rough enough to keep the congregation alert to the sin of comfort. The minister and the magistrate inspected the work. God be praised, it was a fine building. A humble pulpit and simple nave. The ideal place to receive the word of the Lord. Honest wood cut from the Tangle.

'Will you and your wife be able to attend the opening on Sunday, Mr Cavendish?'

The Reverend Molin's obsequious smile was somewhat out of place on his habitually stern face. It was a stupid question, posed only to maintain the momentum of their conversation. The reverend basked in the light of the magistrate's attention.

'But of course, reverend, I would not miss such a holy occasion. God continues to work his miracles in Caxton, reverend, praise Him. The family and I will certainly add our voices to the choir, though sadly my boy is detained elsewhere, in service of the empire.'

'Ah, yes, of course, brave lad, doing his duty no doubt. Let us hope war does not come, Mr Cavendish. We will say a prayer for the boy's safety, and his swift return to the bosom of his family, on Sunday.'

Jeremiah Cavendish fixed the Reverend Molin with withering eyes. They burned through the layers of his platitudes, exposing him for the weak, stupid man he was.

'The war is already here, reverend.'

The last nails had been hammered home as the congregation gathered outside Caxton parish church. Jeremiah Cavendish and his family stood at the front, next to the other notable local dignitaries. Crisp shirts, sober ties, brushed broad-brimmed hats. The glinting chains of office. The villagers in their Sunday best stood behind them in pious ranks. The butcher. The baker. The old undertaker. The smell of moth balls and rose water drifted from the cloth. Bright scarves and spit-shined shoes disturbed the monochrome. Hard earned pretty things were quietly flaunted. The minister delivered an overly long and pompous eulogy to the holy labourers of Caxton. The mayor cut the ribbon. The Reverend Molin led the congregation inside. The last fragment of Elizabeth crouched in the rafters. Jeremiah Cavendish directed his wife and two young daughters to the front pew before positioning himself on the aisle. The church was at capacity, as it always was. The minister mounted the steps to the pulpit.

His sermon was not from a gospel anyone would recognise. It was a creed of fire, gleaned from faded scrolls long since lost. The Reverend Molin called for vigilance.

He called for vengeance and purifying deeds. He praised their fellowship and the magistrate's wisdom. He called for the gallows in the mud and the leaves. Find the sin that hides in the village. Root it out. Bring the accused to the place of judgement. Let the magistrate interpret the word. A beam creaked. The minister paused his sermon. They all looked up. It must be the building settling. The minister continued. Be mindful of those who would spread blasphemy, for they seek to undermine all we have built. Pray for our king. The king of the village. A nail dropped at the feet of the magistrate. The minister stopped, too distracted by the tumbling spike to continue. The magistrate picked up the nail. He examined it, and then turned around to fix the carpenters with his furious gaze. They in turn stared at the floor, hats held between shaking palms. They looked mortified and confused. There was devotion in their work. Pride, too, though it be a sin to show it. Every nail was driven home true and proper. The beams creaked again. Another nail fell. The congregation began to stir. Concerned glances were exchanged. More nails fell. Bolts too. People began to panic. The minister urged calm. The beams began to creak and sway. Plaster and daub now fell with the fittings. The magistrate grabbed his wife and children by the hand and tried to move towards the aisle. A large wooden beam swung down from the ceiling, blocking the way. People ran. People screamed. The air filled with dust and a shower of nails. Sharp pricks pierced skin and skull. Beams creaked and cracked. Splinters cut through cloth and burrowed into limbs. In the beams the wraith slid through the grain.

The essence writhed in the weave as the congregation came apart. But she felt nothing. She was of the Tangle now. Her compass turned on a different circumference. Pity?

What pity did they show her? She began to expand, warping the wood, changing its structure until it shattered. The splinters fell like the shells of the Somme. All around the humble pews they trampled each other in their panic. The last fragment of Elizabeth flowed into the door, tightening its frame until it was wedged into the stone. None would escape. The congregation fell on the door. Clawing and hammering. They piled up, clambering over the fallen. Faces squashed and pulped against the flagstones. Jeremiah Cavendish snatched the ceremonial scissors from the dying hand of the dusty mayor. He stabbed at the bodies that stood in his path. Slashing wildly with open blades. The Reverend Molin stood in his pulpit. Debris clattered around him. He caught the frenzied eye of the magistrate as he cut his way through the faithful. All they had built had come undone. The final splinter of what was once a woman loosened a joist from the transept and sent it across the developing ruins. It impaled the reverend through his chest. Jeremiah Cavendish caught the sound as the reverend gurgled through bubbles of blood. A wild toneless murmur. It ricocheted around the building, rising above the cries of the dying. Could no one else hear it? He tore his eyes from the corpse of the cleric and tried to move through the desperate muddle of people. The murmur turned to a moan. It bent through the frequencies. First a creek. Then a crack. Jeremiah Cavendish looked up. He thought he saw a face looking down from the buckling beams. A familiar face from a hangman's noose.

The ridges of bark were scars on her arms. Branches were arms covered in scars. Torn from her sockets as the villagers snapped. Her fingers were twigs, bent as they fell. The sticks were the fingers pointing to hell.

He remembered the crack of the branch as the lightning struck. Crack. He stood before the Kaiser's demon cavalry in Flanders Fields. He nursed his father, rotten with pox. He watched his dead son eaten by rats. He watched as the graves filled with the flood. He saw the rain and the lightening flash. Crack. Then the roof fell in.

It took four days to dig out all the bodies from the debris. It was the nails, they said. Poor quality fittings, they said. The blacksmith from Appleton was to blame. He was a drinker, they said. They hanged him. Cut his bollocks off too. The king himself came to inspect the wreckage. He said a prayer over the broken beams. Some say he cried. Caxton church was no more. Only ghosts lived there now. In the years that followed, the world made its own ghosts as the bombs fell. When the debris and dust had settled, the soldiers came home. A new world was promised, free of horror and the rule of tyrants. There was work to be done to fix all that had been broken. In Caxton, a young man dressed in the uniform of an army captain took his kitbag from his shoulder and unlocked the door of his old family home. The master was coming. A new flock would follow in time. They would work the land again and prosper. They would build their church on the foundations of the ruins. They would fear the Lord. They would be vigilant. In Caxton Wood the branches rattled together in warning.

Furniture

Elizabeth Duncan had long since ceased to be. Her petty
human grievances had been erased. She was nothing. And
in her nothingness, she was complete. Now she was of the
Tangle. She was of the roots. A zephyr flowing between the
plants of the forest. Everywhere. Nowhere. Like God. Age
was not something that was measured here. There were no
beginnings to mark. Everything was now. Everything was
nothing. But, by human reckoning, thirty-five years had
passed in the wizened wood. This May morning in the year
of their Lord 1974, cells that were once human drifted in the
spores of a fungus. The fresh spring breeze carrying them
over the forest in search of a place to grow. In Hamble's Dell
the spores settled on a human bag. This was a popular spot
for people to discreetly discard their domestic waste, old
mattresses, broken sinks, piles of pornographic magazines.
Cells that were once human detected fragments of old
curiosity stubbornly clinging to the membrane. It was not for
the Tangle, the grotesque parade of events that made up the
lives of those outside. Here in the roots such concerns would
decay in time as all human concerns do. But an obscure layer
of the Tangle was itself still human. It contained its essence.

*Under the loam the fluids combined, joined by the flow
and the surge of the flood, into the roots the blood and
the muscle, torn from the witches born in the mud.*

That occult essence now stirred. Curious and wary. It sank into the discarded bag.

Inside, the heat of decay was beginning to swell, but had not so far grown so potent as to destroy the contents. The essence drifted amongst them, examining each item carefully. Clothes. Women's clothes. It detected a scent clinging to the weave. A perfume designed to imitate the fragrance of a forest flower. Wild approximations of nature. It found an item that looked like a journal. The cover was covered in drawings that suggested daydreams and a potent imagination. Bizarre hieroglyphs like the illuminations of a gospel. Stick figures entwined in exotic relief between the marks. The essence slipped around the words, turning in the curves of the letters to find their meaning.

I am a stranger here. A traveller washed up on the margins of God knows where. This town is like a museum. The locals are polite enough, I guess. Quiet. Andrew? He was charming. Friendly. Like a blank slate. Nothing seems to have stuck to him at all over the years. I'm enjoying showing him. Books. Films. Life. Love. Is it love? We are heading to London for a weekend of dusty bookshops and dangerous dive bars. That's what I'm in for. He says he's never been. He knows so little. I have so much to tell him

We spent the weekend in town. Bed. Plans to elope.
I worry I might be happy.

It curled into a full stop. Love. What was love? When the essence was human it had experienced some unwanted attention. Intimacy forced, but never shared. But they were all under the earth now. It had seen them rotting in the mire. Here in the woods, here in the roots, here in the Tangle, feelings were not named. No love, no anger, no disappointment, no happiness. There were no feelings. Only the sensation of an endless riddle unfolding. The essence slipped around the bag looking for tags and labels. Agatha Denholm. It found her name stitched into the lining of a coat. Names. Names would soon be forgotten. It passed the heart-shaped doodling, the education of a trivial man. The love given freely and the passion for knowledge shared. Now Agatha's words took on a darker weight as the entropy of human relationships took its course. Disappointment, prevarication, betrayal.

I really don't know what I was expecting, I feel so stupid. Of course, he's married. I spotted the family out at the seaside. Kids too. He's just like the others, all those men with their hollow words and empty promises. The vain, shallow sack of a man. I'm such a fool.

This town is hell. I can't go anywhere without pointing fingers and wagging tongues. The atmosphere here. It's suffocating. If only I'd seen through it all. The lies came so easily. Andrew? That's not even his name. He's a Cavendish. Timothy Cavendish. That family. If only I'd known. So charming. So skilled at subterfuge. His father saw to it that I lost my job. That clan. The Cavendishs are trying to destroy me inch by inch. I hear rumours. I should be careful.

Cavendish. When the essence was a human he had hung her from a tree. The magistrate, the magus, the managing director. These were his progeny. If Agatha was in his power she would burn and dangle, just as Elizabeth had.

I just don't think I was made for these times, this town, this time warp. Tradition like a tourniquet. There is no one to turn to. The family rule like tyrants. No one will say a word. No future, no love, no hope. I just can't. I won't. Timothy has agreed to meet in Caxton Wood. Away from prying eyes. I'll tell him what I think. He can't get away with treating me like this. I want nothing from him or his family. Just my reputation and a chance to get out of this stifling prison.

But there was no way out of Caxton. The essence began to decay. Its identity collapsing as another took her place. She had fulfilled her obligation the day she brought the roof down on the parishioners. It was time for her to mutate. The essence drifted out of the bag like smoke. Sliding into the roots. Into the cells. Becoming nothing. Along the knotted highways. The essence. Losing its singularity. Multiplying. Searching for Agatha. The forest sensed a disturbance. An expectant chatter spread; psyche joining body. A new ghost for the wood. The essence bent through the fibres of a young ash tree, travelling along its branches, along the rough bark. It met the fibrous knot of a rope. At the end of the rope, in the mouth of a noose, a body swung like a grim pendulum. Once full of hopes and dreams, but now a simple husk. At her feet was a familiar face. He had changed. This was not the body he had occupied all those years ago, but it was him nonetheless. Another hangman, another Cavendish.

*

Minutes, seconds, hours, days. Pointless notches on the continuum. Meaningless markers set out by humans to convince themselves they were getting somewhere. Agatha stood at the threshold of a new dimension. Her body hung undiscovered in the woodland glade; her assassin had returned to the town. With her death the curious fragment died too. The last splinters of a human consciousness had been tidied away and absorbed. Now there was only the Tangle. Agatha stood in her place. Newly hatched, uncertain and anxious. She had been a woman of the city, of bricks and doors, of couches and beds, roads and traffic lights. She had seldom visited the woods while she was alive and always felt uneasy when she had. Too much muck and the chance of rain. But she was welcome now. In time she would forget the seduction of things, but for now she hovered in the flux between two worlds. She was not yet of the Tangle. She could not pass over the threshold until the bitter anchor she carried was discarded and her duty to the Goddess discharged.

The ridges of bark were scars on her arms. Branches were arms covered in scars. Torn from her sockets as the cruel man snapped. Her fingers were twigs, bent as they fell. The sticks were the fingers pointing to hell.

The machine had replaced the fallibility of human craft, but a few artisans still plied their trade in the town. Their faulty notches came at a premium for those seeking authenticity in their furniture. A group of these artisans were out scouting for materials. Just like their ancestors, they were looking for trees to cut into planks and spokes. Agatha hadn't gone far since her demise, but she was already decaying. Her body had been gradually consumed by the entities of the wood. Bugs. Rats. Microbes. This was the funeral sacrament of the Tangle. A becoming. To nothing. To nowhere. Yet Agatha still was.

She was in the knots of trunks. She was in branches and leaves. She was in the glade when the craftsmen came.

Eyes without sight, vision or focus. No lens or pupil,
motion or locus.

She studied the forms that stood in the clearing. She knew the young Goodridge boys from around town. They were a family of whittlers. So when they arrived in the forest with their axes and chainsaws, she knew their purpose. This was the chance to travel back to the world of men. Back to the town. To step once again on its broken pavements. To find young Tim and do him in. To satisfy the debt he owed. For all the knots. For all the lives cut short. As the Goodridge boys cut, she flowed into the severed trunk and waited.

Bartholomew Goodridge & Sons were Caxton's finest cabinet makers, where the fruits of the forest were turned into works of art in their workshops. They were best known for their beds. In their dextrous hands the wood was carved and bent. Topped with mattresses of exquisite comfort and generous depth. 'You'll feel so good in a Goodridge bed, you'll never want to get up' was how the advert went. The picture was of a laughing woman holding a steaming cup of tea, with an anxious-looking boy in his school uniform about to miss the school bus as his father languished in the comfort of his Goodridge bed. Private schools. Traditional values. The message would have been a calculated slap in the face had it been meant for the world outside. Three-day week. Power cuts and strikes. The country was struggling. But these beds were not designed for outsiders. These beds were not for the sinful backs of city folk. Goodridge beds were for the new aristocracy. The rural plutocrats directing their vassals from remote offices in Caxton's holy shire. Their brokers bought Panamanian bonds while they lived out lives of isolated feudal harmony. That was the way of things. Goodridge beds. For the elect. The summit of the social pyramid, like owning a Rolls-Royce. Roger Goodridge ran his finger over the smooth varnished headboard of their 'Golden Sleigh' model; it was a popular design amongst the country elite. Cavendish senior. A royal stamp of approval. Once he was satisfied that everything was in perfect order, Roger nodded to the foreman to begin preparing the bed for delivery.

'Well, this is marvellous, isn't it, darling?'

Timothy Cavendish patted the mattress like the neck of a horse. Karol Cavendish smiled thinly, holding a neatly folded pile of sheets. Timothy returned her smile with an unconvincing smirk. Their game continued. Gaoler and prisoner. She got what she could for her children, that was her only comfort. Divorce was unthinkable. In these days. In this place. Once the trap was sprung, you were held fast with bonds stronger than the ropes. Just like the ropes he favoured. She could not leave. This town had taken it all: her hope, her money, her will. Patrols kept them safe and the sinful at bay.

The magistrate, the magus, the managing director.

Karol placed the linen on the mattress and patted it wistfully. She knew not to get too attached to it. It would all have to be replaced soon. This was the third new bed in five years. They both knew why. Offerings. Sacrifices. She couldn't face occupying the same space afterwards. Every wrinkle and draft-blown feather was a reminder. A new bed and no questions. No one ever asked questions. In any case, the police would be no help.

The magistrate, the magus, the managing director.

She had never asked him to drive Agatha out of the town.
He said she had left and that he'd never see her again. She
never wanted anything bad to happen to any of them. But
bad things did happen. She sensed it. Her suspicion grew with
every muddy track on the carpet, every late-night bonfire,
every cut on his hand. He did so hate inconvenience.

The sunlight sliced through the gloom, playing over
Karol's face like a nagging child. She stirred, managing to
crank open one eyelid, which lifted like a reluctant garage
door through her Valium haze. Her husband's ill-defined
form lay still beneath the sheets next to her. He must be
asleep, which was strange as he was usually an early riser.
She was dimly aware of his face pointing towards the ceiling.
She wouldn't try to wake him. Time spent without him was
time well spent. Karol gathered her jelly limbs and quietly
shuffled out the door. In the bed, Timothy Cavendish lay as
still as a corpse, his arms and legs frozen and unbending.
His breathing had stopped too. His blood no longer flowed
through his veins, no pulse, no metabolic functions at all. But
he was not dead. He had merely been paused.

Eight hours ago, Timothy had slipped into the fresh new
sheets. Tired after fresh exertions in the wood. Another
escape from the mundane world of respectability he so
despised. He had enjoyed his fun with Agatha, and he was
sorry it had ended. But once the game was up there was
nothing for it but to pack her in. Clean up the mess. Tie up
loose ends. His father would expect it. As he nestled into
the duck down pillow, he thought of her. Her presence was
apparent. He could detect her scent in the smooth wood of
the bed frame, its grain like the soft warmth of her skin.

Agatha's face, too, was as clear as day. It was almost like she was in bed with him. But the film he had so carefully constructed from his memories refused to play. No matter how hard he tried to capture the image of her nakedness she would slip out of his grasp. Instead, she was clad in leaves, her garments the boughs and blossoms of the forest. Flowers sprouted from her eyes; shoots flowed from her fingertips. But her voice, her voice, her voice.

The ridges of bark were scars on her arms. Branches were arms covered in scars. Torn from her sockets as the cruel man snapped. Her fingers were twigs, bent as they fell. The sticks were the fingers pointing to hell.

'Timothy, Ti-mo-thy.'

Whispers.

'Timothy, Ti-mo-thy.'

Agatha floated from the grain of the wood, forming into a mist that drifted over and into him. Into his mouth, into his brain, through the pores of his skin and into his lungs. Timothy Cavendish tried to say something. Something witty and charming. Something seductive and sensual. A vision of a Mayfair hotel room flashed into his consciousness; two naked people in bed smoking. Smoking and fucking. Smoking, drinking and fucking. His silken words replayed at quarter speed like a demonic incantation.

'Room service. Your champagne, Mr Cavendish.'

The waiter's sing-song voice sounded like a dirge. He couldn't move. The mattress began to tear as branches forced their way out of the springs. He tried to jump out of the bed. To break the spell. But he couldn't move. The branches held him down. Agatha's wispy presence twirled around his ears, his eyes, his mouth. The branches curled back into the mattress. Now he was alone in a dark room. It was cold. It smelled of decay and the must of damp earth. He could not move. He tried to scream but his jaw set tight in a grimace. Agatha turned into a whirlwind inside his veins, freezing him in that exact moment, with all hopes of redemption withdrawn and salvation rescinded.

It was nearly midday and Timothy had still not risen. Karol thought she should probably check on him. She had got the children ready for a day out and they were growing restless. Better tell him they were leaving. He liked to know where she was. At all times. But it was strange that he still slept. Had he slipped out during the night? Would they be needing a new bed so soon? Karol climbed the stairs and went into the bedroom. She threw back the still-drawn curtains. Springtime sunshine poured in, illuminating the bed. Timothy was in the same position she had left him in. Head pointing at the ceiling. But now, as the sun strafed the room, she saw his face. His eyes were wild and wide open, with a strange luminescence around the cornea. Karol leaned over him and looked into them.

Karol, it's me! Oh, thank God! Help me get up, I've had some kind of seizure. Bloody awful dreams all night, and now I can't move.

She bent her ear to his slightly open mouth, listening for his breath. But there was none. She moved her ear to his chest, searching for his heartbeat. But there was none. Her fingers sought his pulse. Nothing, not a flicker. He was dead. Karol clicked her fingers in front of his eyes. Nothing.

It's me for Christ's sake, Karol! Can't you hear me?
Stop fucking about and help me!

She shook him, gently at first, and then more vigorously so
that his head rocked back and forth like a rag doll. No doubt
about it, Timothy Cavendish was no more.

'Oh, thank God.'

She leaned over him again, staring hard into his pupils.
She thought she saw something, a hint of a figure swinging
from a tree. It must be a reflection from the outside. Karol
closed his eyelids with her fingers. She had looked into those
treacherous pools enough for one lifetime.

No, Karol! Please, please my darling, I'm here. You can't
leave me like this! Karol! Karol!

The doctor confirmed the diagnosis. A seizure, he said.
Timothy's heart must have stopped in his sleep. He tried
to reassure Karol. I'm sure he felt no pain. Her face was
contorting in what the doctor took to be grief. But it was
rapture she was struggling to contain. His father must not
know. Not until she had time to escape.

The magistrate, the magus, the managing director.

Dr Harris, look at me! Surely you can see me. I'm alive for
Christ's sake! Where are you taking me?

The ambulance arrived to take the body away.

'There shall have to be a post-mortem I'm afraid, Mrs
Cavendish.'

The doctor said it should be a formality as no foul play
was suspected. No hint of a scandal would ever be allowed

near the Cavendish name, they could all be assured of that. The post-mortem was noisy. The pathologist sliced and sawed. Timothy was finding it impossible to articulate his pain by that point. It was really just one long strangled scream. All his parts thrashing about, undulating like a rollercoaster as the doctors cut and scooped. Agatha had long since flowed out of his malign frame. She had passed through the streets one last time but found they had lost their fascination. Instead, she followed the roots. Back to the woods. Back to the glade. Back to the Tangle. There she decayed.

> *Come walk with me to lilac glade, through woodland,*
> *stream and knot.*
> *Come stand beneath the gallows' shade till all weeping*
> *is forgot.*
> *Leave the tears and terrors to the mischief of the town.*
> *Come walk with me to lilac glade, to the oak tree's*
> *shady crown.*
>
> *In darkness now from darkness born, circumference,*
> *length and span.*
> *In lilac glade the wreath and thorn, wove mockeries*
> *of man.*
> *In lilac glade beneath the earth, in death's ecstatic bond.*
> *Come walk with me in lilac shade, to the emptiness beyond.*

The mouldering scent of dark, wet soil filled his nostrils. He had heard that people's senses were often scrambled during bouts of illness. It should pass in time. He opened his eyes. He hoped to God he'd never have to experience such agonies again. Christ, the hallucinations! The pain, like he was being cut open. Timothy stretched out his fingers, feeling the reassuringly familiar grain of smooth wood; there really was no mistaking a Goodridge bed. They always used the finest trunks to make their furniture. He could feel the quality. Timothy patted the wood again and tried to raise himself up from the bed. It was awfully stuffy in the room; he needed some air. His head banged awkwardly against something hard and unyielding. He put his hand up to feel. The finest grain, polished to perfection, smooth and sturdy, built to last. They really were the Rolls-Royce of furniture makers. His eyes focused on a bright brass plaque above his head. Bartholomew Goodridge & Sons, manufacturers of fine caskets and coffins.

Hunts Up

The problem had been years in the making, centuries maybe. Rapacious animals had been allowed to run wild and unchecked. They were ravaging the countryside and spoiling the last pristine enclaves with their malignant presence. They had already devastated the indigenous wildlife. Populations were depleted and their numbers were sinking to near-extinction levels. They marauded at will, protected by ill thought-out laws that had been pushed through the council by do-gooders and bleeding hearts. Enough was enough. Something had to be done about this awful plague. A cull. A cull, that was what was needed. It wouldn't be pleasant. It would certainly be a bloody affair, but the council had decided to approve the action by the narrowest of margins. It would not be cruelly executed. It would be professional and proportionate. The young and the majority of females would be spared. It was the males that were the problem. Vicious things, fearless and brutal, always fighting for territory, never satisfied, permanently hungry. The council meeting broke up. The preparations for the hunt began immediately. Tomorrow the great purge would begin.

The horn blast stirred the village. Hunts up. Today was the day for the chase, for the beating of the scrub with sticks. A day for shooting, trapping, tearing and rending. Hunts up. Caspar yawned as he pulled his boots up over his tweed trousers. The thick material was irritating after a summer of unusually high temperatures, but there was a chill in the early morning air, and besides, he needed something sturdy to protect his legs from the thorny bushes. He would be right in the thick of it today. Caspar had the look of an athlete gone to seed; a vague paunch was encroaching on his belt. Ruddy cheeks and a tousled, blond mop of hair that looked like it had been dumped on his head suggested an upbringing of public-school dinners and compulsory sports. A solid 'chap' one might say. He glanced over to the radiator. Caspar had put the heating on early this year, and he was expecting to see their rotund cat Beryl curled up next to it, but she was nowhere to be seen.

'Is Beryl up there, darling?'

Caspar shouted up to Elspeth, his wife, who was pressing her hunting tunic for today's meet.

'She was out the flap early this morning, funny old thing. Out late last night too. Why?'

'Oh, no reason, just thought she'd be lazing by the radiator, that's all. Do you think she's taken a lover?'

He could hear Elspeth laughing as she swished the iron over her riding clothes. She had gone from public school to Oxford University, into a position with a respectable financial institution, and she was heading for great things. But she had given it all up for a quiet life of rural conservatism. As she pressed the iron through the folds of fabric, she often wondered what might have been. Caspar continued his preparations. He unlocked the cabinet and took out his shotgun, the smell of its freshly oiled muzzle bringing a smile to his face. He turned the gun over in his palms, admiring its intricately tooled barrel. He looked down its length. It was a fine thing. His father had been a keen hunter too; he had bequeathed the gun to Caspar in his will. Caspar had coveted it since childhood, and now it was his most precious possession. Today he would do his father proud. Hunts up.

'Right, I'm off! See you at the Bull for drinks before the ball! Wish me luck!'

'Good luck, darling! Don't forget Johnny is riding with me today. It might be the day for a blooding now the ban's been lifted.'

'Oh, God! Of course, I forgot. I hope you catch a few to make up for lost time! I'm just sad to miss the big day.'

'Don't worry, darling, you have to do your duty. I hope you get a decent brace. Don't forget to keep count. I know what you're like when you get carried away.'

'I won't, I won't. It could be a record tally today. No more bloody quotas and those ghastly men from the council poking about with their forms . . . Oh, and please get a nice picture of Johnny if he gets blooded today. Love you both.'

'Love you too, darling.'

Caspar smiled. Picking up his cartridge belt, he stepped out into the morning mist.

Bly Stone was a beater. A wife beater. A child beater. A dog beater. Today he would thrash the thicket, chivvying out the birds for the hunters to pepper. The work was well paid, easy too. He used to be a farmer until his drinking got the better of him. The foxes got the last of his flock a couple of years ago. Fuckers. Now you could hunt them again, Bly would love to kill one of those bastards. He'd join the hunters in a heartbeat if they'd have him back. But he was sure the incident at the Boxing Day ball hadn't been forgotten. Cunts. He was one of them once: jodhpurs, boots, the lot. Now he was a beater. A man beater. An animal beater. A self-flagellator. He did odd jobs for those who'd trust him. Stinking of booze. Stained with neglect. Most avoided his resentful glares, though some were only a few sherries away from the same state. Those golf club bores. Those landed Land Rover-driving snobs. The middle management team builders were the worst; they came in squadrons at the weekend, jostling for position like a pack of young bucks. Amateurs. Shooting wildly into the air, swigging on fucking hip flasks engraved with stags. Fucking cunts. Bly was one of them once too. He had settled before his time in this rural backwater. Given up the high life of the city to become a sure-fire success in the agricultural business. But the promise of a new life had withered in the soil. Those long nights. No lights. No life. Plenty of pubs. Bly rattled the whiskey bottle to and fro in the weak light of the kitchen window. A slither of golden liquid stained the bottom. He could see it glowing through the green glass. He threw back his head and tipped the bottle. The meagre contents dribbled reluctantly onto his tongue. He closed his eyes and swallowed. He fucking hated himself. Bly took up his threadbare cap, adjusting it carelessly on his unkempt head. A group of local tomcats sat on a wall watching him leave the house. Bly was often roused from his drunken sleep by their endless scrapping, but today it seemed like a truce had been called. They were almost regimental in their stillness as they watched him head up the back lane. Bly dragged himself towards the gathering place with a heavy head full of malice.

Eugene Carlson exuded success, from his John Lobb loafers to his Jermyn Street tweeds. But he couldn't hide his bridge-and-tunnel brashness, as his diamond ear studs testified. His aristocratic pals found him a little gauche; he was an American after all, and a young one too. The older yanks, the industrialists and media moguls, seemed to have adapted a lot more convincingly to the strict social hierarchy of the shires. These young disrupters were a loud and unsophisticated bunch, all booming autotuned dance music and carelessly stolen street slang. One was certain they would be happy to use machine guns at the shoot given half a chance. But seeing as Eugene now owned the country club, it was deemed better to ignore his more vulgar habits. This was the third year he had booked out the whole place and flown the shareholders out of their Manhattan lofts for a weekend of shooting. But this year would be especially cathartic now the local council had lifted the quotas. Something about a cull? Eugene liked the sound of it. It sounded . . . excessive.

He had taken a full plate from the country club buffet. Force of habit, you know? Grab it while you can, right? Still, the coke had taken the edge off his appetite. A morning pick-me-up had been required. Last night had been wild, man. But he needed to stay sharp today. Keep those shareholders happy.

'It's been another great year, guys. Thank you for your faith in me. Thank you for your faith in the company! I gotta say, I am stoked as fuuuck to be here again!'

A small chorus of whoops and a modicum of fist pumping broke out. Eugene felt like a superhero, amped on coke and his own legend. He could do no wrong. He had slayed the competition, cornered the market, bullied the team out of unionising, cut costs to the bone. So what if there were a few lawsuits? He could pay off those attention-seeking bitches. Hey, so you took a bit of persuading to party with the boss. So what? Here's a fucking apartment in Malibu. You don't want it? Fuck you. My lawyers will crush you, drag your sorry ass through the courts until you're penniless. Eugene got what he wanted, when he wanted it. He raised his glass to his nervous-looking staff. There were hesitant whoops and a throaty 'Fuck yeah' from his most loyal lieutenants. Eugene turned to face the gathered shareholders, raising his arms wide in a messianic pose. He carelessly filled his glass, letting the champagne slop down the sides and onto the ancient rug. He downed the champagne and filled the glass again. He sniffed, enjoying the numbing residue that trickled down his throat. He made a speech. Inarticulate. Rambling words. He talked about money. He talked about power and profit. He talked about himself. He talked about killing. More whooping. More clapping. More sniffing.

As Eugene eulogised inside, a large flock of birds drifted in tight formation high over the village. Gilbert Lambeth shaded his eyes. Sixty-five years a twitcher but he had never seen such an odd sight. At this time of year large flocks were not unusual, it was migration season after all, but never would you find such a variety of birds flying together: starlings, rooks, chaffinches and blackbirds wing to wing. Gilbert took out his old notebook and jotted down his observations. His fellow birdwatchers would enjoy mulling over the puzzle at the Bull later, if the landlord would let him in. Today's activities were bound to cause some unfortunate divisions in the village. Now the council had approved the cull, good folk of conscience like Gilbert must act. He was hurrying to the Quaker's meeting house to meet his fellow saboteurs: an eclectic cadre of youthful anarchists, performative hobbyists, Christian animal lovers, aging hippies who had been stranded in the countryside since the 1970s, and those for whom the idea of massacring animals for sport was, well, just wrong. Gilbert was a veteran humanist, carrying the conviction that people might one day metamorphose into something good. As a young man he had marched to Aldermaston, longing for an end to war. He had protested on the streets of London against various forms of injustice, chained himself to fences, sat in front of police vans and military vehicles.

He had been arrested and detained and was on a number of Home Office lists. But Gilbert was, at his core, a good man. A kind and gentle man. Most people in the village loved him. Even those who thought his views to be dangerous Marxist nonsense found it hard to really hate him. He was regularly banned from the Bull, they all were, but it was usually to stop the younger hotheads from starting an argument with the beaters, and things tended to blow over in time. But today would be different. Today things were going to change.

Gilbert knocked on the door of the Quaker house. Young Jack Devlin answered. 'The Devil' they called him. An anti-establishment provocateur. He was against most things and found himself in a near-permanent state of fury. The Devil had been arrested innumerable times, breaking into research facilities, gluing himself to machinery, throwing eggs at political figures. It was embarrassing for his parents, who were both local notaries. They had even diverted a proportion of his inheritance into a makeshift bail fund. But like Gilbert, Jack Devlin was essentially a good boy. He saw the world with the clarity of youth, before disappointment and regret tarnished his optimism.

'Morning, Gilbert! Ready for it? Most of the others are here, just waiting on the lot from town. Josh's bus is knackered or something.'

'Good morning, you young Devil.'

Jack's serious 'direct action' face cracked a little at Gilbert's gentle humour. Jane Bradshaw appeared at the Devil's side. She was his girlfriend. Resourceful. Local. Born and bred in the village. She was less sentimental about the countryside than some of her fellow activists, but she opposed the hunt with just as much vehemence. To her it was class war; against the backdrop of rural poverty and prejudice, she had dragged herself through college, becoming politicised along the way. She wanted to be a lawyer. To take the fight to the powerful and the forces of corporatism that were turning the countryside into just another factory. But for now, she was a mechanic. From an early age she had helped her father repair various farm machines, and now she put her experience to good use at her uncle's garage.

'Ah, and good morning to you, Miss Bradshaw! I do hope the others make it. We will need the numbers if the plan is to succeed.'

'They'll be here Gilbert, no worries, and don't you fret about the plan, it's going to work. There's no way it can fail.'

As the sentence faded on Jane's lips, a rickety camper van lurched around the corner and sputtered to a halt outside the hall. Jane sighed, a sardonic smile playing on her lips as she shook her head.

'I'll get my tools.'

Gilbert and the Devil offered a small round of applause as a ragtag band of saboteurs spilled out of the van, yawning and stretching into the misty morning air. Hunts up.

*

They stood in serried ranks. Experienced hunters next to half-drunk dilettantes. Clashing patterns of country attire and a dull rainbow of gumboots, like a privileged platoon of irregular troops. A variety of weapons crooked over forearms or in the hands of loaders. Some of the city boy adventurers tarried by the outdoor buffet. Trestle tables covered with starched white cloths were filled with steaming tureens of breakfast fare, untouched fruit bowls and trays of chilled champagne. Toasts were loudly proclaimed, backs slapped and hip flasks emptied. Hunts up. Caspar was impatient to start. He looked back disdainfully at the pack of financiers and entrepreneurs. He took the hunt seriously. It was a tradition in his family going back generations. He would not let his father down. Caspar grasped the gun in his hands and looked out over the bracken towards the woods. Though much of the ancient forest had been cleared for crops, there was still a large swathe of the Tangle in this part of the country. Caspar had played there as a child, making camps and fighting campaigns against imagined aggressors in the dips and gullies. He let out a long sigh. His hot breath curling into the cold morning air. He was aware of his heart beating in his chest. Something was wrong. Incorrect. Jarring like a mismatched thread. He watched the beaters heading into the thicket. Off to stir the flocks with their sticks. He tuned into his pulse; he timed its regular throb. What was missing? Then it struck him. Nothing stirred. There was only stillness. He spun around to see the drunken group of Carlson employees balancing flutes of champagne on overflowing plates. Not one hand was raised to waft away troublesome insects. Because there were no insects. No wasps on the jam, no flies on the bread, no mayflies or bumbling bees. Not even the ever-present midges hindered their enjoyment of the breakfast buffet. Caspar knew that the use of insecticides had increased dramatically recently. Perhaps that was it? Everything was changing, too fast, too soon. He would have to change soon too. Change or wither to nothing.

Caspar was shaken from his dreary daydream by the sound of the hunter's horn sounding in the village. Hunts up. It would soon be followed by the clattering of hooves and the baying of the hounds. A venerable country tradition had been restored. An ancient sport that made him feel safe. Some things were worth preserving, he thought. But the expected hubbub was strangely absent. Again the silence began to press around him. Isolating him from all that was familiar with its mutating pressure.

'What are we waiting for . . . ?'

Eugene Carlson was corralling his half-cut employees to the front line.

'Where's Ralph with my gun? Yo, Ralph, let's lock and load, dude.'

A stoical local handed Eugene his loaded weapon.

'It's Robert, sir. Please wait for the signal before you shoot.'

'Thanks a bunch, Ralph.'

Eugene was keen to kill. He winked sleazily at one of his employees. The ranks were finally filled. The chatter and bluster ceased. Now they all became aware of the silence. Puzzled glances were exchanged. Even the most experienced woodsmen seemed uneasy. They focused their eyes on the edge of the forest, trying hard to ignore their apprehension. Soon the silence would be broken by the turbulence of flapping wings. Eugene belched and took aim. Caspar lifted the stock of his gun and took aim too.

'I see something!'

One of the Carlson employees let off a round.

'Wait, don't shoot!'

An alert gamekeeper managed to push the barrel of the gun skyward, leaving the round to sail harmlessly above the trees, just as a group of beaters emerged shrugging from the wood.

'What the fuck?'

Carlson yelled across the bracken as Bly Stone emerged from the treeline, clearing a path with his beater's stick.

'Nothing doing! Not a thing!'

'What's he saying? Fucking clown. What's this guy saying? No birds, what is this bullshit?'

Eugene was not accustomed to disappointment and would not tolerate further inconvenience. He lowered his weapon and took a discreet sniff from his silver cocaine capsule. Caspar rolled his eyes, watching the young entrepreneur make a mockery of country etiquette. Caspar shouted across the scrub.

'What's up, Bly?'

Bly was now only a few feet from the hunters. He stopped and spat on the ground. He hated these cunts.

'Like I said, there's nothing there, in the trees or on the ground. It's like they all fucked off on holiday. Maybe they knew you were coming?'

'It's those bloody sabs!'

Royce Cotterill, master of the hunt, came storming across the lawn from the direction of the village. The kennelman and Elspeth followed in his wake. They were extremely agitated.

'Is everything OK, Eli? Where's Johnny?'

Elspeth shook her head and grimaced, mouthing 'It's OK' to her worried husband. Royce's face was red with fury.

'They've really done it now, those fucking troublemakers! I'll have them all up in front of the judge by lunchtime! This is intolerable!'

'Calm down Royce, what's happened?'

'Those bloody saboteurs have only gone and stolen our horses! Must have broken in last night. Everyone one of them gone. They should be strung up! And that's not all. Oh, no, it's the hounds too! Not one of them left in the kennels. They even took the pups. They'll do time for this!'

The kennelman glowered. Royce Cotterill simmered with rage. He smacked his riding crop against his thigh with a penitent's zeal. Elspeth joined her husband's side, offering a reassuring squeeze to his arm. Her face wore the look of someone used to being around blustering men, a kind of resigned frown.

'I can't do much good here, Caspar. Johnny will be so disappointed if he can't ride with the hunt today. But it's a bit bloody difficult without horses.'

Caspar gave his wife a smile. They were blessed with an ability to see the funny side of even the most unfortunate situations.

'I think I'll just head back to the house, wait for Johnny there, and hopefully head out later. Once they find the bloody things.'

'OK, darling, hopefully see you at the Bull once this is all sorted out.'

She kissed him tenderly on the cheek, more like a mother than a lover, and headed off to find their child. He watched his wife walk across the lawn back towards the village. He felt fortunate to have such an understanding spouse. She was the cement in his carefully constructed life. 'A fine filly' his father had called her. Caspar wouldn't use that kind of language, of course, but underneath it all, though he tried so hard to appear modern, it was really what he felt too.

Royce Cotterill had barely taken a breath since he arrived. His face was like a purple balloon filled with indignation.

'That Jack Devlin and his crusty friends will be behind this, you mark my words. I thought I saw their clapped-out old bus outside the Quaker's hall this morning. Well, I've called the police, they won't get far. I suppose we shall have to just ride out after lunch now.'

A scream cut across the landscape. Beaters, shooters, hunters and waiters snapped their heads towards the woods. The silence was beginning to fracture. Caspar instinctively raised his gun; the others nervously followed his example.

Eugene took another sniff and raised his weapon too. He'd kill the first fucking thing that came out of there. Some of the beaters who had recently emerged plunged back in to find the source of the scream. Bly headed past the line of hunters, looking for a few stray flutes of champagne to pinch from the buffet. The stillness was underpinned by a low rumble, like a far-off storm brooding. Distant but getting closer. Gathering in intensity. Another scream. Closer this time. Eugene let off a round.

'Sir! There are men in those woods.'

Another scream, this time elongated and desperate, like a drowning man at sea being sucked under by the current.

'Fuck this.'

Eugene fired again.

'Wait! For Christ's sake, wait!'

More gunfire. Sporadic and hesitant at first. Then they all opened up at once. Muzzles flashing and smoking with impotent rage. Round after round crashed into the inscrutable heart of the woods. Trees splinted and branches crashed as the projectiles tore into the dark interior. The firing stopped. The stench of cordite and human bowels filled the air. Caspar was shaking, staring wild-eyed down the barrel of his father's gun. Never fire when there are beaters in the field, everyone knew that; it was basic safety. He had let his father down. Tears welled up and trickled down his trembling face. He stared hard at the woods. The whole forest was vibrating. A juddering motion that made the Tangle tremble and shake with perverse ferocity. Then a vast wave came crashing through the undergrowth. The bracken lurched, its stalks pulled by the unseen undertow. Closer. Closer. Hunts up.

*

Gilbert unscrewed his Thermos and took a refreshing sip of tea. Hunt sabotage was much like birdwatching in many ways: long periods of patient waiting with only the briefest flurries of activity to relieve the tedium. All things considered, he enjoyed the anticipation as much as the activity itself. Doing good was something to look forward to. To save a life was a holy thing. Gilbert was always prepared for those long hours; he had a full Thermos and a stout blanket on which to rest. He had chosen a dark weave so as to blend in more effectively with the shrubs. He didn't go in for camouflage and face paint like some of the youngsters, but he did at least attempt to look as drab as possible. He settled down on his blanket and pulled out his binoculars. He scanned the fields. Nothing. No movement. No visible signs of life. Strange. But he was pleased that the animals seemed intent on hiding from the riders. He smiled to himself. They would be greatly delayed today. The plan was working perfectly. He knew it would be unpopular in the village. They had broken a number of laws, both written and unwritten. On this occasion every rule of the game had been bent and snapped. Horses and hounds spirited away and let loose. They would do time for their crime, of that there was no doubt. But the cull must be thwarted at any cost. Phase two of the plan was about to begin.

Gilbert's attention was drawn away from the fields and into the brightening sky. A large flight of birds was wheeling above him in a dizzying display of ever-changing patterns. Gilbert put his binoculars to his eyes. The same odd variety of species that he had noticed earlier. They whirled together in the crisp morning air. He reached for his notebook, momentarily forgetting his vigil. He scribbled down his observations. Fascinating. This week's birdwatchers meeting would certainly be lively, there was so much to discuss.

He wondered if anyone else had noticed these strange formations. Gilbert raised his binoculars again. The dancing flocks were much lower now. As one, they swooped, diving down at great speed, almost touching the ground, before shooting up into the sky again. It was like the attack pattern of a hawk. Perhaps they were foraging? Or hunting. Now the flock was directly over him. Low and close. So low in fact that he didn't need his binoculars any more. Gilbert put them down and began to note each species as they swirled above him. He was struggling to keep up. His pencil scratched frantically on the page. Such was the variety of birds, he was forced to use awkward acronyms and initials to record them all. He recognised the plumage of a chaffinch. Very close now. It swooped over his head, almost knocking his cap off. Gilbert laughed in delight. These beautiful birds felt his love for them. He could sense it. There was nothing to fear from him. He hoped one might choose to perch on his shoulder for a while, perhaps let him stroke its delicate feathers. He watched the chaffinch shoot up into the sky. It twirled up, cresting the current before corkscrewing back down towards him. Gilbert's smile froze. It was going very fast, and he hoped it would not collide with him and hurt itself. He shielded his eyes against the glare of the sun as the bird descended. Closer. Closer. The chaffinch was falling.

'Slow down, little one, slow down.'

The bird stopped a few centimetres away from his face. Flapping its wings to arrest its descent. Gilbert could feel the gentle waves of air flowing from the bird's beating wings. It began to ascend slowly, its tiny black eyes focused on Gilbert's wonder filled pools. Now it was hovering a few metres above his upturned face. He breathed a sigh of relief as his eyes focused on its subtle plumage.

'How wonderful.'

He whispered as the chaffinch folded its wings and
dropped like an arrow. He didn't even have time to raise
his hands before the bird's beak pierced his cornea. A
dull moan escaped the old man's throat. A long note of
incomprehensible pain. The beautiful birds. The beautiful
birds. The chaffinch withdrew its beak from Gilbert's eye,
dragging out bits of vitreous humour as it slid out. The bird
cocked its head and began to peck, drilling into the lens of
Gilbert's eye before tugging the whole thing out of its socket.
The chaffinch cocked its head again, then with one swift
movement it severed the link and flew off with its prize.
Gilbert fell on his back, stunned. In agony. His hand groped
about. Already going into spasms as shock took hold and the
threat of death approached. His fingers lingered in a pool of
tea and blood. With his one good eye, he saw the black cloud
of birds hovering above him. They swooped on the currents
of air. The beautiful birds. The beautiful birds. Then, like a
giant fist, they fell on him. Pecking and rending until all that
remained was the bloody shadow of Gilbert Lambeth on the
scrubland floor.

*

Beryl sauntered into the woodland clearing at the head of
a column of village cats. Every variety of feline from feral
tomcat to pedigree Persian in tight regimental order. They
made their way to their allotted place deep in the heart of
the Tangle. Beryl licked her paw and acknowledged Hector,
pack leader of the village dogs. Hector pricked up his ears
and nodded his greetings. The glade was filling up. The tall,
graceful stags stood at the back. The birds filled the branches.
Long columns of mice, rats and voles entered the clearing

and took up their place near the front. The insects emerged
from the soil. Midges hovered and fireflies lit up the glade.
The first council meeting in several millennia was beginning.
The horses came late, having been only recently freed
from their stables by a mischief of field mice. Their hooves
vibrated on the forest floor as they trotted into the glade.
Athena, dressage champion and queen of the equine herd,
whinnied and tossed her forelock. The wild creatures of the
forest twittered, barked, squeaked and hooted their greetings
to their liberated comrades. Tonight, the struggle for life
was suspended. Ancient relations of prey and hunter were
put aside. Instinct in temporary abeyance. Now they had a
common enemy. A contagion that had been allowed to spread
largely unchecked was threatening to kill them all. The
contagion had once been of the Tangle, just like all of those
gathered in the glade. But it had mutated into something ugly.
Until they evolved the wisdom to see, they would have to be
contained. The animals had done little to resist the haughty
blooming of this infant species. Trusting that soon they would
remember the roots and the humility of life. Only the aloof
and independent bacteria had done anything to frustrate
the misplaced sense of omnipotence these creatures felt. But
then, they were never too fussy about who they killed. A hush
fell on the glade as the owls landed to begin the meeting.
The oldest and wisest bird in the forest had no name. Names
were for the indentured creatures of the village. She hooted
a greeting, welcoming the gathered fellowship, and after a
eulogy for those now extinct, the meeting began.

*

Jane rolled onto her back, absentmindedly playing with
a stalk of grass. Jane and the Devil, well hidden in the

undergrowth, their camouflaged fatigues covered with twigs and leaves to render themselves invisible to the hunt.

'It was weird, Jack. They must have got wind of our plan or something.'

Jane's face scrunched up in thought. Last night's operation had not gone to plan.

'What, so there wasn't a single horse in the stable? Not one?'

'Not even a foal, but the weirdest thing of all was the fucking dogs, man! I couldn't believe they'd managed to smuggle them out of the kennels without us knowing. Fuckers! Still looks like the jokes on them. Whoever hid them seems to have lost them, judging by the angry faces outside the Bull!'

'Ha, ha, classic. I wonder what idiot they put in charge of that! Still, once they've found them, we'll be ready, the plans not fucked yet, not by a long way. I reckon they did us a favour. But where the fuck are they?'

'Fuck knows, man. All I know is that it was one of the strangest missions I've ever been on. There's me all commando-ed up, bolt cutters, the lot, and not a thing to liberate. Even the mice had fucked off.'

They both burst out laughing, rolling together in the long grass like two shrubs.

Some minutes later, Jack 'the Devil' Devlin perched on his elbows and looked through his field glasses.

'Fuck all happening, Janey. Looks like they've proper fucked it. You heard from Gilbert, by the way? I love him, but he's shit with mobile phones. I don't want them slipping through without us knowing.'

'Nah, nothing. I reckon they're still trying to find the horses.'

'They'll be out again soon enough.'

Jack tightened his grip on the binoculars. He wanted this. The plan was too good to fail. Even though he knew some people in the village would never speak to him again, it would be worth it.

'Where are they?'

The Devil was puzzled.

'Ouch, the midges are lively today.'

Jack scratched at a swelling insect bite as a haze of tiny flies darted around his head.

'Argh, little twats.'

He put down the binoculars, using both hands to swoosh away the persistent midges.

'They like you. Must be that aftershave your mum bought you for Christmas.'

Jane was giggling at the sight of her boyfriend trying to fend them off.

'Not a fly on me, mate.'

Jane showed him her insect-free sleeves.

'Must be because you smell so bad. Ouch, fucking hell, they're all at it now!'

'Cheeky twat, serves you right! Shit, look Jack, now the ants want a go.'

Jane was laughing as she pointed at a column of wood ants that had marched out of the broken earth and was now making its way up Jack's leg. He tried to sweep them off, scattering them into the grass. But they kept coming.

'Just what I fucking need. I haven't had a nip since I was a kid. Fuck off, you little twats!'

Jack flicked the ants into the bracken. It seemed his love of animals did not extend as far as the insect kingdom. In answer, the ground darkened as if it had sprung a leak.

A black wave of ants burst out of the earth. They scuttled from every crack and crevice, surging towards the Devil's horizontal frame.

'Fuck's sake! Shit!'

Jack brushed frantically, trying to turn back the tide. He must not give away their position. Not now that the plan was so close to completion. The mass of ants had grown into a thick, unguent wave covering his legs like an oil slick. Their pincers tore through his fatigues and nipped at his flesh. It felt like hot daggers. Hot stabbing daggers. Stabbing. Stabbing. Jane tried to sweep the growing swarm from her boyfriend's body. But her actions only served to excite them more. The tempo of their attack increased to a frenzied pitch.

'Argh!'

The sharp needle of a wasp's sting pierced the skin of his cheek. The wasps began to do their duty. They pierced the young man at will. Then came the hover flies and the bumble bees. They joined with their modest armoury to harry the prey. Hunts up. Jane became frantic. Tears flooding down her face, she swatted and brushed, blew and swept the insects from his tortured body. Yet she had suffered not a single nip or sting. This was a precise and scientific cull, not a massacre. Jack was soon paralysed. His blood flowed with a potent cocktail of venoms and necrotic fluids that dissolved and corrupted every cell they touched. As his insides began to turn to slurry, his swollen body was being consumed by the mass. Spiders wove webs in his wounds and sucked the fluids from his skin. Flies injected their eggs into the cuts; the maggots writhed in congealing pools. Earwigs entered his nostrils and began to mine. Biting. Biting. Biting. Jane tried to brush the insects from Jack's mouth, hoping he could catch a breath through the stings.

'Oh Christ, Jack! Hang on, baby, I'll get help! Oh fuck, get off him, get off!'

An agonised groan escaped the Devil's mouth.

'Oh Jack, I'll get help, I promise, please say something.'

She leaned in to catch his mumbled words, her face in the jumble of spindly legs and hard, armoured bodies. She could hear their clicking and sucking.

'What is it, Jack? Please say something, please, I love you!'

She wasn't sure if she really did love him, but it felt like the last chance she would ever have to say it. Perhaps it would be of some comfort. The groan came again, sounding like the rasp of an old man. She leaned closer to hear. His swollen lips parted and a faint hiss of air escaped like a slow puncture from a bicycle tyre. Then came the mandibles. Jane ran. She ran towards the village and the safety of buildings. Roads and bricks and mortar. She ran as far from the fields as she could. Away from the grass, alive with savage ticks. Away from the pitted ground that hid the caves of malignant arachnids and the many segmented fiends. She ran even as the insects finished their work. She ran as fast as her legs could carry her, leaving the desiccated remains of the Devil to the new masters of the scrub. Behind her, the insects marched across the shrunken frame of Jack Devlin. They formed into thick columns and headed towards the village.

*

Bly gnawed on a chicken leg whilst stuffing a bottle of reasonably fine wine into his coat pocket. It was his reward for putting up with these useless cunts. They were popping off at phantoms on the country club's lawn. He'd beaten these woods for years now, but he'd never seen anything like this. Nothing stirred. He thought it was quite funny,

all this fuss over the cull, all the excitement at being able
to kill again, and not a fucking thing to shoot at. Fucking
funny. He heard another random volley rattle across the
scrubland, but this time it mingled with a scream. Bly
turned towards the woods with only mild interest. The toffs
were getting spooked. Another scream, closer. Now even
the seasoned hunters started to fire wildly into the trees.
Something was coming. Bly put down the chicken leg and
swept up a champagne flute, downing the contents in one
gulp. In the pit of his stomach a feeling of unease began to
rise. A reckoning. Bly tasted a metallic tang in his mouth.
He wiped it with the back of his hand. Blood. He had bitten
through his lip. He felt his cynical composure crumbling as
if a long-postponed debt was finally being called in. What the
fuck was that? A fresh scream, more complex and unsettling
than the last. It pierced the morning air, rippling through
the blue towards the gathered hunters like an invisible belt
of disturbance. Bly steadied his half-pissed frame against the
trestle table. Something was coming. He noticed that posh
cunt Caspar letting off round after round into the wood. He
looked terrified. The rich yank had lost his shit too. If he had
a bazooka, he'd be using it. Bly wanted to run, but a morbid
fascination kept him anchored to the spot. Could this be the
purging wave he secretly longed for?

*

Beryl dragged her pampered bulk through the stalks. She
was carrying a few kilos but she could still move like a cat
half her age. Behind her came the other village cats, flanked
by the beagles and Hector's canine militia. The animal
collective charged. They must carry out the council's grim
instructions. This was the first wave, the stealthy, low-slung

assault squad. The rats, mice, cats and dogs. They flew beneath the tall bracken virtually undetected. Beryl could see the polished boots of a part-time huntsman as they approached the edge of the scrub. Only a small lawn to cross, then they would be upon them. She tensed her muscles and prepared to pounce.

Eugene Carlson was fraying like a pulled cardigan. The coke and booze mingled uneasily with adrenalin, making him feel woozy and nauseous. He tried to focus on his rifle sight.

'Fucking reload, man, fucking reload!'

Robert held the reloaded gun ready, his hand steadier than the frantic pulsing of his heart. Eugene fired at nothing. He threw up on the stock and took the fresh gun from Robert. Wiping the stock, Robert reloaded and waited for Eugene to spit another shot into the void. Eugene wiped the sweat from his eyes. This was not the weekend of bacchanalian excess he had hoped for. He scanned the treeline, desperate for a target. Nothing. Just the disembodied screams of men. Suddenly, too late to react, he noticed the bracken vibrating on the edge of the lawn. Rats, like a volley of torpedoes, shot out from the undergrowth.

'What the fuck, Ralph!'

'It's Robert, sir.'

The rats flowed around their feet, gnawing through their ankles like buzz saws through pine. Robert tumbled to the floor and was soon consumed. Eugene was somehow still standing, held upright by the mass of rats. His mouth hung open, unable to understand how a man of his wealth and position could be so horribly inconvenienced. He tried to blast a hole in the horde with his rifle, but it made little impression. His shins were now being whittled to the bone by razor-sharp teeth. His eyes stared unbelievingly into the scrub as Beryl launched herself from out of the bracken. Her claws glistened in the sun as they plunged into his face. Eugene fell. His head smacked on the earth. Beryl stood over him, her chubby tail swooshing behind her. With one rapid slashing movement she took his eyes.

*

Caspar retreated, using his father's gun like a club. Rats and mice flew off at tangents as he batted them away. He prayed he could hold them back, because if the animal horde was to reach the village . . . God knows. He thought of Elspeth and Johnny waiting for him by the fireside. Toes curling and flexing as the flames warmed their feet. His wife would bring out the biscuits and hot chocolate. Johnny would spoil his appetite. It was shepherd's pie tonight. They would turn to the window, surprised to hear the sound of feet. Was daddy home? Their fragile bodies ripped to shreds on the Chesterfield sofa.

'Bly, help me turn these tables, quickly man!'

Bly was hypnotised by the unfolding horror. He moved automatically, tipping the tables over. Some of the hunters had the same idea and a makeshift stockade sprang up on the lawn. The tide of rats broke on the fortress wall. Caspar was shaking uncontrollably now.

'Oh Christ, oh Christ.'

He fumbled to reload. He could hear his heartbeat booming fast against his ribs. Everything had gone quiet again. The silence pressed.

'Fuck, fuck.'

Caspar risked a glance over the parapet. The animals had gathered in silent ranks around the tables. Cats licked their paws or prowled the perimeter. Dogs obediently sat and sniffed the air, as if waiting for a treat from their master's hand.

'Fuck, fuck, fuck. What are they doing?'

Caspar scanned the gathered animals. Some had once been pets. He recognised many of them from around the village. He had tickled their tummies by the welcoming hearths of local pubs. Thrown them treats at a thousand drinks parties. Patted their muddy heads as he chatted to their owners in the park.

'Good boy, good girl.'

He whispered to himself, as Beryl, slick with gore, inspected the ranks. Caspar wanted to shout her name.

'It's your favourite tonight, girl, yummy mackerel.'

The words died on his lips, mingling with the dying moans of humans.

Bly just stared into the woods.

'They are coming.'

Bly stood up.

'Get down, for fuck's sake, Bly, get down!'

Everyone was shouting at him like he was a disobedient hound.

'What the fuck did you say?'

You cunts. You overprivileged turds. Think you're so much better than me, do you? Bly's face broke into a grotesque grin as he pointed towards the woods. The treeline exploded. Out of the Tangle came the horses, stags, deer, oxen, sheep and pigs. The sound of their hooves thundered over the manicured lawn as they came on across the scrub. Bly carelessly kicked over a flimsy section of barricade and walked towards the oncoming animals.

'Bly, what the fuck are you doing? Come back!'

The rodents made a path. Bly walked down it. In zombie order he staggered forward. The cats and dogs let him pass too. Their noses twitching in anticipation. His tear-filled eyes were transfixed on the stampede. He reached the edge of the lawn as the first horses broke out of the scrub. The deep, dark pools of the horses' eyes swallowed him as they locked gazes. Bly fell to his knees and raised his hands, as if the messiah had finally returned to judge them all. He began to laugh hysterically.

'Oh, thank God.'

Athena's hoof splintered his face. His features instantly rearranging like a distorting mirror. As her hooves connected with the ground, they pushed Bly's broken head into the soil. Hunts up.

Now the siege reached its inevitable climax. Tables were tossed aside, and their defenders dispatched by tooth, hoof and claw. The ground became littered with the disconnected fragments of limbs. Lying severed amongst the blood-stained tweed flotsam like a grotesque tailor's floor. The investors, hunters, weekend hedge fund adventurers, lawyers, advisors and ancillary staff were all carelessly strewn about. All dying by degrees. Moans mixed in with the sound of gnawing. Once the killing had stopped, the rats and pigs had begun to scurry over the corpses, chewing at the flesh of the fallen, even as some still breathed. The battlefield would soon be clear. The first stage of the cull was going to plan. Now they must take care of the village.

Caspar lay broken against the splintered trestle table. His legs jutted out like the useless limbs of a ventriloquist's dummy. Flattened flesh and shattered bone. His entrails glistened, exposed to the morning air through a gaping wound. Next to him a circle of rats and cats were lapping

at the bloody remains of Royce Cotterill. His scarlet tunic
was soaked to a tone that matched his angry face. The top
of his head was missing; the ridges of his brain poked out
through his ill-advised comb-over. Caspar thought he looked
like a discarded sausage. He smiled to himself. Always good
to see the funny side. That's what Elspeth said. Caspar
was struggling to breath. His nose was clogged with broken
bone and congealed blood, so he gulped like a fish. Not long
now, he thought. A comforting softness brushed passed his
shattered cheek. The delicate bones of a cat. Beryl rubbed
herself against him, her tail flexing and waving as she
purred. They were back in the cottage. Hot toast and tea.
Ready to open their Christmas presents. Johnny was very
small, jumping about, remonstrating with his cruel parents.

'Can we open them now, daddy? Please, please! You said
after breakfast!'

'Alright, you little monster!'

Beryl brushed against his legs. Purring. Purring.

'Should we give Beryl her present first, Johnny?'

His breathing was too painful to bear now. Beryl stepped
onto his chest, tail swooshing, body vibrating.

'Hello old girl. Come to see your dad, have you?'

Beryl placed her paw on his lips to silence him. She
turned to survey the horror around them. She cocked her
head and brushed it affectionately against his bruised face.
The purring stopped. Their eyes met. Her eyes were filled
with tears. It is strange to see a cat cry, Caspar thought.
Beryl's claws flashed from her paw, piercing his lips, top and
bottom. She drew his lips together as blood poured down
his clogging airway. Their eyes remained locked even as his
last stuttering attempts at breathing faded to nothing. Beryl
withdrew her claws. Caspar remained inert, propped up like

a forgotten toy. She licked her paw before padding off to join her comrades. Hunts up.

*

Elspeth wasn't sure how, or why, she had been spared. The animals had poured into the village like an apocalyptic whirlwind. Down chimneys, up plug holes and drains, smashing through windows and doors. Every conceivable species and subgenus had swept through the village, killing almost everything in their path. They had stormed the cottage too. Swarming from every crack and crevice. They had pursued her around the house, finally cornering her in the loft conversion. The dogs were snapping at her legs when a fox strolled through their ranks. It climbed her torso, perching on her chest, with a set of snarling jaws only inches from her throat. The urgent hoot of an owl had risen above the clamour. Then as quickly as they had come, they were gone. Elspeth stumbled out into the midday sun. Nothing stirred. All the animals were elsewhere. She wandered in a daze past the village green now littered with the torn remains of her neighbours. She headed for the stream. The gentle brook where Johnny liked to play. Perhaps he was there hiding in a tree? Perhaps they had spared him too. A small boy child too young to hurt a fly. But the flies were in no mood to be hurt by boys, girls, women or men. Now they buzzed over the carrion. The splintered remains of an arrogant breed. Elspeth passed through the brambles, careless of their vengeful pricks. She stumbled through the nettles, but the stings barely registered. She must find her child. By the slopes of the riverbank, he would be skimming stones, he would be making camps, he would be making plans. Where was Johnny? Her beautiful, beautiful boy.

Today was to be his first hunt. His first taste of the chase. Today he would place one faltering step into the adult world. Today he would grow into a man, just like his father: sturdy, proper, correct. Today he would be blooded. Today. Today. Today. Hunts up.

Helen

A single rose on a grave. A barren patch. No grass grew.
No insect settled. On the stone a simple engraving. Timothy
Cavendish.

No motto. No epitaph. No one to mourn him. His father
had died years ago. The last of the patriarchs. The magistrate,
the magus, the managing director. Only one of his two
daughters now lived. Helen. Helen standing here. Brigitte had
married the vicar and died. Helen lived. Helen standing here.

She dropped the rose. As she always did. Every year
without fail. Not out of love. She had hated her father. But
for her mother. She came every year for her. Just to check he
hadn't risen from the grave to spite them. She was a woman
now, like her mother, but stronger. Free of the bonds of her
family and the spell they had cast over Caxton. She had
flourished in her later years. She had moved to the city and
forgotten the oppression of this place. Helen worked hard and
gathered accolades. She added initials to her name. Professor
Helen Cavendish FRS, FRSA, OOG. She was as happy as she
could be, but she never forgot the sadness in her mother's
eyes. That's why she had built the thing. The Happiness
Engine. Everyone would feel the benefits of its wisdom. No
one would have to look that way again. But she was wrong,
and she knew it. Happiness is everything.

God knows how she had ended up back here. But the
town had dragged her home. It was the work. She had been

horrified when the university had announced the location of its latest research facility. But somehow, she had expected it. This place. Brigitte married the vicar and died. Then the world went to shit, and now military flags flew on every street corner. Just another coup d'état. The new regime had taken to her work wholeheartedly. Helen tried to back out, to destroy the files. She told them it would not work. But it was too late. Tomorrow the president would come. Freshly installed as the glorious leader; the figurehead of their bright new future. He would cut the ribbon and the A.B.A.C.U.S. would begin its programme. She stared at the austere headstone and sighed. So much death and so much yet to come. Her sister lay nearby. Cut to ribbons in her potting shed.

Brigitte's death. That's when the doubts had been seeded. Even before she finished her work, she knew her project would fail. But she was already too far in to stop. Those woods. Her sister had been an awful human. But no one would wish that on anyone. The blood. The Tangle. Helen had studied the forest since that day. She had wandered its knotted paths. That's where she found him. The author. Matted beard and dirty clothes. Scratched lenses in plastic frames. Too long in the wild. He was looking for answers too. He had taken notes. Drawn sketches. Bound them all in a book. He let her read his findings. Florid prose full of fanciful conjectures. But there was something in them. They had become friends of a sort. They explored the forest together. She was going to meet the author after the ceremony. She was going help him add some much-needed rigour to his words. She couldn't think in wires and switches anymore. She could only think of the Tangle.

Pond

Under springy loam and layers of hot decay. In the filaments
of leaves and the deep veins of trunks. In stems and roots. In
the dense air of the forest. From the canopy to the core. The
blood of life surges like an insolent torrent. Occasionally it
will settle, forming numinous pools. Cool ponds of inscrutable
depth or dank mires of putrid sludge. These enigmatic lagoons
are an invitation to glimpse another world converging with
our own. A viscous scrying dish to aid time travel and augury.
The wriggling microbes that infest the morass remind the
creatures of the land of their origins. But look closer and it is
possible to see the future stretching out through the murk.
Look closer, good pilgrim. Come closer to the shoreline, good
pilgrim. Gaze into rippling waters. Can you see the happiness
you seek? Are you not deserving of all you desire? Through
will and good fortune, let the world bend to your needs. The
haughty pinnacle of evolution. Staring into the congealing
blood of life. Do my bidding, for I am man. But blood demands
blood. The satisfaction of desire always comes with a price.

Paul Porter waved his phone in the air like a wizard
conjuring the furies. There was no signal in the Tangle. He had
been disconnected from Fuck Finder and his hook-up was now
missing in the bushes and byways of the forest. Things had not
been going well for Paul. He was on his last chance at work.
He had stapled a colleague's finger to the office noticeboard
last week, and he was certain that once his case went to the

tribunal, he would be out of a job again. The boss would be
sorry to see him go; he'd said that. I like you Paul, he'd said.
You're a good guy underneath it all . . . it's just, you know? You
need to calm down when things don't go your way, Paul. He'd
said that. Standing there in his fucking office. He couldn't look
him in the eye. At weekends he moonlighted as a children's
entertainer. Pazz the Magnificent. Balloon animals. Sleight of
hand tricks with cards and coins. His pet rabbit Doris pulled
from a top hat. He was cheap, so he kept a passably full diary.
But one tousle-haired youngster had become too inquisitive
and had snuck under his magic table. The screaming, the hair
pulling, the messy faces and cake fights were all part of the
background hum of children's entertainment. He could tolerate
all that. But this boy had spoiled the fun for everyone. He had
violated the magic code. Without a code you were nothing. Pazz
the Magnificent had delivered an instinctive clout to the side
of the child's head, causing the boy to spill out from behind the
magic tablecloth and into the middle of the birthday party. His
dazed whimpering had swiftly blended into howls of protest.
Angry parents had escorted Pazz the Magnificent off the
premises before he had time to complete his act, leaving balloon
animals deflating in the conservatory. He had begged the
parents, with tears in his eyes. It was a mistake; it would never
happen again. He loved his work, making the little ones laugh.
Conjuring the wonder. Of course, I'm not sorry. If you had some
control over your children, this would never have happened.
I'm a professional. Can't you see? Can't you see? Why can't you
see? He wasn't a violent man. But some people just couldn't
help breaking the spell. He fucking hated them for it.

His ejection from the venerable guild of children's
entertainers had left him with too much time on his hands.
He spent long evenings alone, browsing ever more lurid

material on his computer. Eventually finding himself walking the darker neighbourhoods of the World Wide Web. As he brooded, with his resentment gnawing at him, so his desire for unorthodox diversions began to blossom. Passwords and encryptions. Keys, pseudonyms and dubious avatars became his obsession. Pazz the Magnificent was reborn as a sexual adventurer. Fuck Finder was a really great app. User-friendly. A five-star operation. He had met some very interesting people on it. But though he had certainly been put through his paces, no one had really warranted a return visit. He rarely gave more than 3 stars. His rating was low too. Detached, too rough, morose, those were some of the more helpful comments. He was beginning to think he might end up with the one or two-star amateurs and borderline offenders. Then Pan1977 popped up. The notification he'd received this morning was so stimulating that he had forgone his usual caution and headed into the dark interior of the woods. There was a promise of erotic delights of a more specialist variety than he was accustomed to. He rarely found anyone willing to satisfy his needs. Even the most open-minded correspondents tended to baulk at his more outré requests. But not Pan1977. They had offered some of the most dynamic suggestions for pleasure he had ever come across, and without prompting too. Normally he had to deftly pirouette around the subject, looking for the right moment to up the ante. But Pan1977 had jumped straight in. It was as if they had read Paul's mind. There were activities on the menu he never knew had a name. Pan1977's profile picture was a little blurry. But somehow, the indistinct figure with the lively imagination simply became more attractive in the shadows. He pushed on through the bush. Hard and focused.

Paul trembled as he brushed aside the branches. Pan1977 was somewhere in the woods, dancing their delicate reels amongst the flowers. He was certain. Pazz the Magnificent aroused. Pazz the Magnificent, risen and ready. Pazz the Magnificent, the elemental force of passion. He snagged his lightweight cardigan on a thorn bush. He cursed, hoping that Pan1977 hadn't noticed his awkward entanglement. A crackle of twigs alerted him to movement ahead. He quickened his pace. Soon. Soon. The light in the wood began to intensify. The grey-green shadows taking on golden epaulettes. Rays of sunlight pierced the crown of the trees as the forest thinned. Paul found himself emerging into a clearing of flower-dappled grass. Bright and sumptuous. A shimmering pond nestled in its centre. He had lived in and around Caxton Wood all his life, but he had never come across a pond before. Not even in his most adventurous childhood wanderings. Maybe it was one of those bucolic features the corporation had recently added. Alongside the woodchip picnic area and the folksy neopagan carvings that dotted the paths. The corporation had attempted to entice townsfolk to the forest. To sell them expensive parking adjacent to their crude parody of nature. This must be one of those features. It was too perfect to be real.

He scanned the banks. This would make a delightful spot to fuck away the afternoon. It was well chosen. He smiled and stretched out his fingers, entwining them in a web as he bent back his palms. His knuckles cracked as a twig snapped. He thought he could hear laughter. Light and playful. A game? Oh, how wonderful! Paul tore off his cardigan, twirling it around his head like a demented helicopter, before carelessly letting it fly. The afternoon sun was reaching its zenith, bathing the clearing with a dazzling warmth that penetrated his pasty skin and soaked into his bones. He unbuttoned his shirt, leaving him in vest, slacks and sensible shoes. He extended his arms in a Christ-like pose and shouted.

'I am here!'

His voice echoed in the clearing. Spinning endlessly around the glade like a scream in a cave. Paul was surprised. It was a fearful sound. Not at all what he was expecting. His voice kept ringing and swirling, bouncing off the banks of the pond. The gentle laughter he had heard earlier skittered across the surface like a water boatman. Blending into his own mournful tone. Gradually his echo dissolved into the summer afternoon chatter. Birdsong and cricket clicks replaced the ghostly boom. He relaxed somewhat. A smile returned to his face as his thoughts again turned to sensual exploration. He stepped closer to the water's edge and began to walk around the circumference of the pond. Hoping to catch site of Pan1977 in the rushes. The corporation really had done a marvellous job with this pond. It was so idyllic it was almost ridiculous. The green saucers of the water lilies were crowned with bright pink blooms, over which kaleidoscopic dragonflies hovered. Thick grasses and exotic ferns bowed over the surface like obedient butlers, providing shade for the sleek water voles, who occasionally poked their twitching noses into the air. The water was crystal clear, like polished glass. Paul stared into it. Pazz the Magnificent stared back.

He threw off his shoes and pulled down his slacks. In vest and pants he stepped into the water. Pazz the Baptist. Into the cleansing waters he waded. The cool, cool waters. The sensation was breathtaking. He went further into the pond, letting the water creep up his thighs. He waded further in. The feeling of well-being ratcheting up in intensity as

he pushed back the supple water. The water caressed his
cock like a gentle lover. The sensation was unmistakable.
Fingers, palms, pressure. Paul closed his eyes and let himself
get carried further and further into the pond. Hands were
all over him now. Rubbing, tugging. The water was soon
past his shoulders, rising over his neck. Paul hardly noticed
that his head had disappeared under the surface. The hands
increased the vigour of their caresses. He thought he might
cum in the perfect pool. He opened his eyes. He was at the
bottom of the pond. But the water was so clear it was like
daylight on the surface. The caresses of the invisible hands
were reaching their crescendo. He realised in his ecstasy
that he was not alone. A vague shape was forming from the
bubbles of his breath. A figure of staggering beauty emerged
from the bubbles and floated before him. Neither male nor
female. Nor an amalgamation of both. But something new.
He could not describe this apparition with his stunted human
vocabulary. Was this Pan1977? A god? An angel? A demon?
He reached out to touch the creature as it swam around him.
But it was already inside him. Its hands were the hands of the
water. The beautiful, beautiful touch. The exquisite lightness.
The water hands suddenly tightened their grip, becoming
more aggressive. Just how he liked it. The current swirled
hard around his parts until it felt like his cock might be torn
clean off. He gasped in pleasure as he came. His seed mixing
with blood, as finally his member was uprooted like a leek.
Spinning softly in the current before settling on the bottom.
Blood blossomed from the wound. Paul's smile was so wide he
thought his jaw might crack. The cool cleansing water rushed
into him, filling his lungs until they burst. His eyes, wide
with joy, were fixed on the face of the beautiful creature as
he passed from the world of men into the next. As he stared,

the creature's eyes turned from emerald green pools to beams
of burning red fire. Still beautiful. But now it was a terrible
beauty. He drew his last breath. Sucking in more water until
he was full. As he inhaled, the water thickened to a glutinous
tar, encasing every fibre of the unfortunate ex-children's
entertainer. He tried to scream but it was too late. The water
hardened in his cells. Petrifying him from the inside. The
blood of life sucked back into the Tangle.

*

Hilda Wilton struggled to the nearest bench with her phone
wedged between her chin and collarbone. Breathless in
the growing summer heat, she hurriedly deposited her dry
cleaning and medical bag. There was a do on tonight. Smart
frocks and ties.

'Dr Wilton.'

She answered with as much professionalism as she could
muster as her dress slipped from the hanger into cigarette
ash and dust.

'Fuck, sorry, no, nothing . . . must be a crossed line.'

She winced. This wasn't the 1930s. A look of relief
mixed with a resigned eye roll as she finally recognised the
caller's voice.

'Sergeant Harker, yes, yes, no, I didn't recognise your
voice, apologies, ye, ha, yes, erm, how may I help you this
morning, sergeant?'

She removed the phone from under her chin and quickly
sat on the bench. The blood drained from her face and a hint
of discomfort flickered in her eyes.

'Yes, I understand, sergeant. I know the spot. I'll get to you
as soon as possible. Don't touch the body, if you please. Yes,
yes, sorry, I realise you know that, yes, OK, thank you . . .'

She absentmindedly cancelled the call, letting her dry-cleaned dress fall back into the dust and ash.

For nearly thirty years she had avoided the woods. A short stroll in the park, skirting the edges of the Tangle, was as near as she would get. Naturally there had been quite a number of cases in the scrubland. She would try to avoid those calls too. How she had dodged them until today was anyone's guess. She had a feeling that people knew not to call on her for those jobs. The ones in the woods. They were good like that. Occasionally she would catch a whisper, a glance or a sudden awkward silence when she entered the room. The girl from the woods. That's what the newspapers had called her. Thirty years ago. Dangling by her legs. Staring at her lover's bloodshot eyes as they swung in the branches. The scuttling sound of those things. Pinching and cutting. The blur of blue as a policeman ran into the clearing to save them. The screams as the scuttling things cut him down. Severed limbs and stretched sinews. The swaying of the branches. The DI, in her calm, resigned way, pierced and rendered so they might live. She remembered running through the woods, stumbling into the day and a thousand flashing lights. Cameras, questions, blankets and tea. No one believed them, of course. She had spent a year in a psychiatric ward. Her lover had thrown himself off Ardlington viaduct. Push it down, they had said. The hysterical delusions, the hallucinations, they weren't real. Tam Stamp had done them all. The harmless hippy of the woods. He had killed all those people. Cut them up and rearranged them in that hideous stinking sculpture. He had killed himself before the trial. That was good. Case closed. Except she knew he hadn't done it. The scuttling things, the woodland spiders, the creatures of the Tangle. She had been an exemplary inmate and had grown interested in medicine during her time there. It was something real and tangible, something she could understand. Perhaps if she studied hard, she could fix the pain, in others, if not herself. Years of study and heartache. Now here she was, Dr Hilda Wilton, attached to Caxton CID, trembling on a bench.

Hilda sat in her car, staring at the dials on her dashboard. The last anchor of the human dimension. The spindly legs, clicking, piercing, cutting. The neat uniformity of the fuel gauge. The blood and sinew ripped and pulled. The machined perfection of the steering wheel. The headless torso in the leaves. She shuddered, closed her eyes and gulped down the conditioned air. Trembling slightly, she stepped out of the car.

'Sorry for dragging you into this one, Dr Wilton.'

The DI looked embarrassed and uneasy. She didn't like having to adopt such a formal tone with a childhood friend, but at least it was her on this job and not one of her macho co-workers. Hilda offered her a nervous smile by way of reassurance and nodded decisively towards the woods. They began to march towards the trees, the doctor's strides disguising her unease.

'This is a strange one, doc. I don't want to pre-empt your findings, but it looks like the victim drowned in the middle of the wood. That's not all, but I'll wait until you see the body before I speculate further.'

'Very wise, Claire. Let me be the judge of the cause of death, eh?'

Hilda regretted snapping at her friend. Claire Hammond was a good detective and a better friend. The vision of another DI. In another time, imploring her to run as a branch pierced her chest. She placed her hand on Claire's shoulder. Claire placed hers on top, squeezing it gently. She understood that this was not easy for the doctor. They pushed back the flaps of the forensic tent and joined the team who were standing over the victim. As soon as she saw the corpse, every nerve in her body told her to run. Get out of the woods, it's happening again. She swayed slightly. Claire steadied her.

'Are you OK?' she whispered. 'I'm right here behind you, take your time.'

Hilda tried to smile, hoping to force some confidence back into her face. But the smile froze and contorted into a grimace. Claire squeezed her arm gently. The doctor turned, acknowledged the officers in the tent and silently went to work.

She had done her best to leave the forensic tent with dignity but had noticeably lurched through the flaps. She gulped mouthfuls of heavy woodland air as she tumbled into the glade. She had seen worse: car crashes, industrial accidents, victims of fire. No, a drowned man with a missing phallus was nothing to get worked up about. It was this place. This fucking wood. Miles from any water. No signs of the body having been dragged or deposited here from elsewhere. But she was certain it was a case of drowning. This place. Always there, on the edge of her consciousness, the edge of her every moment. She steadied herself on a tent pole and tried to regain her composure. The structure vibrated at her touch. She would be better off leaning on one of the sturdy trees that were dotted about the glade. But she wouldn't touch the trunks. Things dwelt in the bark that she'd rather forget. The trees towered over her, their uncanny presence like a terrible echo from a past she had hoped to escape. She had to get out. That terrible harvest. That gruesome workshop. That beautiful furniture. She looked nervously at the trunks, half expecting the creatures to emerge. Glistening pincers and sharp wooden claws. But instead, there was stillness.

She took her hand from the tent pole. But there was no tent.
No police. No forensics. Just the body of a drowned man, and
silence. Her breath froze in her throat as if she was being
gently throttled. She looked at the drowned man prone on the
leaves. Stillness. Like a tomb. The drowned man on a slab.
The drowned man walking on arachnid legs. Click. Clack.
A sound began to drone around the trees. At first the sound
was nothing but a discordant hiss, barely discernible above
her own internal hum. But the hiss began to swell, engulfing
the frequencies of the forest until it was all she could hear.
She thought she might be losing her mind. She clasped
her ears, wanting to rip them off, to escape the cascading
vibration. The sound began to change from hiss to harmony.
The structure of the wood shifted. Layers were peeled back
and exposed. Her breathing became slow and steady. Music
replaced the static hiss. Delicate chords of simple beauty
rang out in the treetops. Its soothing tones, reassuring
somehow. This was the woodland of her childhood, before
those scuttling things had taken her. A subtle shift in key
alerted her to the movement of water. Between the branches
of a spreading ash, she saw a waterfall dropping silently into a
rocky pool. The incongruity of the sight didn't disturb her one
bit. In fact, she expected it. She looked around to where the
crime scene tent had once been. The drowned man was there.
The drowned man stood and began to walk, brushing past
her as he headed towards the waterfall. She began to walk
with him, over the soft forest floor as the strange symphony
continued to swirl around her. In the middle of the silent flow,
she saw a figure. The water bent around the figure like the
current of air in a wind tunnel. The creature was part human,
part rock. It looked like the naked torso of the deceased
Detective Inspector. Thirty years in the past, standing under

the falling waters. The figure signalled with a stony hand. The drowned man walked into the waterfall and disappeared.

'Come on, Hilda, let me buy you a drink.'

Hilda Wilton turned around slowly as her friend emerged from the forensic tent. She had a look of concern on her face. She gently took hold of the troubled doctor, and arm in arm they walked out of the woods.

*

Pazz the Magnificent lay on the mortuary slab, his ribcage open like a Viking blood eagle. His skull was unscrewed, with his brain nestling in it like a bag of fossilised worms. Various organs had been removed to be weighed and examined. His cock was missing. Dr Wilton walked around the excavated corpse, tapping her pen against her lips in thought. Her diagnosis of death by drowning had been correct. But it wasn't water she found filling his lungs, but instead a kind of black pumice. It resembled the solidified volcanic material more often found in and around active volcanoes, rather than inside the bodies of ex-children's entertainers. It was flecked with glowing red streaks that seemed to indicate part of the rock had not yet fully cooled. Yet it was not only cold to the touch, it was freezing. This was unusual. But, in her way, Dr Wilton had expected this too. She was haunted. Haunted by a space that would never let her go. The vison in the forest. The silently dropping waterfall and the ghost in its midst were all signs on a journey. Spectral signifiers of something missing. Part of her lost in the woods, longing to return. She wanted it back.

*

Hilda scanned the local papers. Hilda scanned the airwaves. Hilda was looking for stories. Events that seemed out of the ordinary. Unorthodox occurrences. Anything relating to old Caxton Wood. She studied its history, taking out every book on the subject from Caxton library. She poured over cuttings torn from old magazines. She bookmarked scratchy videos made by amateur naturists and low-rent historians. The wood she had avoided for over thirty years became her obsession. She had said nothing to her friends. Claire Hammond had called to see if she was OK. That day in the woods. Everything was so fucked up. But the doctor had seemed unnaturally still. Claire was worried about her. I'm good. I'm good. She said nothing of her late-night ramblings, her daily incursions into the Tangle. For years she had politely declined the invitations, all those picnics and languid summer strolls. People knew not to ask the girl from the woods. But now she looked for every opportunity to wander the twisting paths of the forest. Holidays owed, lunch breaks stretched, weekend plans cancelled or rearranged. Time was for the Tangle. The rough stone hand under the silent waterfall. The drowned figure. She walked the paths, hoping for the visions to return. In that gloomy glade with the gelded man under the tarpaulin. The wood had spoken to her through its indistinct signs. It was an offering. A chance. She must subjugate her fear and surrender.

The days were long and the nights were cold. In the deep black interior, she crept. The forest was never the same. Each visit was different. Familiar routes changed direction or were obliterated by the shifting foliage. It was hard to get her bearings. She found herself going over the same ground again and again. Her impatience only made the task harder, as if every irritable blow to a dangling stem caused the density of the vegetation to increase. So, instead, she found herself quietly standing under the trees. Eyes closed and focused.

She would reach out her palms to touch the trunks. Just like Sarah did. Sarah, the sacrifice. As the capillaries of her palms penetrated her skin, she thought she sensed tiny vibrations pulsing through the bark. The pulse was weak, barely perceptible. But, bit by bit, the path became clearer. Until one day she found it. It was getting late. Darkness was coming. But the light still clung to the sky like a fading stain. She had gone through her ritual as usual, eyes closed, breathing steady, intention set. This time the tingling sensation seemed more pronounced, as if her fingertips were being pricked by warm needles. The pulse was clearer. Beating with a disordered syncopation. Click. Clack. Clack. She opened her eyes. Her pupils as black as Dante's well. She heard the chime of harmonic chords. She was back. She gently pushed the branches aside and stepped forward.

The ancient ash, scion of the original root, swayed in its glade. It noticed a human figure stumbling in the twilight. A vaguely familiar creature. It had been here before, years ago, or was it only moments ago? What was it doing? It looked lost, all its kind did. They were dying, slowly, and soon they would be gone. But that was for later. This figure seemed sympathetic somehow. Like some of the others who had since joined with the Tangle. The ash stirred as the figure pressed its hands on the bark. It was her. Once the ash had been a craftsman. She had been one of the components. But she was faulty. The ash had found a better fit. The ash had taken only what it needed. But there was a residue. A surplus. Hilda pressed her palm firmly against the ridges of the bark. This was the place. The glade where she had been bound and tied all those years ago. Moments from death. Hanging by her bleeding ankles as those *things* cut and sliced. Tears rolled down her cheeks and her breath came in rasping sobs.

The memories were too great to contain. They threatened to overwhelm her. But she wouldn't run this time. She pressed on the bark. Inside, the faint memory of DI Sarah Ward pressed back. Hilda looked for news, Hilda looked for stories, Hilda looked for signs. She had forgotten something in the bark. Something lost. But the connection was still too weak. The door remained closed. The ash stirred. At the boarder of the Tangle, another figure was staggering into the forest, looking for satisfaction.

*

Baxter Long watched the doctor lock her car and walk off down the track that led to the woods. He had met her on a couple of occasions. He had even been a patient of hers for a short time. When the Caxton Harriers' regular medic had been on administrative leave. He remembered her penetrating gaze. She was nice, but odd. She had sorted his ankle out, no problem. He had seen her here, at this exact spot, every day for the last fortnight. Different times of the day for different lengths of time, but every day without fail. He knew because he was here every fucking day too. He always waited until the doctor drove away. He didn't want there to be any chance of anyone seeing him. Not that anyone would recognise him.

His once-taught belly hung like a deflated rubber ring over his cargo pants. The fact that he was wearing cargo pants at all was testimony to how low his standards had fallen. Once, he'd worn tailored suits or box-fresh kit with a sponsor's logo. The Caxton Harriers had been heroes of track and field. Gold medal winners. The others were anyway. Faces in the papers. Baxter obscured. Blurred in the back line. Arms around celebrities. Baxter at the peripheries. Not quite. Nearly. Reflected glory. Gold traded for bronze.

Now he made unenthusiastic kids feel bad about themselves
in his Saturday morning 'Sport can be fun with Baxter Long'
sessions. He would shout words of discouragement from the
sidelines, then give them the benefit of his insight on their
shoddy performance. They were more like extended eulogies
on how close he had been to fame than instructive lessons
on fitness. He despised them all. Especially the parents with
their autograph books. Ironic snaps for laughs at his expense.
His bitterness was quickly consuming him. Booze and pills
kept him going, but he had been close to calling it a day.
Three weeks ago, he had taken a rope into the forest. He had
trudged through Caxton Wood to find a tree worthy of his
corpse. He had threaded the knot and was about to cast it
over a branch when the waters had risen.

She was taking too long. Something must have detained
the doctor. He couldn't wait any longer, his desire was too
great. Baxter would risk it. The forest was large enough, so
he doubted their paths would cross. Not if he was careful. He
opened the door and stretched; his joints clicked painfully
as he pulled himself out of the seat. He was wearing his
Caxton Harriers kit. It was stretched over his torso like the
skin of an overinflated balloon. The medal flapped on a faded
ribbon around his neck. He closed the door, threw the rope
across his shoulder and set off towards the forest. Baxter
stepped stealthily through the undergrowth, watching for
signs of walkers or fucking couples. The wood was deserted.
He whistled the theme tune to a weekend sports programme
that the Harriers had once featured on regularly. He stopped
and looked around again. This felt like a good spot. It was
never the same, but he always had a feeling when he was in
the right place. It had to be deep inside the wood, well off
the beaten track. Private and secluded so that his ceremony

would not be interrupted. Not that he would be embarrassed if he was discovered, far from it. He imagined people would be very impressed if they came across him while he was in full flow. He just felt the time wasn't quite right to share his rebirth. People wouldn't understand. He wasn't sure he did.

Baxter threw the rope over the branch and held the noose in his hands, pulling it gently open. He placed it over his head, then looked for a place to tie the rope off. He had discovered that he had to fully intend to go through with it before the waters came. It was essential that the experience was authentic. Soon everything was prepared. He stood poised. His eyes closed. He tensed, ready to step. Sure enough, after a few seconds, he felt the cold sensation of water running over his naked feet. He let the water rise further and further up his legs until it passed his loins. Only then could he be sure. He cautiously opened his eyes. A broad smile spread across his face. Once again, the hidden reservoirs of the forest had risen from the soil to save him. He was soon waste deep in a radiant pool. The cold waters had warmed to a pleasingly refreshing temperature. He wriggled his toes in the soft mud, waiting for the transformation he knew was coming. He glanced around the shoreline that had formed around the nascent pond. It was beautiful. As the water rose, he watched the brightly coloured insects settle on the leaves. They turned their compound eyes towards him. Baxter Long waved at them. The insects waved back. Their mandibles were now mouths. The pads of their feet became hands. The chirruping of the crickets turned to roars of adulation, willing Baxter on. The lilies rose, forming towering stands filled with excited spectators. The water flowed over his shoulders. His toes were no longer wriggling in the mud. Instead, he could feel the soft inside of a running shoe and the firm surface of a running track. The water covered his head, and yet he could still breath freely. The crowd roared. Baxter approached the start, waving again at the crowd as he crouched. He readied himself to spring out of the blocks. A stickleback transformed into a portly steward. Sun hat and flannels. He raised his fin and fired the starting pistol. The crowd roared as Baxter ran. He had never moved with such supple ease; the rest of the ghostly field was left floundering in his wake. The crowd were on their feet as he crossed the finish line. A new world record!

Baxter had set several world records that month. His accolades accumulating in his psychic trophy cabinet. Every day he walked through the woods. Every day enacting the same grotesque subterfuge. Every day the waters came. Every day he ran, jumped and threw his way into the record books as the packed stands cheered him on. Baxter emerged from the pond, the water falling from him and returning to the pool like mercury skittering across a laboratory bench. He breathed in deeply and prepared to enact another round as the pond retreated into the soil, just as it always did. This time he would stun the crowds with his prowess in the javelin. He stretched out his arm and simulated a throw. But outside of the water his arm clicked awkwardly. He cursed and rubbed his shoulder. The ache lingered in his joints as he picked up the rope. As he was bending down, he thought he caught sight of a figure on the other side of the clearing.

*

Hilda was huddled on all fours in the dirt and leaves. The dust of the forest that had stained her cheeks was criss-crossed with dark valleys carved out by streams of tears. She reached up and clawed at the trunk of the ash tree, pulling herself to her feet. The vague tingle continued. Inside the trunk, the impression of DI Ward pushed against the bark. The time was approaching. Hilda's eyes began to focus through the multi-faceted lens of her tears. Before her eyes, the glade was transformed. The muted browns and dark shadows were now complemented by a rainbow of colour. Flowers bloomed in an impossible variety; their pungent bouquet filled the air. Pin-sharp tones blended, creating an unlikely harmony. A chaotic arcadia. A shimmering pond rippled gently in the centre of the clearing. It was magnificent. Across the far side of the pond, she could see the figure of a man. She recognised him but couldn't quite place him. Was it from work, or the pages of a magazine? He was dressed in ill-fitting sports kit. He was throwing a rope over the branch of a tree. His presence was jarring in the bucolic disorder. She saw that he had tied a noose in the rope. He put his head through the noose. He was going to hang himself. She called out to him, but her words rebounded. Ricocheting off an impenetrable membrane. Do no harm. She began to run across the clearing towards the pond, shouting noiselessly at the man as she ran. She reached the shoreline, waving her arms, trying to attract the man's attention. Close, closer, so close she could almost touch him. She reached out to grab the stranger as he adjusted the rope around his neck. He was preparing to jump. Her fingers glanced against the nylon material of his athletics kit, causing a tiny static charge to leap from her fingertips. Then he was gone. Hilda was left clinging to thin air, looking out over the gentle pond. The sound began to rise again. From hiss to harmony. Do no harm.

Under the water the crowds were silent. Baxter waved. He beamed, waiting for the swelling roar to engulf him. But there was only silence. He looked up at the stands in surprise. A thousand blank eyes stared sightlessly back. The crowd stood like a zombie horde. Crooked necks on withered bodies. As if hell had been emptied and dumped on the terraces. This had never happened before. Something was not right. But Baxter could not stop now. Perhaps when he launched the javelin and it again broke all records, as he was certain it would, the crowd would transform, as it had from insect to human. His kit felt awkward and tight. He looked down in dismay as his paunch poked out from under his vest. The crowd stared blankly. He walked across the stadium towards the marked-out runway. The firm track was beginning to lose its integrity. Pools began to appear in the asphalt. His feet squelched as his pumps took on water. He hastily grabbed a javelin from the competition rack and began to mark out his run-up. The pools spread and merged. Dark brown sludge and claggy slime mingled into a horrible ooze that slowly flowed across the field. Baxter drew back his arm. All suppleness was gone. Now only the desperate ache of regret remained clinging to his muscles. Tears welled in his eyes. He had asked too much of the Tangle. His desires would never be satisfied, he knew that now. But it was too late. He ran through the foul mud and let the javelin fly. For a few seconds it described a beautiful arc in an azure sky. The zombie crowd watched its progress. The faintest flicker of life cut across their decaying faces like a badly tuned TV momentarily finding its signal. But as the arc itself began to decay, so the crowd began to devolve into a host of gibbering shadows. Baxter watched the javelin's flight. There would be no world record today. His world was at an end. A terrible howl began to rise from the stands. The javelin stopped in mid-descent and began to turn. Through tears made thick by earth and mud, Baxter watched the javelin travel remorselessly back to the source. Guttural groans filled the dissolving stadium as the stands reverted to mud and silt. The jutting jaws of flies broke through the rotten skin of spectators. All around, the illusion was fading and a dark unreality was taking its place. The javelin seemed to meander through the gloom, travelling at a painfully slow speed. He could see its sparkling metal tip revolving like a satellite. Turning. Turning. The only bright thing in the thickening darkness. He closed his eyes as the tip of the javelin found its target. Burrowing slowly through the sinews of his neck. The revolving spike turned to the branch of the ash as it carried him silently into the black depths of the pond.

*

The blood of life seeped back into the forest floor. Its consistency stiffened by the will of the lost. Into the roots the glutinous ichor flowed. The ash. Queen of the forest. Ruler of the third lunar month. Scion of the original root. Sucked up the blood. Into the bark. Into the leaves. Take only what you need. There was a surplus. A residue. The shimmering drone faded. Hilda stared after its receding echo. At her feet was the body of a man. The will, the longing, the horror. She knelt down to feel for a pulse. But there was none. The ash stirred. The surplus. The residue. Hilda let out a sigh. He looked so defeated in his ill-fitting sports gear. She caught sight of something glistening in the dead leaves. She left the side of the dead athlete and went to study the source. It was a medal. She picked it up, turning it over in her hand. The will, the longing, the horror. She bent over the body and placed the medal carefully around the dead man's neck. She laid it out neatly on his chest. She bowed her head and tried to conjure solemn words. But words were for the living. She looked again at the empty shell of the man. The ash tree stirred. The will, the way, the longing, the horror. Hilda touched the bark as her eulogy died on her lips. The horror would never end, but nor would the beauty. The surplus. The residue. Take only what you need. A silent spark flew. The ash returned what it had taken. The surplus. The residue. Hilda felt nothing as the spark passed into her. She would feel nothing until it was too late to feel anything at all. She would feel nothing, because it gave her nothing. The void was her gift. The emptiness its offering. She pulled her phone from her pocket and called the emergency services.

'In the woods. My name? Oh yes, Hilda Wilton, Dr Hilda Wilton.'

She ended the call and returned the phone to her pocket. As she removed her hand, Hilda studied it with interest. She noted the growing prominence of her veins and the subtle shading left by the soil of the woods, which made her skin look like parchment. She raised her hand to her face and felt her faulty flesh, letting her fingers linger in the pits and crevices. The hint of a smile formed at the edges of her mouth as she turned towards the direction of the town. Take only what you need.

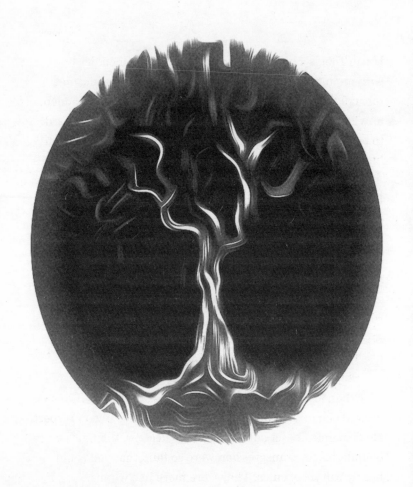

Apple Blossom

Uncle Tobias's hand gripped young Ethan's shoulders
with an inappropriate firmness. The odour of a dedicated
tobacco habit drifted from his fingers. A hint of a forbidden,
unwholesome world that Ethan's mother had tried so hard
to protect him from. But his mother now lay on the chiffon
lining of Lassiter Funeral Home's second-cheapest coffin.
A rough box of wood, six feet down and a short lifetime away.
Ethan stared down at the box, hoping that if he wished hard
enough, he could conjure up one last word of comfort from
his dearly departed mother. Something to make it alright.
Something reassuring like a game of windmills. He imagined
his mother spinning him around, his legs parallel to the
ground, her hands holding his arms as he flew. Round and
round. Round and round. Ethan smiled. Ethan laughed.
A sudden thud and the pressure of Uncle Tobias's reeking
hand snapped him out of his happy dream.

'Stop that, boy.'

Ethan looked up at his guardian, his face falling into a
mute blend of grief and fear. Uncle Tobias was big on respect.
He demanded strict adherence to his decrees, though the
boundaries for transgression were so fluid that you could
hardly call them rules. They were more like whims. A
constantly shifting set of demands, deliberately designed to
be impossible to fulfil. Only the punishments had a terrible
monotonous predictability to them. His mother had hated

Uncle Tobias. A second thud drew Ethan's attention back to the grave. Flowers were falling on his mother's coffin. Thud. Bright flowers on freshly cut stems, sundered from living plants, sacrifices in this strange human ritual. They would decay in the tomb too. Thud. Thud. White petals covered the lid of the coffin like forlorn confetti. Apple blossom. His mother's favourite.

One by one the mourners cast their blooms into the grave, pausing to nod awkward condolences at Ethan and his unwanted foster parents. Uncle Tobias returned their condolences with a curt nod of his own. His hand momentarily left Ethan's shoulder to direct his wife. Aunt Janet. An almost invisible presence in the household. A vague spectre who only materialised when called by his tyrannical uncle. She too was subject to his arbitrary brutality. Isolated and cowed. Soon he would do the same to Ethan. Uncle Tobias pushed his wife forward. He wanted to show a united front. He wanted to show the world that he was the master of the family now that his sainted sister-in-law was gone. She was always scheming, pouring poison into his wife's ear, trying to undermine his authority, trying to prize her away from him. Well not any more. Aunt Janet shuffled forward, acknowledging the mourners with an uncertain smile. Her hand brushed against Ethan's. She glanced down at his confused face and, for a few seconds, a tender look played across her features. The tar-clogged voice of Uncle Tobias broke the conspirators' bond.

'Time to go home. These parasites will be getting pissed at my expense, I suppose. They'll be no wake for us. She's dead and buried and that's that.'

He attempted to guide them back to the car as the gravediggers began to fill the pit. Grubby topsoil shot through with broken masonry and plastic bottle caps tumbled onto the cheap coffin. Thud. Thud. Ethan shrugged off his uncle's hand; he didn't want to leave his mother in such a disgusting hole.

'Wake up, wake up!'

Ethan ran to the edge of the grave. The gravediggers stopped their shovelling and bowed their heads, unsure as to what action was most appropriate. Uncle Tobias grabbed Ethan by his arm, dragging him away from the lip of the grave.

'Come here, you little swine.'

'Don't let him take me!'

'I'll have none of your nonsense, you little shit.'

Uncle Tobias cuffed the boy around the ear. Ethan let out a cry. Some of the departing mourners looked back with anxious faces. Then headed in the direction of the Bull, mumbling to themselves.

'No, I won't go! You can't make me.'

Uncle Tobias slapped the boy hard around the face. His head lurched viciously. Stars sputtered and flashed before his eyes. Such violence. Another cry. But not from Ethan's mouth this time. A mournful note that seemed to stretch and elongate, extending to the point of impossible intensity until it splintered and faded into the early evening air. But no one turned this time. Only the gravediggers seemed aware of the rupture. They looked from the grave to the man and back again. Ethan struggled free from his uncle's grip and ran to the grave. The scream had come from there, he was sure. Why could no one else hear it? He looked down into the pit. Apple blossom blooms peaked out from beneath the soil. Their sweet odour mixing with the damp decay of the earth. He was in an orchard on the edge of a pleasant meadow. His mother chased him around the trees as he giggled and ran. 'I'm going to get you, I'm going to get you, the tickle monster is coming, the tickle monster is coming.' The monster is coming. He fell, he floated, he drifted into the darkness.

Ethan was face down in the soil. Ethan was at the bottom of the grave. His small body flat on his mother's coffin. In his hand he grasped a twig of apple blossom. He looked up, resting his chin on the wooden lid of the coffin. He twirled the stem around between his fingers. The blossom seemed to sparkle in the gloomy surroundings, its perfume pulling him back, back to happier times. Ethan felt a soothing warmth emanating from the coffin. The grave became a womb. Suddenly he became aware of rough hands thrust under his arms as the gravediggers dragged him up. He caught sight of their sympathetic faces as they hauled him to the surface. His uncle waited at the edge. His face had no sympathy; it was red and furious. Uncle Tobias unfolded his arms and snatched Ethan from the gravediggers' embrace without the courtesy of a thank you. Wrenching the apple blossom from Ethan's hand he tossed it on the floor and dragged him towards the car. Aunt Janet followed a few steps behind.

*

The punishments were severe and frequent. In Caxton town's charmless suburbs. Behind the walls of the 1920s detached house. Beyond the off-road parking bay. Inside the pebble-dashed walls. Torture was undertaken with an obsessive attention to detail. Tasks were long and repetitive. Failure to complete them satisfactorily was certain. Even the slightest inaccuracy in the outcome would lead to further repetitions. Tasks, chores, duties. All were gateways to Uncle Tobias's real pleasures: torment. He was a skilled and ruthless operator, running the house like a gulag. Weekends were particularly difficult for Ethan. With work put aside, Uncle Tobias could really indulge himself. There was rarely a let-up in the cycle of punishments, and Ethan would often flop into bed sore and exhausted. As the sun went down and the neighbourhood made its way to bed, Ethan would pull the covers up close, waiting for the creak of the stairs. The sign that his uncle was paying him one of his frequent night-time visits.

Breakfasts were fraught. Uncle Tobias liked to leave the house promptly at 7.25 a.m. He had timed the journey to work perfectly: thirty-five minutes door to door. His routine never altered. But Ethan was a new and unwelcome obstacle to his daily timetable. He was chivvied relentlessly from the moment he woke until his departure for the school bus at 7.20 a.m. No slacking. No dawdling. At 7.23 a.m. Uncle Tobias would lock the door, leaving Aunt Janet imprisoned inside. She had access to the garden, of course. He wasn't a monster. Besides she could keep the garden nice and tidy. Just the way he liked it. The talk of the cul-de-sac. The beautiful garden behind the house of infamy.

Ethan's route to the bus stop never varied. He would walk steadily along the neat footpaths, past the prim and proper flower beds of suffocating ordinariness that bordered the unremarkable gardens of unremarkable people. This was a suburbia of bitter, thwarted ambitions and disappointment. On the way to Long Lane the path opened up into a grassy verge, rising on each side and dotted with shrubs. At the crest of the slope was a small copse of trees. The sentinels of the Tangle. The edge of the matted woods. Ethan used to play there, beyond the borders of the known world, deep in the twisting domain of living things. Every day as he walked past, he could feel its nagging vibration. Under the asphalt, in the cracks of crumbling paving stones. The roots.

At 07.10 a.m. precisely the Bakelite phone clattered into its cradle. This had never happened before. Uncle Tobias looked more than surprised. He hated to be inconvenienced. Fury contorted his jowls, but his phone manner remained faultless.

'Of course, Mr Barrowman, I understand. It's never happened before. No, of course, that's no excuse. I will leave immediately.'

Uncle Tobias replaced the receiver. He continued to utter a steady flow of foul invective as he gathered up his jacket and briefcase. Ethan had never seen his uncle look so uncomfortable. The beast was rattled. He struggled to keep a smile from his face.

'You.'

Uncle Tobias jabbed his finger at Aunt Janet.

'You, you don't . . . don't do . . . just don't do anything. And you.'

In lieu of instructions, Uncle Tobias clipped Ethan around the ear as he headed towards the front door. He watched his uncle's bulk slide across the hallway like a malevolent shadow. The door slammed, causing the teacups to chime against each other as the house shook with his uncle's transmitted fury.

For a few seconds, a dense silence settled in the kitchen. Ethan and his aunt were momentarily free. The kitchen appliances hummed, their electrical cadence absorbing the pair's attention for want of a more familiar focus. Aunt Janet broke the silence.

'I have something for you.'

The sound of her voice surprised Ethan. Like the faltering sentences of a small child, or the cracked dialogue of a hermit recently returned to civilisation. A fresh sentence formed on her lips, but she sucked the words back down. She went out into the hallway. Ethan could see her reaching into her outdoor coat. She pulled an object from the inside pocket. He could see a faint smile play across her pale lips. Aunt Janet was holding something in her hand. He could just make out its spindly silhouette in the ochre glow. It was a sprig of apple blossom. His apple blossom. Aunt Janet returned to the kitchen holding the sprig in front of her like the cross at the head of a pilgrim's progress.

'I went back to get it for you, the day of your mother's funeral.'

His mother's funeral had been weeks ago, and yet the sprig of blossom looked as fresh as the day it was cast into her grave. The petals were firm but delicate. They looked like eyes. His mother's eyes. A drop of water dripped from one of the petals like a tear. It hovered in the static between leaf and floor. Inside its delicate membrane Ethan could see his mother's face smiling back at him. He floated through the static, sinking through the membrane. A whisper drifted across the distance. Words of comfort. Words of prophecy. The teardrop hit the floor.

'You best get to school, Ethan. You don't want to be late.'

*

Ethan's days became uncharacteristically eventful. Not that anything happened. It was more that his moods shifted and pitched in a way that he had almost forgotten. Since his mother's death he had existed on a blank plane of numbness. It was best to press his feelings down. But now he felt something. His sorrow hadn't diminished, but now, at least, he was experiencing something akin to hope, that most human of illusions. Ethan kept the blossom close. He felt the twigs against his torso; they felt like comforting fingers, stroking. Stroking. Often he would take the blossom out and examine it. He took in every detail, every knot, every curve of every shoot. It remained unchanged. Even in the tight confines of his pocket, with all the attendant clutter pressing around it, the blossom never diminished in any way. It was constant, like his mother's love. But the laws of entropy were clear: the apple blossom must decay. As the days passed, his anxiety grew. Decay or discovery, one was inevitable. If his uncle was to find the blossom, he would lose it forever. He must find a safe hiding place.

Monday morning. A dread day for most children, but for Ethan school at least provided a few hours away from the cycle of horror. Breakfast had proceeded with the same military precision. The rustle of his uncle's newspaper, the occasional clink of knife on porcelain, the randomly barked orders, the habitual hum of the morning. Ethan had been somewhat surprised to see his aunt when he returned from school the day the blossom came. He thought she might have taken the opportunity to run. But she had stayed. She had stayed for Ethan. They exchanged the briefest of glances as he left the house. A conspirators' nod.

The walk to the bus was routine enough. Monday held as little surprise as any other day. As he walked, Ethan took the sprig of blossom out of his pocket and examined it again. Every day it somehow seemed fresher and more fascinating. He held it up to the sun. The light caught the petals and radiated out. He paused on the path where it opened out into the green valley of grass. He looked from bough to bank. The soft sound of the grave drifted down the verge. It came from the Tangle. It was a melody, like the songs his mother used to sing to him.

Come walk with me to lilac glade, through woodland, stream and knot.

Come stand beneath the gallows' shade till all weeping
     is forgot.
Leave the tears and terrors to the mischief of the town.
Come walk with me to lilac glade, to the oak tree's
     shady crown.

In darkness now from darkness born, circumference,
     length and span.
In lilac glade the wreath and thorn, wove mockeries
     of man.
In lilac glade beneath the earth, in death's ecstatic bond.
Come walk with me in lilac shade, to the emptiness beyond.

Ethan left the path. The soil seemed to writhe as his feet
touched the grass. Like the rippling tide in the shallows.
Like a shoal turning on the currents. He neither walked nor
climbed. He was carried. The bent back of St Christopher, the
torn arms of Simon of Cyrene. The nameless saints carried
him. The Tangle carried him. Ethan reached the top of the
bank. He was no longer in Caxton's drab suburbs; he was in
the borderless hinterland of nowhere. He entered the wood.
As he stepped, the jumble of roots parted. His sense of time
was forgotten, his location became irrelevant. Further and
further. Until he was deep inside the Tangle. The path grew
wider, flowing like a river into a bright clearing. Shafts of
sunlight penetrated the canopy in mottled columns. Ethan
was deposited in the glade. It felt cloistered and safe. Around
him the chatter of birds was tuned to the melody of the
forest's conjuring rite. Rise sweet child. Rise sweet boy. He
felt the blossom in his hand turn, as if it were attempting to
escape his grip. It was unmistakable, the bough was moving.
It was drawn towards the soil. The sprig of blossom began

to writhe, its bark no longer soft and comforting, but harsh. Biting. Covered with thorns. Ethan dropped the sprig as if he'd been stung. Tears welled in his eyes. His blossom. His beautiful blossom. The blossom drifted slowly down to the forest floor. When it hit, he knew. His tears stopped in an instant. A smile, like the grin of the happy child he once was, shattered the sadness. He began to run around the glade in an ecstatic circle. Ridiculous, stupid, without reason or purpose. Alive again, if only for a few moments. He fell, breathless, to his knees, next to the fallen blossom. He began digging in the soil with his small boy hands, clogging his nails, staining his school uniform with dark streaks. Soon he had created an impressive hole. Ethan planted the blossom inside. He tidied the loose earth around the stem. The earth hugged around the stalk. The trees of the glade bent low over the bough, then sprang back to create a perfect circle in the canopy. The sunlight poured in. Ethan stood and smiled. This would be a good place. The blossom would be safe here. Time spun back to its recognised pattern. The dimensions shimmered, shrank and vanished, retreating to their former concealed locations. Ethan was alone on the path. On the road up ahead, he could see the bus pulling out of the stop. He would be late.

That night was the longest in Ethan's short memory. A grim procession of punishment, belittlement and abuse. But he did not cry. He made no sounds of lamentation or sorrow. He was not there. He thought of the beautiful blossom, even as his uncle misused him.

Ethan ran for the bus the next day, he must not be late again. The dull throb of his bruises offered their counsel. There is no time, Ethan. There is no time. He sighed and dejectedly dragged his sore, battered body along the path. He reached the bus stop. But no one was there. Not one familiar uniform, not one classmate or fellow student. Had he missed it again? Had the school changed the timetable and not told him? He stood for a few minutes looking at his shoes, trying hard to think of a way of escaping the horror he knew was coming.

'Ethan, is that you? Oh, my dear boy, whatever are you doing waiting here?'

It was Mrs Krebbs, the drama teacher, driving past in her mini. Mrs Krebbs pulled the car over and shouted theatrically to Ethan from across the other side of the road. She was a 'fun' adult, an actor in her youth. She lived a few doors down from his uncle's house. Ethan had seen her pruning her privet. He looked embarrassed and continued to stare at his shoes.

'Why, the school is closed for the morning . . . I thought everyone knew . . . Asbestos removal in the science block . . . You best get home . . . We are starting after morning break today, though I don't know for the life of me why we don't just have the whole day off . . . That would be lovely, wouldn't it!'

Ethan managed a shy nod. Mrs Krebbs sensed she was wasting her time and skills on the young boy. She waved, wound up her window and drove off. It took him a few seconds to appreciate the opportunity that this unplanned break presented. His uncle was at work, his aunt wouldn't expect him home for hours. He turned towards the path and headed for the glade.

Ethan ran up the verge and hesitated. The scenery looked commonplace and derivative. His heart sank. He must find the path across the threshold. His mind sought the summoning spell.

Come walk with me to lilac glade, through woodland,
    stream and knot.

*Come stand beneath the gallows' shade till all weeping
is forgot.*

Bit by bit he began to see the landscape fold, becoming richer
and more complex. Colours multiplied. Variety blossomed
on the edge. The gateway opened before him. A smile broke
out on his face as he entered the wood. He was carried along
the path in the same way, but something was different.
This time the sound of the forest was muted like a lullaby.
The hush was oppressive. The welcome he had felt the day
before was not as warm, as if his appearance was somehow
ill timed. As he went deeper into the Tangle his feelings of
awkwardness grew. Eventually he arrived at the glade. It too
was different. Disturbed. As if it had been hastily rearranged.
He remembered his mother running around frantically, trying
to plump up cushions and hide the dirty teacups when his
granny turned up unannounced one afternoon. She did that
a lot before the end. Ethan stepped into the clearing. The
trees had closed their crown once more. The light was soft
and subdued. The sound had dropped to a hum. His eyes
began to widen. Everything was upside down, back to front.
Wrong. Wrong. Where was the blossom? It had gone. He
looked around frantically. Nothing. The young bough lost.
Stolen, broken, dead. Gone. They had promised to keep it
safe. The trees. They had promised. He began to feel anger
swelling inside. He had never been so angry. He had been
betrayed. Abandoned. Ethan sank to his knees. He would lie
here and wait for the end. No one cared. Not a single person
alive or dead. A branch creaked. Ethan started. Had his uncle
found him? Let him come, there was nothing left for him to
take. But it was only the trees that stirred. He studied the
gnarled branch that swayed and groaned in the breeze.

Its movement was unnatural. Here in the heart of nature, far from the regularity of men, this branch was pointing. It was unmistakable. The sticks, the bulbs, the leaves, all pointing. Pointing to a spot on the forest floor. Ethan wiped his eyes with his dirty sleeve and followed the line. A subtle light played across the figure of a plant. A sapling. An apple tree. Ethan clapped his hands and began to laugh. This was no tomb; it was a nursery. He approached the delicate plant. It was stretching and flexing its stems, feeling its growing potency as the sap rose. Ethan pressed his hands on the young bark. A whisper echoed around the glade. A voice as familiar as his own.

Come walk with me to lilac glade, through woodland,
*   stream and knot.*
Come stand beneath the gallows' shade till all weeping
*   is forgot.*
Leave the tears and terrors to the mischief of the town.
Come walk with me to lilac glade, to the oak tree's
*   shady crown.*

In darkness now from darkness born, circumference,
*   length and span.*
In lilac glade the wreath and thorn, wove mockeries
*   of man.*
In lilac glade beneath the earth, in death's ecstatic bond.
Come walk with me in lilac shade, to the emptiness beyond.

The day went quickly. All he could think about was the apple tree. Nothing could dislodge the joy from his heart. At 4 p.m. the bell sounded for the end of the school day; he ran for the bus. He jumped out at the top of Long Lane and ran down

the path. The verge rose up to meet the Tangle. He rose with
it. At the summit the gate opened, and he stepped inside.
He glided through the undergrowth until he reached the
glade. His own sacred grove where the spheres intersected.
The clearing chimed with the chatter of living things. At its
centre was the miraculous sapling. It had matured and grown.
Sapling no more. Here was the tree. Somehow, though he
knew it was impossible, Ethan was not surprised. The forest
floor wore garlands of blossom that gathered in bright arcs
where it had fallen. On the branches of the tree, the flowers
had been replaced by sparkling green apples. He marvelled
at their perfection: their skin was taught and shiny, with
the slightest hint of dew glistening on their unblemished
roundness. He reached up and plucked one from a low-
hanging bough. The trees seemed to ripple around him as
he took a bite into the apple. It was the most delicious thing
he had ever tasted, a subtle sweetness that insinuated itself
into every nerve and cell. Just that one bite filled him with
a feeling of extraordinary well-being, as if the flesh of the
apple had been transubstantiated. He took another bite. The
flesh contained a code. In its juice, a message that trickled
down his throat. As it seeped into him, the meaning of the
code was revealed. He was small, too small to understand the
shapes and colours of this new world. The voice, the pulse, the
beating heart. His mother guiding him towards his essence.
First steps, first words. Words coaxed from his developing
mind by his mother's love. He grew, mushrooming from the
sack of sinews and skin into a person. The voice, the pulse,
the tutor's hand. He was a boy, this boy, any boy, any girl,
neither, nor, nothing. He was nothing. As the juice reached
his heart he was erased and reset. He was Ethan, he was no
one. Now he was of the Tangle. The familiar whisper floated

around him. Dripping from the skin of the apple, flowing in the sap of the wood. The sound drifted into his small boy ears. The cipher decoded. The plan set in motion. He looked up into the canopy as it loomed over him, and he smiled.

*

Ethan tumbled through the door, propelled by his uncle's reeking hand. He was obliged to wait for his return every day, no matter the weather. He must be standing ready for his uncle to unlock the stockade. He had been talking to his aunt through the letter box, passing messages to her from the Tangle. He could see her fractured silhouette through mottled glass as she bent down. She had sounded delighted at his tale, though he sensed some incredulity in her hesitant replies. But now his uncle had returned, silence had descended once more.

'What have you got in your pockets, you little shit? You'll ruin that coat and I'm not buying you another one!'

Uncle Tobias clipped him around the ear in a thoughtless reflex and stuck his hand into Ethan's pocket.

'Apples?'

Uncle Tobias's face momentarily broke from his usual scowl.

'I like apples, oh yes. Apple pie with custard, oh yes, yes indeed. Janet, I shall have apple pie after the meat.'

Uncle Tobias licked his lips, letting a globule of saliva roll down his chin.

'None for the boy. That'll teach him for mistreating his clothes so appallingly.'

Uncle Tobias clipped him again. But it lacked his usual accuracy and merely ruffled Ethan's hair.

Ethan's stomach complained. Protesting with a low frequency rumble. Uncle Tobias clouted him again. His uncle had made him watch as he inhaled a vast plate of greasy

meat and potatoes. Ethan had nothing. This was merely
a warm-up for later punishments. Uncle Tobias belched
and farted simultaneously, a skill that Ethan had always
marvelled at. That lumbering turd. Clout. Ethan's smile was
undimmed. Clout.

'What do you look so fucking happy about?'

Uncle Tobias bellowed, his foul breath smothering Ethan
as his uncle's furious face hovered inches from his nose. Clout.
But his smile remained undiminished. Uncle Tobias looked
confused. He raised his hand to strike again, but the scent of
a freshly baked apple pie stopped his swing. Ethan and Uncle
Tobias both turned their heads towards the oven. Trails of
perfumed steam drifted across the kitchen. Uncle Tobias's
mouth flopped open, drool cascading down his grotesque jaw.
Ethan's smile widened, his cheeks struggling to contain it.
He turned to look at his uncle. His gaoler. His tormentor.
He took in every detail of his face, every foul crevice and pit.
Ethan's smile straightened as he concentrated. He looked
more intently now. Into his sweat-filled pores. Into his greasy
follicles. Ethan studied him like a specimen of putrid fungus.

'Oh my, Janet, that sm—sm—smells . . . Oh my.'

Uncle Tobias struggled to form the words as the pie
made its way to the table. His yellow eyes bulged. His flabby
tongue flicked. He loudly cleared his throat, preparing the
passage for the coming pie. He clipped Ethan around the ear
absentmindedly. Ethan felt nothing. Ethan was still studying
his pustulant uncle.

'Not a crumb for you, little shit, not a fucking crumb.'

He wanted to clout him again, but the scent of the pie was
too much. Uncle Tobias grabbed his spoon in his grubby fist.
He plunged it into the golden crust.

'Oh my.'

Uncle Tobias's voice was no louder than a whisper. His faced glowed in the light of the exposed fruit that lay hidden beneath the golden crust. Sumptuous and glistening in the embrace of his aunt's best Pyrex. The ambrosial scent peaking in intensity. A subtle vibration pulsed through Uncle Tobias's flabby frame as he dug his spoon into the pie. His eyes widened. His first bite. The juice seething in the crust. The taste. Too much. Too profound in its depth and variety for any pallet to make sense of. Ethan stared intently; he could see his uncle's synapses sparking as he chewed. His brain struggling to process the signals. There was the briefest of pauses after the first mouthful, as if Uncle Tobias momentarily sensed the nature of the fruit. But he was not of the Tangle. Greed was the maxim that guided his kind. There was a blur of spoon and hand. Uncle Tobias shovelled the pie into his corpulent maw with mechanical diligence. Ethan thought his uncle might suffocate, such was the rate at which he filled his mouth. A series of stuttering snorts kept his lungs full as he continued his relentless binge. The pie dish sat empty. Not a single crumb remained. He had claimed the prize. He could savour the victory. Uncle Tobias lent back in his chair and let out a long, elongated belch. Ethan relaxed too. The flat line of concentration bent back into a smile.

His uncle was breathless and bloated. His nose had started to run. Uncle Tobias produced his handkerchief and blew hard.

'Damn itchy nose, must be the dust. Don't you ever clean up around here, Janet?'

Aunt Janet looked at her husband with a newly discovered defiance. The whispers at the letter box. The childish babble of Ethan's fantastic story. She sensed prophesy at work, even as she stewed the apples. Janet had kneaded the flour into the perfect disguise. The crust was the sheath. The apples the dagger. She was an assassin. Uncle Tobias let out a belch like the chorus of hell.

'I said, don't you ever dust this fucking kitchen?'

Uncle Tobias grabbed at her arm as she was collecting the empty dish. Aunt Janet wrenched her arm from his grip.

'No.'

One word. With all the power of a sermon. The pie dish clattered to the floor. Ethan laughed. Uncle Tobias's eyes darted between Ethan and his wife. What was this? Mutiny?

'What the fuck are you laughing at, little shit? Pick that up! Pick it up this instant!'

'What's wrong with your nose, Uncle Tobias?'

Ethan enquired through stuttering laughter. Aunt Janet's hand went to her mouth as she saw the joke begin to reveal its punchline. Her laugh harmonised with her nephew's.

'Oh, yes! What is it, Tobias? What's wrong with your nose?'

Uncle Tobias began to unravel. His power over his captives waning fast. His hand shot up to his left nostril. Something was growing through the mucus. He tugged at the blockage. A slender green shoot sprouted from his nostril, unfurling in the yellow light of the kitchen. It writhed and thrashed in the air like a new-born serpent hatched from the egg. Uncle Tobias tugged at the shoot. It kept coming. He let out a groan. Ethan laughed again. Now a second tendril was sprouting from his right nostril. Uncle Tobias's voice became a congested snarl.

'What's haaaarrrgpening!'

Ethan was on his feet now. Laughing and clapping as he jumped up and down on the spot. Janet tilted her head and enjoyed the view, like a proud parent at the school nativity play. Uncle Tobias went to punch them for their impudence. A branch exploded out of his thigh. Uncle Tobias screamed as the gnarly frond entwined itself around his leg and fixed him fast to the chair.

'Do something! Get a knife, cut me out! Cut me out!'

His last words were strangled in his throat as a thick branch crept out of his gullet. Small twigs edged across his lips, clamping his mouth shut. Ethan stopped jumping and clapping. He watched in fascination. The whisper in the woods played in a loop. Aunt Janet's arm reached out over Ethan's shoulder, pulling him into her side. He buried himself in her embrace. They stood in silence, as if they were watching an eclipse or a beautiful sunset. Uncle Tobias's eyes were wide with ignorant indignation. Too late had he realised his fragility and weakness. A thin branch flicked his eye out, stretching the optical nerve taut until it snapped, leaving Uncle Tobias's eyeball skewered to the stick like a strange fruit. His chest burst. His trunk became the trunk of a tree. Roots where his legs had been, spreading across the lino floor, burrowing into the soil beneath the suburban hell. Uncle Tobias's features were barely discernible through the spreading foliage. Contorted with confusion and disbelief, defeated, broken, stretched and smashed. At last, his skull snapped. The canopy spread out across the ceiling, broken fragments of skull and flesh hung from the twigs. As the flourishing of the tree slowed, small green buds emerged from shoots. One by one, they opened. Into blossom. Apple blossom.

Janet sighed. Cupping a flower gently in her palm, she inhaled the delicate scent.

'What a beautiful tree, Ethan.'

'Yes, Aunty, what a beautiful tree.'

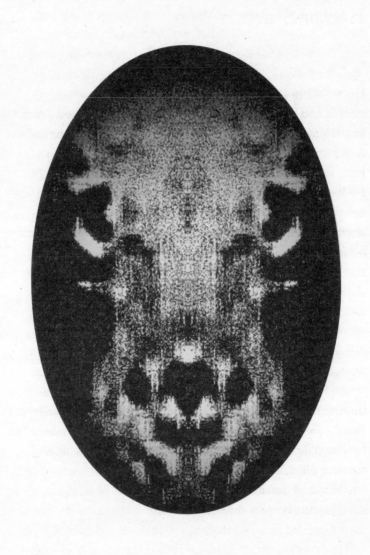

Hector Starts a War

Hector was a hound. A hybrid. A variety chocolate box of
strains and blood lines. A mutt, a mongrel, a mixture. A good
boy. Dumped in the Tangle by a pack of ridiculous humans.
As a puppy, his early life was difficult, but not without joy.
He tumbled in the leaves and found food in the forest.
Friends too. Many of the animals living in the wood were
helpful. Those not intent on eating him anyways. But he was
no wolf, and he struggled to survive in the rough and tumble
of the Tangle. Nevertheless, he found a way to grow into a
reasonably robust dog. His fur was matted, and his muzzle
was a mess. But he had learned wisdom from the woods: how
to hide, how to hunt, which berries were good to eat, and
which ones would kill him. But the first lesson was a warning.
Avoid men. They were the deadliest of all the animals. Killers,
the lot of them.

But Hector was a dog. His species had grown attached to
these mean bipeds. Back in time, humans had lived in the
Tangle too. Hector's ancestors had watched them from the
bushes. The humans would gather in small groups around
burning piles of wood and leaves. They would incinerate the
animals they had killed over the fire. They were rapacious,
slaughtering beyond their needs. They inhabited the skins of
their prey and polished their bones to decorate themselves
and their dwellings. The dogs watched them. They seemed
cruel and taciturn, they seldom mixed with the other animals,

and often killed simply for pleasure. But a few of them seemed nice enough. Some of the dogs ventured down to the humans' nest. Probing the perimeter. At first, they were met with a flurry of stones and angry grunts. But as time went on, they were gradually accepted at the burning piles the humans huddled around. It was warm there. There was food too. Bones too big to wear as ornaments, or too small to make effective clubs, were discarded around the fire. Perfect for the dogs. Over time, a symbiotic relationship began to build between them; the dogs would guard, fetch and kill for the humans, and the humans would in turn provide a degree of comfort for the dogs. It was a good deal. Most of the time.

Hector knew something of humans. Some were kind, at least some he had met. They would stroke his fur and tickle his stomach, giving him treats or playing games that they seemed to take great delight in. Endlessly throwing balls was one thing humans seemed fond of. Hector would run and drop, run and drop, over and over again. They were very sweet, but, by and large, pretty dumb. Their senses were stunted. Their bodies were weak. They blustered about blindly breaking things, never noticing what it was they were breaking. Most of creation was closed to them. As they enjoyed their daily strolls, Hector would take in all the fascinating scents along the path. He could travel through time by smell alone, sensing all the animals that had passed that way before. To him, each scent was a gateway to enlightenment. A message, a signature. He felt the great web of life flowing through the air, and the possibilities of future events encoded in the olfactory flow. While he immersed himself in the richness of experience, the humans would jabber dumbly to each other, carelessly thwacking broken sticks on the surrounding foliage. His first humans had been physically faulty too. Microbes had found them wanting and they had perished. The next humans he encountered were fucking horrendous. By some unfortunate happenstance he found himself passed like some bound chattel to this benighted family. Brutal, arrogant, corrupt and even more stupid than the last lot. Though he was only a small puppy he was far wiser than these idiots. His short time with them was unpleasant; he was bashed and abused, starved, beaten and eventually dumped. That's how he found himself in the Tangle.

On a clear day in spring Hector was playing in the long grass that sprang up in disorderly clumps in the woodland clearings. He was sniffing the recently blossomed flowers, sensing the patterns of the coming months, when he was alerted to a familiar scent drifting on the breeze. The scent of carbolic, compounds, components and manufactured things. The scent of humans. Hector froze. What variety of Homo sapiens was trudging through the woods? Hector ran to the safety of a thicket and sniffed the air. His ears pricked up. The sound of laughter. Soft and joyous, without a hint of malice. The naïve chattering of simple creatures. They sounded harmless enough at least. Hector sniffed the air again. Food. Humans called it a picnic. Hector was starving; his ability to hunt was impaired by his inexperience and inappropriate colouring. Filth could not hide his yellow fur. Hector made a tentative step out of the thicket and whimpered to get their attention. Sympathy was one emotion humans possessed, though only in its most unsophisticated form. The human chatter stopped. He could smell them coming closer. Hector barked uncertainly, having not uttered a sound for several weeks. The human chatter started up again. Hector detected concern in their tone. He barked again, this time with more urgency.

'Oh look, Mummy, it's a little dog! Oh my, poor thing, look at the state of it.'

'Must be starving. Give it something from the hamper, Dad.'

So it was that Hector found himself in the spartan surroundings of the St Hamilton Street Municipal Dog Pound. The first few days felt like a continuation of the indignities he had suffered as a puppy. Their first act had been to cut off his balls. The operation left him in a stupor for days, but after time the pain of loss faded somewhat. Hector would deal with the now; there was no point worrying about might-have-beens. In the pound the possibilities for interesting scent experiences were limited, but the food was good, and the other inmates were pleasant enough. They were a ragtag pack of strays and abused canines who had been rescued from the clutches of various unsympathetic humans. Barely understandable, but sadly familiar, tales of neglect and violence formed the backstory to most of the residents, but strangely few felt any lasting resentment. There were, after all, still a few good humans. The ones that helped and the ones that needed the dogs' help in turn. Hector was hoping for a place to lay his paws. A soft couch and a warm fire. Just like the fire his ancestors had gathered around all those millennia ago. On a late spring morning, the Tangle provided.

He was woken early by the swoosh of a broom and the scraping of a ladder on the concrete floor of the cell block. The good humans were scrubbing the whole place top to bottom with more vigour than usual. Hector and some of his fellow hounds poked their noses through the bars to get a better idea of what was going on. They were putting up bunting and flags. Very strange. Next, a crew of gruff-looking humans came in. They ran thick cables which snaked along the floor to anglepoised lamps. A man came in with a large camera and positioned it to focus on the area where the beams of light met. Hector barked across the central walkway to one of his comrades. A flustered-looking guy with a clipboard cocked his head in Hector's direction.

'Hope these mutts keep their yaps shut when the big man gives his speech.'

A group of serious-looking men joined the flustered-looking man. They were wide and stocky, with dark shades, dark suits, stony faces. They started to check the place over, shining flashlights into the shadows. He sniffed their scent. Military, cordite, sweat and boot polish. Guard humans. After a while they all filed out, except a couple of the serious ones who stood in silence with their chests puffed out. Their fists, hanging at crotch level, balled into their palms. Occasionally one of them would put his hand to his ear. Hector could make out the buzz of chatter in the guard's earpiece. He was receiving commands. Stay. Fetch. Good boy.

'Big Bird is in transit. Standby.'

'We have visual. Unit 2 standby.'

'Roger, roger.'

'Big Bird arrival imminent. Standby.'

'Groundhog, we are go. All units stay sharp.'

Hector could smell the wild gaggle of humans before they had got anywhere near the kennels. They gave off a confusing stench, ranging from obsequiousness to violent overconfidence. His ears pricked up as the rabble approached. Some of the former guard dogs began to alert out of habit. A member of staff and the flustered human ran ahead of the pack and tried to calm them.

'It's OK, boys, nothing to get excited about. It's just the president.'

The president? Hector snaffled up the treats the flustered man had thrown into his pen as the mob of humans burst into the kennel. Cameras flashed and voices clashed. The dogs barked in unison.

'Mr president, will you be increasing funding to animal welfare groups in the next budget?'

'Mr president, did you have a dog growing up, sir?'

'Mr president, will you be letting the kids name the dog?'

'Mr president, is there a poop scoop in your briefing room?'

Laughter skittered around the group like a wasp at a window. All their bodies seemed to be focused in one direction. Hector couldn't quite see the subject of their attention, but he could smell him. He had the scent of frailty and misplaced hubris. He smelled of fear. The pack of reporters, bodyguards and the bigwigs from the dog pound charity began to move along the kennel, stopping to inspect each inmate in turn. The artificial click-clack of camera shutters stuttered down the line of cages. They were getting closer to Hector's pen. He could see the arched backsides of the reporters as they reversed along the row. Then there he was. The president, apparent leader of the ecstatic technocratic regime.

'This one is very special, Mr president. He was found living in the woods all alone, poor thing. He was a terrible mess when he was brought in, but as you can see, our team did a marvellous job fixing him up.'

Hector cocked his head. Who me? They're talking about me. The president came closer to the bars. Hector could see him clearly now, and his first impressions had been correct: his looks matched his scent. Around sixty years old, with a sadness about him that lingered behind his eyes, seeping through his veneer of confidence. He was conservatively dressed, as were all the humans in his pack. But he looked like he would be more comfortable in a fishing vest and plaid shirt. He was a simple man, dull even, and any spark of vivacity or charm was superficial. He looked scared. Hector felt sorry for him and put up his paw to comfort the frightened human.

'Aw look, he likes you, Mr president.'

The president broke into a smile.

'It certainly looks that way, hey boy.'

He locked eyes with Hector and offered him his hand to sniff. So the president knew dogs, it seemed. Hector sniffed. Mid-price cologne. A faint smell of tobacco. Probably a secret smoker. A woman's fragrance. Traces of childish things. Maybe two or three children, one quite young, the others just shy of their teens. He married late, or maybe remarried? The stale sweat lingered on his pores. He was busy: the fading odour of hand soap meant he hadn't had time to adequately rinse. He perspired a lot due to the effort expended supressing his uncertainty. Out of his depth. A political patsy controlled by more self-assured operators. Hector licked his hand.

'Hector! Don't lick the president!'

'That's OK, I like the little chap.'

The president scratched Hector behind the ears. He wagged his tail and rotated his head in a semi-circle to get the full effect of the presidential scratching. The president definitely knew dogs.

Flashbulbs popped like corn in a pot as the president held Hector up for all the world to see. Hector dutifully licked his face to the rapture of the gawping humans.

'Will he get his own bodyguard, Mr president?'

'What about his security clearance, Mr president? How can you be sure he isn't a spy!'

More laughter from the press pack. Hector wagged his tale, happy to see the humans happy. The flustered human hurried them out to a waiting convoy of limousines as the gaggle of reporters continued their chatter. The door of the president's limousine closed with an airtight thunk. Hector was now government property.

*

The presidential palace was a wonderful place for time travelling. The accumulated scents of centuries clung to every cushion, cornice and skirting board. Fascinating to think of all those generations of leaders and their followers who had deposited their memories in the fabric of the building. Hector sniffed everything, intoxicated by the complexity of the place, so much grander than his previous homes. They had smelled of defeat, anger and resignation. This place smelled of power. But under the top note was the acrid odour of misplaced confidence. Almost all human dwellings had it, but in this building it was overwhelming. Hector pretty much had the run of the place and enjoyed checking in on the various departments of government to see if they were happy. He would pad into offices, tail wagging. Most were glad to see him, but some were too glum to raise a smile. These humans seemed to be suffering terribly. Hector thought it cruel and unfair that they had to be so afflicted. He wished he could help them. Sometimes he would claim a small victory; rolling on his back or raising a paw seemed to crack even the steeliest of malcontents. Those moments were heaven for Hector. To see the curl of the mouth and the light twinkling behind the sadness. Even the most brutal humans could be capable of love, he thought.

Some of the humans were a particular mystery to Hector. The ones with the medals lashed to their tunics like Pantone strips. The ones with tombstone teeth and permanent suntans. The ones with the impersonal statistics and growth forecasts. They loved Hector. They ruffled his fur. 'Good boy, good boy.' But they hated other humans. The president was forever banging the table when they came around to visit. Hector would hide under the desk. Inhaling the conflict as the pheromones darted across the Cabinet Room. The vice president and his coterie of advisors would often be called in to steer the argument to some kind of conclusion. But Hector sensed the president wasn't always convinced by the outcome. The familiar scent of defeat and uncertainty lingered in his wake as he paced the presidential quarters. Occasionally he would slump down on the sofa. Hector would hop up, doing his best to coax a smile from the unhappy man.

'Hey boy, you don't know how lucky you are. Not a care in the world, eh boy?'

Hector humoured the dumb commander-in-chief by wagging his tale and licking his face. He really had no idea. Hector's life was full of worry, but he never let it overwhelm him. To say he lived in the now was too simple. In the Tangle, all things lived in the past, present and future simultaneously. Aware of the ebb and flow of events, but never confident of their outcome. Life was more pleasantly surprising like that. Humans were a perplexing anomaly in the flow of all things. They were forever disrupting the balance. They were heedless of warnings, however dramatic. They had invented a universe for themselves. Setting parameters of their own invention. Creating subdivisions, charts and categories that always placed them at the apex. Like precocious youths who won't be told, they swaggered and tutted their way to disaster. Still, he liked them. Perhaps these humans would mutate into something more benign in time.

These thorny issues were beginning to play on Hector's mind as he scampered along the corridors of power. Everyone here seemed so stressed and unhappy. One afternoon in high summer, when they should all have been out taking in the air, a particularly stern group of humans entered the presidential offices. Curtains were closed, and all but the president's closest confidants were ushered out of the room. Hector curled up under the desk as usual, listening to the cascade of chatter. He sniffed the air to discern its meaning.

'Mr president, we believe this will be an important addition to our arsenal and a major deterrent for the hostiles. Our intelligence suggests we are years ahead of them with this particular technology, sir.'

'OK, OK, I've read the briefing, Colonel Hyacinth. I know you guys at defence are keen to green-light this project . . . project . . . what are you calling it again?

'Project Good Boy, sir.'

Hector's ears pricked up.

'Good Boy, I understand. So, like, be a good boy or you're all gonna get it, right?'

'Something like that, sir, yes.'

One of the group of very stern-looking men had a metal briefcase handcuffed to his wrist. The colonel clicked his fingers and the briefcase man inserted an odd-looking key into the lock. A dim light emanated from inside. The colonel continued.

'Project Good Boy is a pathogen delivery system that will dump a virus designed to nullify the hostiles' geno-specific capability to offer battlefield countermeasures, or, for the non-combatant component of their possible response vector to coalesce into a coherent resistance module, right down their gizzards, sir.'

Hector smelled confusion.

'Thank you, colonel. Perhaps you could clarify a few points for me.'

'It kills them, sir.'

'All of them?'

'Yessir, every last one of them.'

'That sounds very effective, colonel. How does this weapon work exactly?'

'The genome specificity is modulated . . .'

'In layman's terms, if you please.'

'Yes sir, sorry sir. Project Good Boy targets the specific sociogenetic make-up of the hostiles, splitting them apart at the subatomic level, rendering them inert, sir.'

'Inert, eh? Sounds nasty. How do we know it won't do the same to us, colonel?'

'Well sir, our scientists assure me that the hostiles are different from us, sir, like a different species. More like animals than bona fide human beings.'

Hector smelled bullshit and rolled onto his back. He began to groom himself, paying particular attention to the scar where his ball sack had once been. *'More like animals.'* He licked his paws and tuned into the chatter again.

'Are you sure about that, colonel? I've met a number of the hostiles and they seemed pretty similar to me. Are you sure this race bomb will work? I'd sure hate to wave that thing around if it ended up killing us all.'

'Absolutely, Mr president. They've run the numbers and conducted all the tests. It seems we are superior in every way to the enemy. We have nothing to fear from these patriotic germs, Mr president, sir, of that I can assure you.'

'That *is* reassuring, colonel. What do you make of it, Newt?'

The president turned to the vice president, who was listening patiently in the shadows.

'I recommend green-lighting the project. The science is clear. We cannot afford to slip behind in the pathogen arms race, Jack.'

'Very well. Keep me informed of your progress, colonel.'

The stern humans saluted and marched out of the office. Hector emerged from the desk and sniffed the floor as they left. The odour of overconfidence clung to the carpets like tobacco smoke on a woollen jumper. He detected the scent of the pathogen too. Despite their best efforts, the germs could not be contained. Their faulty human senses had failed to detect the subtle depths of the microbes' being. They were safe enough. For now. The quantity was too low to cause any significant harm. Hector was happy for that. He sniffed the air. Just as he thought. Bullshit. In fact this particular pathogen, though rare, was not unfamiliar in the Tangle. It lurked in the hidden substrata of the forest. The other animals acknowledged it and left it in peace. But somehow the humans had chivvied it out in their eagerness to find fresh ways to kill. The pathogen was not happy about the disturbance and had mutated into its most aggressive form in response. Hector barked a warning. It was deadly. They should put it back where they found it.

'You need to go outside? Hey Jasper, can you take the dog around the grounds? Poor guy probably needs a pee.'

'Certainly, Mr President. Come on boy, do you want to play catch outside?'

The ball was fun. He'd done his best. Hector followed the aide into the gardens of the presidential compound. He looked like he needed to play fetch. Hector wondered if he'd ever really understand these creatures. If only they could just say what they wanted.

*

The following year was a difficult one for the president and his friends. The hostiles had been doing things and going places the president wasn't happy about. There had been threats issued and people had been killed. Hector heard it all, curled up under the president's desk. He wanted to help them, but so far they hadn't listened to his advice. One morning the sternest of all the president's staff ran into the meeting room, smelling of panic.

'Mr president, our intelligence suggests the hostiles are massing on the border, sir. Satellites confirm a massive troop build-up at their forward bases. We are advising you move to a safe location immediately, sir.'

'Initiate the Carthusian Complex.'

'Yes, sir, isolation at a secure location for all key staff. We recommend urgency, sir.'

Hector ran across the lawn as the president waved to the group of photographers who were permanently camped outside the compound. A flurry of indistinct questions drifted across the lawn. The words were scattered by the rotation of a helicopter's blades, making them sound like the script from an experimental theatre piece. The president fixed a smile and waved, as various aides flung important government documents into the chopper. The stern man with the briefcase handcuffed to his wrist stood a few metres away. He had become a permanent fixture in recent months, since Project Good Boy had been successfully completed. The president ducked his head as the draft of the helicopter blades sucked up his hair like a family of curious snakes coaxed from a basket. He sat between two burly guards. Hector jumped onto his lap and licked his face reassuringly. He knew how much the president hated flying.

The bunker had few scents of interest. No history, fully sanitised, vacuum sealed. But it did have one advantage: its seclusion. The Carthusian Complex was situated in the remotest part of the country, housed deep within the rock of a mountain. The secret hatch opened up onto a rolling green meadow, dotted with wildflowers and low shrubs. At its boarder the Tangle blended into the lawn. Bush became thicket became forest. Whilst the president strolled with his advisors, deep in conference, Hector would run into the woods. It was a relief to be amongst the chaos of nature. The wild proliferation of scents and the stories those perfumes told. Hector made enquiries whilst he was there. What was the best way to help his troubled human friends? How could he make them happy? They were suffering terribly. The Tangle would know. He found answers in the roots and in the secret places where the microbes dwelt. Some decisions were very hard to make, he thought.

'So the hostiles haven't agreed to any of our terms? What does that mean, Newt, in terms of our response?'

'The hostiles aren't happy, that's for sure. We need to be decisive, Jack. The gloves are off now, I'm afraid.'

'I have to agree with the vice president. We must take action, sir, and, of course, we always have Project Good Boy.'

Colonel Hyacinth nodded at the stern man with the briefcase. The stern man returned his nod with a whip-crack nod of his own.

'I'll hear no more talk of Project Good Boy, not until every possible angle has been tried, and that's an order, Colonel Hyacinth!'

'Yes, *sir*!'

Colonel Hyacinth offered a salute to his commander-in-chief, whilst giving the vice president a sly side-eye. *'The hostiles aren't happy.'* No one was happy, Hector thought. He felt sad.

The following days took on the same familiar pattern. The bad news mounted, and the threat of conflict loomed ever larger. Hector padded around the sterile corridors. His visits to the Tangle were becoming less frequent as security was stepped up at the base. But the diagnosis had been painfully clear.

'Mr president, I really must urge you to deploy Project Good Boy, sir, before the hostiles have a chance to overrun us. They have a nearly two-to-one advantage in battle tanks and a three-to-one ratio in heavy bombers. We just can't sustain the losses likely in a conflict situation, sir.'

'Thank you for your advice, Colonel Hyacinth, but we are not actually at war.'

'For now, Jack, but how long can this stand off last? There's happiness to think of, happiness is everything, God damn it!'

The vice president banged his fist down on the conference room table, disrupting the plastic models of ships, tanks and aeroplanes that were dotted about a map of the world. The humans looked awful. Pale yellowing skin, dark rings and heavy bags like refuse sacks, dangling under blood shot eyes. They had barely eaten. Once corpulent men now looked like withered scarecrows dressed for Halloween. Jackets had been long discarded, revealing shirts stained with sweat patches and collars black with grime. Hector was as concerned as any dog would be. He had tried his best capering. Sit. Good boy. But he had only been greeted by increasing hostility. The humans were reverting to type. There was a limit to his patience. The Tangle had warned him. Back when he was only a pup, it had warned him. Avoid the humans. They were difficult. You couldn't teach them a thing. Don't waste your time Hector. It had warned him. They are too much responsibility.

'Mr president, the folks in the cities are in a bad way. One thousand dead today from lack of food, and another five hundred killed in rioting. Sir, we have to do something!'

'Hyacinth's right, Jack. It's time to deploy Project Good Boy.'

The president's eyes filled with tears. He hadn't slept for days. The pressure was just too much for a simple man like him. Hector saw him in his plaid shirt, casting a line into a woodland river. Hector scampering over the rocks looking for sticks to chew.

'I'm so tired, Newt, so fucking tired.'

'OK, OK, Jack, you get some sleep. We'll make the decision once you've had a chance to rest.'

The vice president shot Colonel Hyacinth a conspiratorial look. Hyacinth in turn nodded to the briefcase guy.

'Get the president a sleeping pill, won't you?'

The vice president clicked his fingers. An aide appeared with a glass of water and a white tablet. The president took the glass distractedly, took a sip and swallowed the pill. The bodyguards snapped to attention and escorted the president to his quarters. Hector lingered under the briefing room table.

'Right, you, get that thing over here.'

The stern briefcase human clicked his heels together and gave an inappropriate salute.

'Jesus, Hyacinth, where'd you get this guy?'

'He's a patriot, sir.'

The stern, patriotic briefcase guy placed the briefcase on the table, just above the spot where Hector was curled up.

'Who's got the key?'

'Fuck. The president has the key, around his neck, sir.'

'What, there's only one key?'

'No sir, but you need two keys to arm the device . . . the other is in the base commander's safe.'

'OK, Hyacinth, fetch me that key. I'll try and get the other one off the president's neck. He's gonna be in la la land right

now, those pills are strong. Get to it, Hyacinth, and take
the briefcase guy with you in case anyone starts any funny
business.'

'Sir, yes, sir.'

The angry humans left the briefing room, trailing their
angry scent behind them. They went looking for the launch
keys. But they would not find them.

Hector padded over to his place of precious things. He
nuzzled the items he had acquired during his time in the
bunker. A couple of tennis balls, the drill sergeant's slipper, a
bone from the canteen and two Project Good Boy launch keys.

*

For days he had watched the humans unravel. Their
appearance becoming progressively more dishevelled. The
mood turning ever sourer and more aggressive. He had done
all he could, but the Tangle was right, there was little to be
done for these troubled creatures. Hector pawed at one of
his tennis balls, enjoying watching its erratic orbit around
the place of precious things. He was putting off his decision.
He had a responsibility. He knew that. Things would only
get worse for his friends if he did nothing. Things had really
begun to unravel in the bunker. Hector thought it wise to
remove the dangerous items from the base and put them in a
safe place, so his friends wouldn't come to any harm. Tennis
balls were a terrible trip hazard. Old bones unhygienic.
Launch keys? Well, they were the most dangerous of all.
Who knew what harm they could do if he let them play with
those? Removing the president's key had been easy; he was
easily distracted. He had placed it over the chair in his room
while he was changing into his last clean shirt. The president
was so exhausted that he quite forgot he was supposed to be

wearing it. The base commander was a little trickier, but still, simple enough. Hector had waited until the safe was open. The base commander was quite an amiable fellow. He loved Hector and had remained on good terms with him, even as the others became more taciturn. Hector had simply nosed his ball across the floor. Barked. Then lifted the key from the safe as the base commander went to retrieve the ball. Shutting the door of the safe and patting Hector on the head, he was none the wiser.

They would be back soon. The angry humans and the vice president. Hector tugged at the threads of the tennis ball. He rolled onto his back and wiggled about on the floor, enjoying the roughness on his fur. He sprang up, dropping the ball and letting it roll back to the place of precious things. He padded over and picked up the launch keys in his mouth. They clinked together, sounding like milk bottles in a shopping bag. He scampered over to the briefing table. He tried to pull himself up, but his legs were too little. He reversed a few steps and jumped. The briefcase was open, just as the humans had left it. The inside was sparse. Just two key holes with two green lights above them. A button in the middle. A red button. A big red button. Hector dropped one of the keys on the tabletop. Taking the remaining key, he padded over to the briefcase and, tilting is head deftly to one side, he pushed the key into the hole and turned it. The green light lit up. *All those pasty, sweaty faces, they looked so sick, what can be done? Thousands dying of hunger. Riots. Violence.* Hector picked up the remaining key and repeated the process. The green light went on. *The hostiles are not happy Mr president, the people are not happy Mr president, we must act Jack. Project Good Boy.* Now the red button lit up, winking like a sailor on shore leave.

There was nothing to be done. Everything had been tried. It was a mercy. A mercy for all concerned. What kind of life would they have? Those sunken, sad eyes. It was heartbreaking. Such a good boy. I guess we're all going to miss you, but when all's said and done, you wouldn't want them to suffer any more, would you?

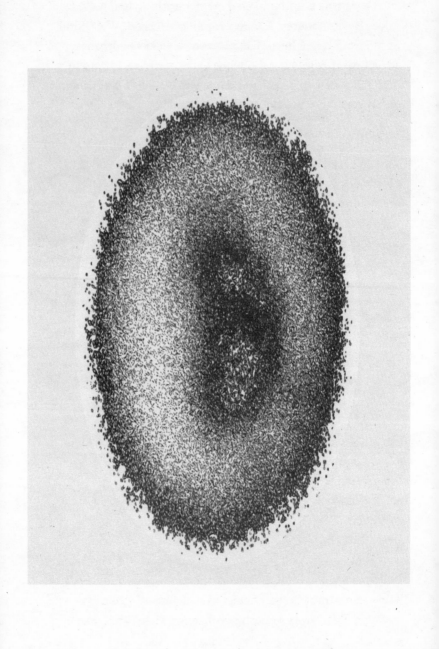

Water Holds Memory

A soft strip of pulverised rock. Dull yellow, blending to grey. Where the rotting stems of stranded seaweed decayed on the edge of land and sea. Forgotten by the tides. They lay like wounded soldiers left to die on a battlefield. Picked over by crabs and gulls. Staring into the foam through lidless eyes, never to return. The beach. A soft strip of pulverised rock. The beach was a graveyard for immutable stone and the certainties of solid ground. Where the water mocked the illusion of permanence. This was the front line in a conflict that had raged longer than any human memory; even the rocks themselves struggled to remember its beginning. But no one came here any more. It was once a place of pilgrimage for the animals of the land. Gazing from the brink into the green folds of another world, perched on the precipice of their habit. Wishing for fins and gills. In the summer months the rites and the frolics of the season used to fill the beach with laughter. Crowds of people had broken the seal between soil and sea, splashing over a charnel pit, an aeon in the making. But now no one came. The council said it was an oil spill. Dangerous chemicals they said. Local gossips offered more lurid explanations. Nothing substantiated beyond idle chatter over the market stall, but everyone knew someone who knew someone who had heard from someone else about a rumour. There was something uncanny about that beach,

whispers in the sand, a feeling of unease; that was what
really kept people away.

Over time the beach faded from memory. The gossips
passed away, taking their stories with them. Years turned to
decades, the beach brooding in its isolation, untroubled by
visitors or the eyes of man. It was a remote spot. No cafés
or amusement arcades, no pubs or sea front restaurants.
The few refreshment huts that used to cling to the humble
promenade had long since packed up and moved on. The
promenade too had gone, battered by storms, never to be
repaired, its brittle skeleton finally sucked back into the
sea. There was no sign of humanity now. Even the lane,
once thronging with holidaymakers filing their way down
to the water's edge, had been reclaimed by the forest.
Now an ambiguous woodland trail was the only means of
access. Trodden down by foraging deer, thin and indistinct
in places, it wove through the woods, stopping just short
of the bay where the beach crouched like a cornered stag.
From the sea the beach was almost invisible, its shallow
gradient hiding it from all but the keenest lookout. It rose
in a gentle slope to a craggy chine, an uneven spine that
looked like the work of a careless butcher. The chine, in
turn, dropped down to a thin border of coarse grass where
the promenade had once stood. The Tangle tumbled down
to its edge, with its wind-blown trees standing like stern
sentinels against the aggression of the waves. Beyond the
Tangle the world of men began.

*

Vince rode his bicycle. He swept down the empty lanes.
The lane morphed as his imagination transformed it.
Perspectives of time and space were temporary borders

to be shifted at will. Behind him was the town. Its bland
avenues and decaying crescents providing only the dreariest
of backdrops. Its predictable edges and crumbling cornices
were nothing more than a faded tableau of misplaced
confidence that was slowly decomposing. Vince peddled
hard inland to escape its baleful orbit. As the town began
to fade from view he felt a liberating lightness, like an
acrobat whose partner has recently dismounted from their
shoulders. He stood on the pedals, coasting along the quiet
country roads, stretched limbs in other dimensions. He was
no country boy. He was born and raised in the city. Ten years
in the rough 'n' tumble. Ten years of postcode scraps and big
lads with knives. The nearest he'd come to the countryside
was the petting zoo in the city park. Tired-looking goats,
threadbare chickens and a lonely llama. The currents of
gentrification had carried his parents out of the city and
deposited them in a coastal town that had seen better days.
It was cheaper here, they had a yard too, but there wasn't
much to do, even the pound shop had closed down. Outside
the border of the town the greenery stretched into eternity.
Vince had never seen so much open space. Even though
large swathes of it were fenced off, marked private or under
the plough, there was still room enough for his imagination
to trespass. His agile consciousness filled the landscape,
probing the layers that were hidden to older minds. Out
here, in the controlled wildness, he was alone.

It was midsummer. It was hot. Very hot. The kind of
searing heat that triggered government health warnings
and kept sensible folk inside. These types of weather events
were no longer rare or even surprising any more. Vince took
them in his stride. He wore a cap, as his mum had insisted.
It had his favourite band's logo stitched to the front; it had

been his dad's, from his raver days. The sun battered him like a schoolyard bully. Drenched with sweat and panting in the thick air, Vince pulled his bicycle over to the side of the road and took a swig from his water bottle. Conditions were hard, but the thought of returning to the town seemed to place unwanted borders around his fantasies. He had further to go, more to see, frontiers to cross. He was far from home now, at the outer boundaries of his world. But he was tired and in need of rest. His parents would not be home for hours yet. The pot was yet to be stirred and the bread remained uncut. He had time before tea. Time. Time. Supressing the pangs of hunger and the nagging of weary limbs, he pushed his bicycle off the road. Vince noticed a wood. He hadn't seen it before. The wood was just there. Suddenly. It was as if it had burst out of the ground like the flourishing of an untapped well. The wood looked like an oasis of variety at the end of a series of monochrome fields. The shade would be delicious. He pushed his bicycle down a stony track. The wood shimmered like a mirage. From where he stood, it looked wild and deregulated, every conceivable species of tree and shrub jumbled together in a disorderly clump. It was hard to gauge its dimensions; the perspective kept shifting, as if the wood was hopping along the edge of the field, retreating to the horizon before surging back across the field. It reminded Vince of the waves on the seafront.

As he got nearer, the wood quickly expanded, taking in the whole horizon. The motion was fluid, silent, unfathomable. The movement was impossible to quantify. Try as he might, his perception was too faulty to judge it correctly. Distance, height, volume, all seemed like inadequate units of measurement for the uncanny flux of the forest. It was spreading out. Surrounding him. Branches and shoots spiralling in all directions. Until he was suddenly standing in the middle of its tight weave. Boy. Bicycle. Alone. The track he had been walking down was consumed by the vegetation. His bicycle tyres began to bounce over the roots that spread like veins under the surface. As he walked, the wood throbbed and pulsed like a lung. But despite this sudden change in the rules of nature, fear was entirely absent from Vince's mind. He was calm. The wood was peaceful. The wood was cool. The wood was full of soothing sounds. Time was moving at a different pace; he could feel it. The melodies of birdsong skittered around the trees in a harmonious sequence. The buzz of insects pitched down to a hypnotic drone as they described languid orbits around his head. Pollen, sparkling in the shafts of sunlight that pierced the canopy, seemed to hang effortlessly in the air, as if the laws of gravity had been momentarily relaxed.

Vince pushed on through the wood, finding the path easy to follow. Direction soon became meaningless. He had no idea where he was going, so he let his feet get carried by the path. He caught a sound. Familiar and yet out of place. The boom of surf. That was impossible. He had been heading away from the sea. He always made for the hinterland during the daylight hours. The seaside was for the evenings. The beach was quieter and more interesting in the twilight, when the contrast between land and sea was less pronounced. But here he was, pulled back to the shore. The sudden collapse of geographical logic was easy to understand; it often happened to him, only not in the tangible world of touch and taste. It was more an ease with the mutable nature of things that played out in his waking dreams. His parents too had once had the gift, though the ageing process had gradually eroded the wonder. But this was the first time he had seen the spell performed in the real world. It was beautiful. Vince noticed the trees beginning to thin before him, parting like the curtains at the start of a play. The sun streamed into the wood. The wood stopped abruptly on a ragged border of coarse grass. Hesitant trees recoiled from the grass as if they had skidded to a halt on the edge of a hidden precipice. Beyond the grassy border a ragged chine was the last defence from the sand. A band of brutalised rock merging with the sea beyond. This was the battlefront. Life on land may have crawled from those salty depths, but now that it had grown apart from the womb it would suffocate if it were to trespass any further, as surely as a child returned to its amniotic sac.

Vince shared none of the forest's reticence; like most humans, part of him wanted desperately to return to the sea. He pushed his bike over the border, bumping over the chine and onto the coarse sand. Looking behind him, he felt the forest recede, mirroring the movement of the waves. The tide was going out. The beach had a forbidding density. The hot air was heavy with anticipation, as if awaiting the coming of the storm and the ozone crackle. The pleasant coolness of the wood was forgotten in the cauldron of the bay. A demon heat rose and hovered above the sand in shimmering waves. Vince took off his T-shirt, kicked off his shoes and rolled up the legs of his trousers. He felt the hot sting of the sand on the soles of his feet, scorching like a penitent's spike. Vince dropped his bicycle carelessly onto the sand. He began to hop over the beach towards the coolness at the water's edge. Moving further and further from the certainties of the land. The damp sediment, dark grey from the lick of the sea, soothed his feet. Vince waited for the waves to return. The initial shock of the cold ocean as it splashed up his ankles; the transmitted snap as his muscles contracted; the simple pleasure of a contrasting set of uncomfortable sensations, confusing his equilibrium. Paddling in the sea was as close to heaven as anyone was ever likely to get. Evolution in reverse. The simple crossing of dimensions. The innocent refusal to be hemmed in by liveable terrain. The thrill of danger as uncertainty played its hand. One misstep, one unexpected surge, was all it would take to drag him under.

Vince focused on the approaching wave as it formed in the channel. A ripple, growing fast as the water was forced up and over the shallows until it became a thundering torrent of tumbling devils. Stretching their tangled limbs towards the land. They ran across the shingle, only to stumble as the beach asserted itself once more. Forcing the demons back into the sea, leaving only their withered aquatic arms to vainly claw at the sand as the ocean retreated. The wave stopped short of his wriggling toes. Vince risked a further step. A fresh wave was forming out at sea. He shuffled forward, hoping to feel the soothing sting of the water on his legs. The wave came on in the same old way. The white-flecked ridge grew again. As he knew it would. But this time it seemed to ascend faster, almost angrily. Vince felt the urge to run. But the sand had sealed around his bare feet like manacles. The serpent wave rose. Slipping rapidly up the shore. But as it was poised to strike, it slowed. It became almost static. He could see the wall of water above him. Frozen. The wave had none of the qualities of water he was familiar with, none of the sparkling froth one might expect. Instead, it was a viscid ooze. Glistening and malevolent, undulating along its length. Vince thought he could see faces bulging from

the surface like prisoners pressed against the bars of an
overcrowded jail. Fractures began to appear in his world.
Small glimpses into a hidden mechanism. He could see the
formless cogs grinding. Cold. Unconcerned. Relentless.
This moment of disconnection lasted only a fraction of a
second before the wave reverted back into its more familiar
form. It broke on the beach and scampered up the sand.
Slopping around his ankles and splashing up his shins. The
feeling was sensational. He quivered with delight as the
shock travelled up his body. The sun above him renewed its
attack. Vince splashed into the water, letting the waves dash
against his torso, tasting the brackish tang of the water on
his lips. He felt the weight of the heat lift from him. As his
body gradually became acclimatised to the chill of the ocean
he started to risk further forays into the surge. Rubbing
the water onto his shoulders, splashing it on his face until
it stung his eyes. As his confidence grew, so his desire to
explore the depths blossomed. The bottom of the ocean.
The undersea fiefdom of eccentric monsters and astonishing
things. He was diver. He was submariner. Vince plunged
into the approaching wave.

> *Root of the land, hidden by earth, sown by the seed,*
> *born by the flood.*
> *Drowned by the wave that sundered the rock, the sea*
> *and the salt, the skin and the blood.*

The sound of the world suddenly shrank away. As if all the
frequencies had been crushed under enormous pressure.
He was an intruder returning to the deep after an absence
of millennia. However, the sea was already familiar with his
kind. Long ago it had spat his ancestors out onto the land.

They had returned millions of years later in vessels that floated on the surface. They had caused mischief in the sea, as was their habit. The sea had been forced to remind them that they were creatures of the soil now. It smashed their boats and ravaged their ports. But still they came. Vince pushed himself like a torpedo out of the foaming mess. As he floated above the waves he thought he saw figures on the beach. He tried to twist his body as he flew. But the forces of attraction were too great, and he fell back into the swell. He sank down, inelegantly writhing as water rushed up his nose. Sudden panic overtook him. He was an imposter, he could not function here. He pushed himself back to the surface. Gasping and sputtering. This time he managed to get to his feet. Steadying himself on the seabed, he brushed the wet hair from his face. He scanned the beach. There was no one there. He looked up and down its length. He was sure he had seen something. Nothing. Still its presence dangled there. Like a broken body in a gibbet, hovering over the sand.

Those few moments above the waves made him shiver. His body had adapted to the temperature of the sea, and he found himself unwilling to leave it. Now it was the land that seemed alien to him. That shimmering presence. Vince dived back down into the water, neither fish nor boy. Trapped between two worlds. The sounds of the beach retuned to a womb-like frequency, but something had changed. The layers peeled back. Molecules bonded in unfamiliar sequence. This was the seldom glimpsed dimension that only occasionally intersected with our own. Vince was held fast. Water. Not water. This was how things really were. Thick. Clinging. He thought he would drown in the clag. It clasped him tight, unwilling to cede an inch. Instead he moved like seaweed, finding himself rooted to the bed, his legs like stems bending in the current. This was how it would end. Stuck fast and drowning. His lungs cried out for air. The mechanisms of his body clicked and spun. Despite the precariousness of his predicament, his mouth opened, seeking the breeze. This is how it would end. But the flood never came. Instead he found he could breathe easily. The viscous liquid filled and nourished his veins. He swayed like a weed. A dark shadow passed over him. The keel of a boat. Sounds, slowed down to a wrenching grind, echoed around the gelatinous medium. Vince put his fingers in his ears, but he had no fingers, no ears either. The sound was continuing to bloom, growing steadily louder. He tried to translate the vibration into something intelligible. He thought he recognised screams. Grunts. Wailing. The noise of conflict.

Eyes without sight, vision or focus. No lens or pupil, motion or locus.

He looked up to the surface, though he had no eyes. He saw smoke drifting in the air. Vince's lungs began to ache, his throat contracted. He was human again. He fought his way back to the surface, the thick liquid thinning as he swam. His mind signalled caution, but his body demanded air. Vince pushed his face through the skin of the water. It was dark. On the beach it was night, and the beach was not empty.

A long, wooden ship was anchored in the shallows. It was of an ancient design, with a prow that curled up into a barbaric dragon's head. Vince recognised it from his history lessons: a Viking ship. Screams eddied across the waves, curling around his partly submerged skull. His eyes were frozen open, stinging with the salt but unable to close.

Figures milled around the shore. He could see unwilling
women being dragged towards the longboats, their faces
streaked with blood and tears, arms stretched back to the
land as if grasping at some invisible thread that would
secure them to their homes. On the sand, blood ran in black
rivers that sucked the light from the risen moon. It flowed
from the cuts and severed limbs of men. Monks dressed
in their sodden habits were kneeling on the sand. Gruff
warriors stood over them, sorting those deemed useful from
those to be left in pieces on the shore. Axes swung and
swords swept like scythes. Heads rolled. The lamentations
of the monks spiralled into the sky. Waiting for a reply. The
wrong question. Always the wrong question.

Vince's head throbbed. Part sea, part blood. The horror
fascinated him; he was transfixed by the hypnotic swing of
the axe and the mantras of despair rising from the victims.
The vision was too compelling, too unbelievable. Those
screams. Those fractured arias. They were real enough.
He submerged himself further, hoping that the water would
muffle the cries, but it only seemed to channel them all the
more, until it felt as if the screams were inside his head. He
had received no instruction from his parents, no guidance
on how to deal with such matters. Spectres. Time travel.
Don't talk to strangers. Call us if you think you are in
danger. His telephone was in his trouser pocket, in a pile
of his clothes lying next to his bicycle. This certainly felt
like an emergency. He should call someone. Vince poked
his eyes above the swell and looked to see if his bicycle was
still on the beach. He had left it just short of the craggy
chine, in the area where a Viking warrior was currently
disembowelling an unfortunate cleric. The steam from
his gushing viscera described an arc around where the

handlebars should be. There was no sign of his bicycle. Vince hung in the ooze.

The current began to take him closer to the boat. The Vikings were hefting loot and battered captives into its shallow hull. He tried to paddle away from its looming form, but the current was too strong to resist. These irresistible eddies. They had sprung from the depths quite suddenly, dragging him along like the line of a fisherman's rod. He whirled helplessly towards the dragon boat, spinning around like a leaf, unable to reverse his course. As he got closer he could see a statuesque warrior emerging from the hull. His imposing frame raised itself above the gunwales. He was enormous. Vince sailed impotently towards him. The warrior raised his axe, dripping with gore and sorrow. Vince was close enough to see his face. An unholy beard carried fragments of skin and brain in its matted weave. His eyes were black, empty sockets in which only a demon light flickered. The warrior raised his axe above his head. His horned helmet silhouetted in the moonlight like Baphomet risen from hell. The stench of wet fur assailed his nostrils. The goat god is risen. The goat god is risen. Vince forced himself under the waves, pushing against the current with all his strength. His lungs burned. He pushed and thrust. Trying to move through the thick water. His body was weak. His body was frail. He needed air. He began to rise through the murk. Vince closed his eyes as he floated to the surface. He hoped for a swift end. A quick, sharp bite from the warrior's axe. It would be over in seconds. He awaited his fate. But no blow came. Vince opened his eyes, expecting to see the cloven hooves of the warrior devil above him. But all he saw was a wispy cloud dissolving in the summer breeze.

The wave broke the stone, the salt sowed the soil.
The wood fled the shore as the serpent uncoiled.

Vince was cold and exhausted. Had it been minutes, hours,
days, or years since he had stepped on dry land? With feeble
strokes and laboured kicks he approached the shallows.
His tired and bloodshot eyes tried to focus on the beach.
His bicycle and neatly stacked clothes were where he had
left them. He felt relieved to find objects occupying their
expected places. A gentle wave broke over his head. Vince
spat out brine and blew the sodden wisps of hair from
his eyes. As he looked up he could see translucent figures
parading across the sand. Glamorous ladies twirling parasols
on a ghostly promenade. Moustachioed gentlemen in striped
bathing costumes preening in front of modestly attired
girls. All shimmering and transparent in the summer heat.
Another wave broke over his head. A strangled cry rose
from the surf to his left. Close. Vince turned to the source.
A small child, no older than five, struggling, in trouble,
clearly drowning. The figures rushed to the water's edge
but seemed unable to enter. Vince was closer. Could he save
the boy? Vince was only a child himself, could he carry the
burden? He swam in a rapid crawl towards the drowning
child. He was so close to the boy now that he could see the
hope of salvation in the child's eyes. The boy reached out
his hand, his fingers stretching across the swell, trying to
connect with Vince's own outstretched hand. Their fingers
met. For a few seconds the barrier was breached, two worlds
fusing in a dreadful symmetry. An ectoplasmic shock darted
up Vince's arm. His eyes were the boy's eyes, scanning the
beach for his parents. Too young to be in this deep. Lacking
the skill to stay afloat in such choppy seas. They would never

forgive themselves, he thought, as the water cascaded into his lungs. The figures on the beach vibrated in the haze and began to spin. They spun faster and faster until they became tornados of sand, their features stretching in the torrent, pulling their bodies up into the sky. The spinning stopped. A fine mist of dust settled back onto the beach. The boy faded into waves. Vince shouted in confusion as he floundered in the tide. Spinning around looking for the child. Diving down again and again until his weak boy arms gave out. The waves pushed him up the shallows and deposited him onto the beach. He lifted his head from the sand, spitting out grit and seaweed. He was alone.

*

Vince woke from another night of fitful sleep. Tangled in his sweat-drenched sheets. Every time his eyes closed, the visions returned. He was hanging in the ectoplasm. Axes, blood, the screams of butchered bodies. The helpless fingers of a child slipping through his own. His body had only succumbed to sleep in the early morning, when his mind had momentarily paused. These snatched moments of sleep provided no rest, just confusing fragments of changing states. He caught his reflection in the mirror as he dragged himself out of bed. He was carrying heavy bags under his eyes, his skin looked grey, a winter tone on a summer's day. Vince avoided the sunlight. He avoided the beach.

His parents were worried. Why would a boy so young be so anxious? It was the summer holidays, a time for adventure, a time for fun. But for the last three weeks Vince had become quiet and withdrawn. At weekends he sat inside. Even as the temperature soared, Vince stayed in his room;

his friends would pop by, but all he did was shout down that he was not well and needed to rest. Never mention the sea. They knew that now. Vince had grown to hate the sea. Mum and Dad tried, but fared no better, though they attempted to coax him down with bribes and incentives. But Vince could not be persuaded. Perhaps they should call the doctor?

Three weeks became four. Four dragged into five. But, at last, the nightmares became more manageable. His mind had begun to file them away. Memories to be laughed at in later years as childish fancies or youthful illusions. His parents were full of such stories, shared fables that hinted at insights that had now faded from their memories. Haunted homes. Creatures in closets. Figures in the trunks of trees. All these stories were true. But such ideas were too inconvenient to be allowed to rub shoulders with more agreeable facts, so they were filed away as well. Vince began to make cautious trips into the outside world. He began with a visit to the backyard. All the phantoms were there, as he suspected they would be. The next day he made it as far as the shops; the ghosts on the high street clattered on their melancholy routes. Sightless eyes and spectral limbs. Endlessly looping. Vince became accustomed to the apparitions. He always suspected they were there, occupying the indistinct folds and creases of the town. He knew others could see them too but had chosen to blot them out. He wasn't troubled by these stranded spirits and lost souls; it was the beach that refused to let him go. Its cruel tangled net had wrapped itself around him. Vince hacked at it every day. Stay away from the ocean. Stay away. But the Tangle needed allies, emissaries, ambassadors to convey its message to the beach. It began to work its way back into the fabric of his world.

Who will carry the weight of the golden seed to the shore?
Who will brave the tide and the ocean's savage maw?
Who will pay the price the waves will surely ask?
Who will ride the swell in the tempest's icy blast?

These were the last days of the Anthropocene, when the summer never ended. The Tangle lay low under the scorching torch of the sun. Outwardly withered, but truly only resting. Waiting for the heat death and the passing of the mantle. For the evolution of sense or the funeral dirge. These were the last days of innocence, when all the elements had gathered together, fusing into something new, something terrible. In these last days, Vince sweltered in his room or in the scant shade offered by his yard. Anything. Any fraction of relief was better than the beach. Between the cracks the weeds broke through. Spreading invisible scents and seeds throughout his home. They planted themselves in the dust of his room, into the cracked toys of his childhood. The spores fused with the fabric of his clothes and bore down into the fibres of the food he ate. Time to rise young man. Time to hatch. One Wednesday in August the pressure was too much to bear. The mercury had popped off the scale, and his parents were out at work as usual. Vince found himself alone with his thoughts and the presence that surrounded him. These were the last days of childhood; the urge to live was too strong. The back roads and fields, the hedges and ditches, all needed to be explored and occupied. The Tangle was calling him back to finish the games he must play before weariness and responsibility made them seem foolish to him. These were the last days for good boys and girls. Before the mysteries of the world sunk back into the bark, locked away for eternity. These were the last days for Vince. For now, he must live.

Who will carry the weight of the golden seed to the shore?
Who will brave the tide and the oceans savage maw?
Who will pay the price the waves will surely ask?
Who will ride the swell in the tempest's icy blast?

Vince pushed his bicycle out of the garage, where it had languished these last few weeks. A few tenacious cobwebs clung to the spokes. The dozier spiders tumbled off and ran for cover into the flower beds as he wheeled the bicycle out. He began a silent countdown. He adjusted his rucksack on his back. He checked his route out of the town. Vince was using his father's old Ordnance Survey Map. He didn't want there to be any chance of ending up on the beach again, no quick routes to avoid roadworks or time-saving deviations favoured by the satellite navigation. He needed a dependable path inland. Vince selected winding B roads and seldom-trodden tracks that all led in one direction: away from the sea. 5-4-3-2-1. The countdown to a childhood's end. He supressed his nascent adolescent feelings and put his trust in the Fates. It would be good to be back in the folds of the forest again. Away from the oppression of the town and the cauldron of his home. Away from the thick air of his room. Away from the boom of the surf. Vince put his feet to the peddles.

The country lanes were like leafy veins criss-crossing the rolling landscape. They followed an ambiguous route. Old packhorse trails and eccentric shepherding paths were their templates. Along these winding byways the arms of roadside shrubs arched from densely weaved hedges. Reaching high above the road they embraced in the middle of the lane, forming dark tunnels that provided welcome shade from the glaring sun. In these spaces his mind was free to wander.

He peddled fast, his chin close to the handlebars. How like a blood cell he was, sucked by the current into the land. His imagination filled the cracks and peeled back the cataracts. He could see the tramping progress of carts and heavy horses, bent-backed villagers seeding the soil. He could smell the sweat of their labours and taste the juice of sweet fruits sampled as they harvested the crop. Timeless at last, he felt the occupants of long-lamented eras returning to their homes. Some joyful and content, singing and clapping down the lanes, others resentful for lives cut short or wasted on whimsy. He could feel the bones of highwaymen hung from gibbets of iron. He could hear the crows call as they pecked the last strands of flesh from their faces. Sightless, they called to him as he cycled by. Let him pass. He will never linger here again. Vince flowed, and in this silent passage the beach was quite forgotten.

He had cycled for maybe an hour or more when he came to a fork in the road. He stopped to check his father's map. He must not take the seaward route. He must not falter. The map was confusing, too many lines and bewildering gradients. He was tempted to try his phone, though he was suspicious of its intentions. But there was no signal out here. There was a sign, however. It was old and carved in wood, not a modern council sign, all fluorescent and eye catching. It was a wizened post. Weather beaten. It had a gnarled trunk that held two roughly hewn arrows at its summit, each with a name carved into them. The letters were in a spidery script, painted in black pitch, almost impossible to read against the knotted wood. Vince had to squint to make them out: right, Ambleton; left, Caxton. He checked the map, shaking it out in the thick air, trying to decipher its meaning. The road to Ambleton would take him back to where he began. It described a warped circle that joined up stranded islands of twee cottages until it was reabsorbed by the network of roundabouts and carriageways that ran back to the town along the coast road. The sea. He must stay away from the sea. In contrast, the road to Caxton was relatively free of interruption. It meandered through Caxton Wood until it reached the town on the other side. That would be the safest route. He had been to Caxton Wood with the school on a history field trip. Vince had found the trip fascinating, though the darkness of the wood had unsettled him; it was dense and full of shadows. Whispers rose in its glades and gullies. He could hear those whispers now, hanging in the heat haze. He must stick to the road. But that wood? On the other side was Caxton. An island of manufactured things. It wasn't a bad spot, a collection of villages that had blended together over the years. It had all the usual vestiges of old-world charm: Tudor cottages, the ruins of the old church and the remains of a roman fort. Generations of local youths had scrawled on the crumbling battlements, 'Trevor Hines is a twat', 'Caxton rucking machine', 'Barry loves Helen', with crudely drawn genitalia adding to the romance of words. There was the hint of the now too. Poorly translated, as the town planners tried to move with the times. Buildings that smacked of committees and compromise were hidden amongst the heritage, like the embarrassing results of an after-school craft lesson brought home by proud children. Function flexed in the Central Business District. There were car parks with supermarkets at their centre, mini roundabouts and bypasses, a shopping centre too. He could shelter there a while. Perhaps skim stones in the lazy river that ran under the medieval bridge. Add his notch to the wisdom carved into the stones of the fort. Then he'd double back through Ambleton and be at home in time for tea.

The climb was hard. Vince stood on the peddles to achieve the torque he needed. He slowly climbed the hill. Once he reached the crest, he could see the road slicing an incision through the vale, right into the heart of Caxton Wood. He paused at the top of the hill, looking down into the dark blob of the forest. It pulsed to its own rhythm. The trees moving to and fro against the breeze, even though he could feel none. The sight was mesmerising. Inviting. Pollen, seeds and spores, the genesis of flax, all the elements of reproduction and renewal, swirled in the air around his faulty frame. Doubts ebbed and flowed. His breath pulled the particles into him. They spread through his cells like a vaccine, increasing their potency with every inhalation. Doubt turned to senseless calm. The trees swayed against the phantom breeze. He turned to look at the world he had left behind. The road that led home. Beyond the hamlets and hedges, across the fields and farms, under the drains and pipes, over the roofs of houses clinging to the land was the sea. Vince pushed off and sailed into the mouth of the entity.

The descent was effortless. Like a helpless fly sucked into a whirlpool, Vince was drawn into the wood. He sailed closer to the edge. The sun's rays lost their strength. All light, all heat was absorbed and annihilated. He shivered as he crossed the horizon. Vince took his feet off the peddles and freewheeled along the dented country lane, separated from the seasons and the passage of time. It was cold, the muted chatter of birds and the soft creak of ancient trunks the only sound. The road was out of place in the wood, like a surgical pin thoughtlessly lost in an unwilling patient. Vince was a stranger. His mind wandered through the knot of branches.

There were no apparitions of humanity here. No wraiths called from their rest by his passing. The voices he heard were of a far more ancient vintage. Deeper and deeper he drifted, caught on the currents that drew him like a magnet to some hidden terminus. Vince tacked across the lane, careless of bends and blind corners. There was no human traffic here. He was alone. Vince knew from the map that Caxton Wood was not large, having shrunk from its former vastness over the centuries. It should take him no more than thirty minutes to cross it. Yet he felt like he had been in the forest for hours. He looked at his watch. It had stopped.

He felt uneasy. He felt separated. Separated from the tangible. His mind groped for anchors: his room, his yard, his parents. Here amongst the sticks, here in the Tangle, there was no place for parents. He must turn back. He had miscalculated; the journey through the wood was taking too long. No time. No time. No time to carve his name into the ramparts of the fort, no time to skim stones or explore the grey courtyards of Caxton town. No time. He stopped and swung his bicycle round in the dark lane. The canopy pressed around him, arching over his head, forming a black dome like a starless night sky. The heat began to rise. The cold tomb-like air began to thicken into a viscous heat. In front of him the road home was quickly swallowed by the forest. There was no way through. No chance of return. He spun around and peddled fast. He must get out of the darkness. The road bent and swerved around impossible angles and improbable inclines. Vince peddled harder. Sweat began to pore down his face as the thermometer climbed. The heat was crushing. His breath came in stuttering gulps as he pushed himself along the pitiless highway. Ahead, all he could see was an endless tunnel of trees. He concentrated on his feet, willing them to push the peddles faster. His white plimsolls blurred like pistons, laces snapping like snakes. His legs began to fill with lactic pools, corroding and painful. He tried to concentrate on the passing of distance by focusing on the road beneath his wheels. He imagined the darkness lifting as he exited the forest. He willed the sun to return to brighten the lane. Soon, it must be soon. As he stared, the road beneath his wheels melted, morphing from the hard, concrete certainties of tar and stone chip into a dark, forbidding liquid. He looked around him, trying to find some natural marker by which he could fasten his sanity. As his eyes penetrated the gloom, the dense knot of the forest began to unwind. Vince could hardly breath now, the air was solid. He thought he could see light up ahead. Was he out of the wood at last? He peddled faster, though he could no longer feel the peddles. The branches continued to unwind; the unbroken blue of the summer sky began to break through the melting canopy. He felt a breeze cooling his sweat-drenched brow. The relief was magnificent. He closed his eyes and enjoyed the sharp chill as the currents of fresh air broke against his body. It was like plunging into the ocean.

Who will carry the weight of the golden seed to the shore?
Who will brave the tide and the ocean's savage maw?
Who will pay the price the waves will surely ask?
Who will ride the swell in the tempest's icy blast?

His legs moved with the same regular, piston-like motion. But he was no longer connected to the peddles. His hands no longer curled round the plastic grips of the handlebars. His fingers no longer summoned the brittle ring of the bell.

He was no longer cycling. He was paddling. Vince's eyes
sprang open with sudden horror. He was in the ocean. He
floundered in the waves, eyes fixed on the endless horizon,
unwilling to look behind him. What strange vortex had
spat him out into this? He began to long for the terror of
the forest. At least it wasn't . . . *this*. This haunted pool.
He began to shiver, the cool refreshing sensation changing
quickly into a bone-deep cold. His clothes ballooned in the
swell, then clung to him like icy limpets as the air escaped.
His lips turned a corpse-like purple. His skin mottled. He
spat into the water and cursed. The maps had failed. He was
back. He was alone. He knew it would be there, even before
he finally plucked up the courage to turn around. The beach.
That haunted ribbon of broken, pulverised rock.

Vince pushed back the water and waited for the waves.
Deep inside him, the seeds and spores began to write their
message in the molecules of his body. Through pores and
glands it gradually seeped into the water to be collected
by the tide and carried back to the emptiness of the core.
Vince stared out to sea as the first wave formed. It came on
like a regiment of cavalry, slow at first, but then growing
in confidence as it approached the bobbing boy. It was only
a few feet away and already Vince could see the turquoise
lustre of the wave fade to a dour grey. The supple flow of
the water replaced by the dense solidity of a malignant
effluent. The wave hit, sending him under. Beneath the
surface the thickness continued. Strong eddies of churning
goo spun Vince around in slow motion, filling his nostrils
with slime. He held his breath, willing the rotation to stop
long enough for him to come up for air. The liquid turned
with agonising indifference, but at last he completed his
cycle. Vince spluttered to the surface as the wave rolled

past him. The sky turned from day into night. It was raining hard, and a gale of enormous ferocity blew as the rain lashed down. His instinct said live. At least there was a chance that way. He turned towards the beach and attempted to swim back to land. The storm surge kept pulling him back, pushing him sideways or dragging him under. Progress was difficult. The message reached the core. The emptiness considered its response.

On the beach Vince could see lanterns flickering through the gloom and figures running about on the sand, engaged in frenzied activity. A barrel floated past him, then a tea crate, fragments of broken wood. Vince grabbed at a piece of timber as it floated by. He clung on to it as the sea continued to rise and fall with a nauseating strength. The broken plank had the feel of a cured ship's timber, perhaps part of a damaged hull. A shipwreck? A body floated past dressed in the tattered uniform of an ordinary seaman from the eighteenth century, with ripped canvas pantaloons and a striped marinière. He recognised the costume from his history books. He followed the body towards the shore. He could hear shouting now. The lanterns were clearer too. The scurrying figures on the sand were forming ant-like columns, running from the shallows up the beach, then to carts yoked to sullen donkeys. The figures were loading barrels, crates and boxes into the carts. A cry rose to Vince's right, another sailor, but this one very much alive. Vince watched him swim with painful difficulty towards the figures on the beach. The figures paused their salvage as the exhausted sailor dragged himself ashore. Two men put down the crate they had been hefting and ran towards the desperate seaman who was attempting to raise his battered body from the surf. Vince was glad the sailor had made it.

One of the men took the sailor under the arm and pulled him up, steadying him against the breaking waves. The other man drew a knife from his belt and cut the sailor's throat. They let him fall back into the water as he gasped for air through the grim incision. Vince began to swim as hard as he could away from the shore. All along the beach, similar acts were being committed on floundering survivors. With knives, cudgels or the application of hands on exhausted heads, thrusting them back into the waves to drown, not one was to be saved. All that was to leave the beach that night was the wrecker's loot.

Vince trod water in the cantankerous swell as another wave formed out at sea. The wave rose in the same turbulent fashion. A haunted mountain of dull, grey sludge crashing over him. Sucking him down and spinning him about in its dark undertow. When he surfaced this time, the sky was shot through with the lilac hue of dawn. The sea was calm and still. There was an unnatural silence pressing down around him as he floated uncertainly offshore. In the atoms of the sea the council debated. Treaties and compromises. Looking for a balance. Vince wrinkled his nostrils as an acrid smell drifted across the waves, invading his throat with its corrosive vapour. He recognised the unrefined odour of gasoline. He began to notice the surface of the sea; it was covered with a film of oil. Great globules of thick crude floated like ponderous jellyfish in the contaminated brine. He began to swim cautiously towards the shore, the oil gathering on his clothes and skin as he swam. He became heavy with the clinging load and was struggling to move his limbs as the current carried him further in. Vince wanted to free himself from the reeking sea. But that beach. That beach was death. On the sand there were no spectral figures or phantom bathers, but something worse. The dying squadrons of seabirds, their feathers coloured black with bitumen, struggling to take flight, away from the horror, away from land. Oil saturated the waving claws of suffocating crabs, their shells caked in clotted tumours of spilled crude. Gasping fish poisoned by chemical waste, struggling for life on the polluted shore. This was hell. Hell for all things living. The idiot waste of a childish race littered the oceans and scarred the land, leaving carrion rotting in the wastes as its only monument. Down in the deep, the spores joined with the drops of the ocean. New formulas were spliced in the cauldron and sent back into the world.

The wave broke the stone, the salt sowed the soil.
The wood fled the shore as the serpent uncoiled.
Now the sea is calm, its fury spent at last.
The land has brought the sacrifice, broken sail and mast.

The wave rose in the dark to claim the sacrifice.
The gift was wisely chosen, the land must pay the price.
The broken bones of sailors, from vessels cruelly torn.
Their souls sing incantations, in emptiness reborn.

The reckoning rose in the gathering wave. This time the swell swept in a vast wall of black water, higher than any building, temple or folly. Vince resigned himself to the end. He thought of his smiling parents, of sunny days laughing in his pram as they pushed him around the park, feeding the ducks, licking an ice cream. He thought of his friends, he thought of their games, their stories, their comforting arms lifting him from the gravel when he fell, their encouragement when he tried new tricks. He remembered his parents' old flat, his neighbours waving as he walked past, him waving back, their eyes meeting in a bond of unbroken community. He remembered the cruelty too. Then the wave hit. He had expected to be tossed about by the undertow, to be cruelly battered and tormented before finally succumbing to the tide. But there was no movement, no current. There was nothing. The blank emptiness of pure absence. It was as if the water was now beyond all comprehension, in a dimension where the contradictions of being and nothingness were settled in a void of complete indifference. The relation of all non-relativity. In this place, though it had no location, laws, rules and equations meant nothing, and all mankind's absurd fumbling was annihilated and reborn. This was the divine dimension.

The laughter of a seagull woke Vince from a dream. The dream of life. He lifted his head from the sand and pushed his soggy locks from his eyes. He was on the beach again. But not the beach. It felt like an exorcised space, with all the ghosts finally laid to rest, mingling with the particles where they belonged. The day was warm, but a pleasant breeze gave it a freshness that made it close to perfect. He sat up and examined himself. No bruises, no cuts, he felt strangely rested and whole. He noticed that his clothes had gone, but he wasn't unduly concerned. He got to his feet and began to walk along the shoreline. The water lapped up the sand in a gentle cascade. Azure blue, clear, clean. Vince felt a vibration from the land and turned to its source. The Tangle blended effortlessly into the beach, as if the sea and land were two different states of the same substance, its limits impossible to determine. It was green and lush, spotted with dots of colour from a thousand exotic flowers that exploded in the thick canopy. The vibration was life. The chatter of the forest, a chaotic symphony with no key, filled the air with its disorganised music. Vince walked up the beach, drawn by the strange melody. The sand, soft beneath his toes, gave way to grass-covered loam. His nose twitched as it registered the scent of the extravagant blooms. Unfamiliar species with unfamiliar fragrances. He entered the Tangle. Vince was an emissary, a pilgrim, absolved in the waters, no longer in need of redemption, no longer seeking the way, for there was no path to follow, no maps to guide him. He was nowhere.

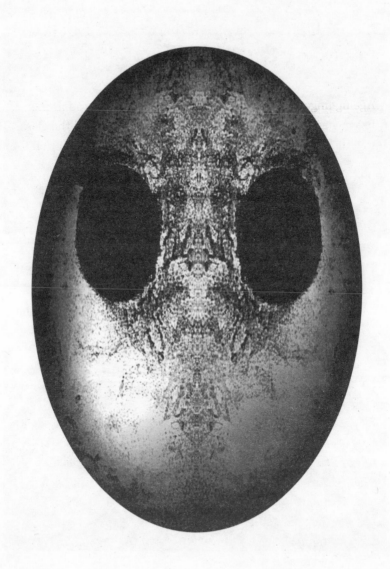

Send Us a Thought, Oh Dark Lord

Ageing fingers bent by the cruelty of time curled around the
heavy glass. Ageing hands wrinkled into ridges lifted the glass
to a thin, furrowed mouth. Ageing gums with an absence of
teeth sucked at the liquid. Nectar or poison, she could not tell.
It was just another glass. Like all the others. She placed the
glass back on the table and stared into the fire. The flames
licked over the hissing logs; smoke blossomed in the grate.
Hilda Wilton was old once. Perhaps it was now? She had
worked here as a young girl. Pulling pints. Breaking up fights.
She had met her first and last boyfriend here. They were
lovers. Then he died. Cut into components for the ash tree's
beautiful furniture. It was too much, he'd jumped off the
viaduct. Then there was the Tangle. Now she was here.

The Bull was buzzing. The large television screens that
had been recently installed to the annoyance of the older
clientele were the subject of the whole pub's attention. A
local girl done good. There she was on the screen. Professor
Helen Cavendish. From a long line of Cavendishs. Caxton's
most ancient clan. She drank in the Bull, so the landlord
said. Nice girl, he said. They all did. Not like the rest of that
cursed line. Not like her father. He'd died young. Good thing
for him they didn't have the death penalty then or he'd
have swung for what he did. That's what they said anyway.
Those bold enough to whisper. She was a scientist. Local girl
done good. Head of a team of scientists. They'd cracked it.

Made a computer, better than all the other computers. She was going to watch the president of the new regime switch it on. Everything was going to be alright when he did. The A.B.A.C.U.S. they called it. Here he is now, the president. Quiet everyone. Like the fucking moon landing this is. That's what they said.

Hilda stared into the flames. She had sat here for hours, or was it days? The comfortable Queen Anne chair, one of a pair. A permanent fixture in the Bull public house. She had just arrived. She had just this minute sat down. No one ever saw her come in, no one ever saw her leave. She was always here. Always now. Don't let her glass run dry. It's unlucky. That's what they said. Hilda stared into the flames. She turned her head slightly. Her friend was there. He was always there. She tried to smile, but she'd forgotten how. Erwan turned his head towards her. Their black eyes locked, and a silent message was passed. On the screen the crowds waved as the president's motorcade arrived. Flags with crooked insignia flew. The president addressed the crowds and glad-handed dignitaries. The president mounted the steps of a grand building reeking with overconfidence. He strode with purpose towards a brighter future. He had ribbons to cut.

Erwan sucked in the liquid. Don't let his drink run dry. It's unlucky. That's what they said. They stared into the fire and waited.

Eyes without sight, vision or focus. No lens or pupil, motion or locus.

The broken body of an astronaut lay in a crumpled pile at the foot of the stage. His neck had been twisted 180 degrees. His glassy, dead eyes gazed at the vaulted roof of the Museum of Ignorance. An old man dressed in eccentric attire skipped down the steps. He wore the peaked military-style cap of a museum employee on his head. Two tufts of orange hair jutted insolently from the sides. On his feet he wore a pair of mismatching shoes.

'Oh, what a shame,' he said, closing the astronaut's eyelids. 'He was such a dainty thinker in all matters scientific. Quite a curious sort too, though he obviously wasn't looking in the right places on this occasion. We shall all miss him terribly.'

The old man smiled. The smile grew into a laugh. Then a scream that spiralled into a piercing shriek filled every corner of the museum.

They'd keep the pub open late tonight. Everything was on the up. The new regime was harsh but fair. They all said so. You can't make an omelette without cracking a few eggs, they said. Besides, this new A.B.A.C.U.S. would sort everything out. No problem. The Happiness Engine, that's what they were calling it. Happiness is everything.

The old man's cap began to tear. His clothes split. His shoe leather ripped and buckled as the wiry malignance burst from his wizened frame. Blood and sinew dangled from his skeleton. The dripping figure stretching to its full height, flexing its talon-tipped limbs. The Mesmeriser gathered up the broken corpse of the astronaut in its wasted arms and began to ascend the dais. Once at the summit it absorbed the essence into its core, leaving an empty skin at its feet. The Mesmeriser sat on its throne, gazing down at the exhibition hall of the Museum of Ignorance and all its dusty trinkets.

There she was. The local girl done good. She was showing the president the flashing read out. The A.B.A.C.U.S. whirred. The president was delighted. Medals were pressed on chests. The drinkers in the Bull cheered. I knew her when she was a little girl. I knew she was destined for great things. That's what they said. Despite all the tragedy. They said. Her father. She was so young. The ropes in the woods. They whispered. The name Cavendish had death hanging from every letter. She was different. That's what they said.

Hilda and Erwan. Sucked at the liquid. Don't let their glasses run dry. It's unlucky. That's what they said. They watched the flames fuck up the wood. Its fiery tongue lashing the grain. They watched the fire and waited.

A lost dandy glided between the exhibits. Citizen Kavendish Jeremiah, looking for thrills. The Mesmeriser pulled a thought from its skull and twirled the archaic script around in the air. The words revolved. Faster and faster until they merged into one solid black ball. The Mesmeriser spun the globe on the tip of its foul nail. Suns, stars and galaxies began to form around the spinning globe. Vast, infinite expanses of cosmic objects spread out around a single point. Then the spinning stopped. The Mesmeriser flicked the thought out into the vastness it had created. To become just another speck.

The president cut the ribbon.

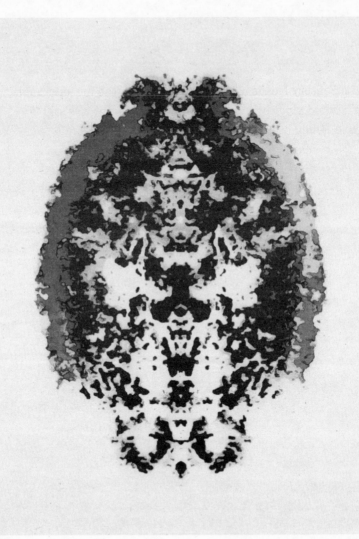

Outer Town Dissolution

His Sensory Nexus Mask lay discarded on the museum table, a muffled ping the only discernible sign that it was still functioning. Kavendish stroked his bare skin. Taking the time to reacquaint himself with his own flesh. His skin felt rough compared to the celluloid certainties of the mask. It felt flawed, faulty, frail.

In front of him was a book. Its pages were full of stories. It was empty. His hands felt the rough wooden surface. The words nagged at the edges. It was as if he had uncorked an intoxicating poison. Its complicated vapours were now drifting into him. The slow exhilaration began to seep into his veins. The figures from the photograph mocked him. Her face. His face. You simple fool. You pointless fraud. Kavendish tried to turn his eyes away, but a taloned hand grasped his cheeks and forced him to look. The questions rose like smoke. Somewhere there was night. Somewhere there were moons and stars. Somewhere there was trouble, violence and disturbance. Somewhere there were unruly roots. Somewhere there were mysteries.

Kavendish worried; he never worried, he hated it. He felt divided. Professor Helen Cavendish. A scholar. A creator. The creator. The A.B.A.C.U.S. Yet her doubts had flourished. Something had fractured her certainty. She had found it in the woods. But by then it was too late. There were secrets in this book, secrets that would disrupt the Great Equilibrium and leave it in a garbled mess. Kavendish's world of unrestrained pleasure was a dank, windowless prison. But now, after reading these few tattered pages, it seemed as if a great crack was forming in the walls of his cell. Illuminating his confinement. He was curious. It was electrifying. Kavendish gathered the book and loose photographs and stuffed them into his pockets. He was committing the first crime in centuries.

The pavement was warm and clean, bathed in the light of the never-setting sun. The rays bounced off the sparkling glass of a neighbouring building, projecting the reflection of the Museum of Ignorance onto its surface. Kavendish felt the museum loom behind him. The stolen book weighed heavily in his pocket. He felt confused and unhappy. The most dangerous emotion. The only crime. The only possible act of sedition. He glanced up again at the reflection of the museum; it wasn't too late to return the book. The burden was too much. He just wanted to be happy. He turned to return. But the reflection was gone. There was no museum. Just an endless piazza surrounded by absurd fuck pads. His Sensory Nexus Mask pinged back into life. He was transparent once more. The screen filled with vast plumes of data. Kavendish blinked furiously. His Kudos Quotient was low. He had been away too long.

He needed to think. What a horrible prospect. Kavendish began to walk slowly across the piazza. His face frozen in an unconvincing grin. His Kudos Quotient showed some modest improvement. The Service Citizens who had been so diligently tending to the sidewalks were returning their brooms and sanitation equipment to the storage facilities and heading for the transports. A Discipline Drone monitored their progress.

I hope you have had a productive day, Citizens. I hope your service has brought you happiness. I hope your leisure time will be joyful. I hope you had a productive day . . .

The drone's voice faded into the distance as it shadowed the line. The visions of the twisting roots still lingered in Kavendish's mind as he watched it disappear. The city suddenly seemed ridiculous to him. All this energy, all of mankind's ingenuity, squandered on vacuous projects and funnelled into ludicrous architecture. All these vulgar buildings cluttering the skyline with their demented spires. Behind their elaborate frontages was a decadent, duped population wanking itself into oblivion.

Kavendish found himself by the river again. The pneumatic pavement following its path toward the glass bridge and the park at its terminus. Kavendish took some solace from the river. It flowed outside of time. Separate from the follies of the city that it bisected. As civilisations rose and fell, the river continued to carve its way to the ocean; and when all our ingenuity was exhausted and our buildings had returned to the soil from whence they sprang, the river would keep flowing. Relentless and unimpressed.

The hoots of a monkey troop announced Kavendish's arrival at the park. He entered through an arch of lush foliage and took the anti-clockwise path. The genetically modelled animals moved amongst the foliage. Their chatter diminishing as they alone sensed the onset of darkness. It was only humans that gibbered and frolicked in their artificial day, though there were no Aristoians to be seen at present. The Service Citizens were returning to the transports. Kavendish would soon be alone. Something caught his eye. A twisting pillar, like a drill reversing from the ground. A rough tower was emerging from the manicured lawn of the park. It was a tree. The same tree. Unfolding in the vanquished twilight. Casting shadows where none should fall. Its canopy sprang open like a magician's bouquet.

Kavendish was no longer on the path. Though he hadn't moved a step. He was under the canopy. It was dark. The bright, trimmed lawns of the park had vanished. In its place was a rugged floor of broken twigs and dead leaves. He was in a forest. All around him. The Tangle. Thick with trees and tightly meshed shrubs. It was uncivilised and inhuman. He felt his face. His Sensory Nexus Mask was gone. Quotients were irrelevant. The sounds of the modified animals had tuned to the cautious chatter of wild things. The rustle of creatures running for cover added an unfamiliar cadence to the warning calls. In this dimension the animals feared man. Kavendish stepped gingerly on the uneven surface. This was not the way of things. He approached the gnarled trunk of the monstrous tree. It resembled a bent, malignant figure. Its branches the tentacles of a great leviathan. His impulse to touch the black bark was uncontrollable. His manicured fingers crept from his tense, balled fist and made contact with the skin of the tree.

The face of the professor. His face. Her face. So like his own, and yet not him. The mouth opening and closing, words forming. Kavendish let his fingers linger on the knots of the bark. Rough bark. Rough skin. The wood penetrated his flesh, sending out tendrils into his body. Wily shoots wriggled into veins, travelling at great speed through his nervous system. Speech centres, motor functions, his eyes. The figure of the professor stood before him. Her mouth opening and closing. Kavendish leaned towards her. They joined and travelled again.

*

238

He jumped on a pneumatic pavement that led across the river. He followed a group of Service Citizens who were heading for the transports. They were leaving the city. He would leave with them. Out of the maze of spires. Into the Tangle. They appeared to be heading towards a large stone arch that lay a few blocks from the riverbank. The arch was at the top of a boulevard lined with perfectly pruned poplars, which led to a quite fantastic structure Kavendish had never noticed before.

London Terminal 1.

A baroque masterwork of demented genius. A garish and exuberant collection of ornate carvings. Depicting all manner of dryads, nymphs and mythical beasts frozen in ecstatic poses. A network of bright, brass girders weaved between them like the trail left by a huge mechanical snail. The effect was painful on the eye. Two Discipline Drones hovered over the entrance.

Kavendish bowed his head and followed the Service Citizens inside. The interior of the transport hub mirrored the madness outside. Two wide platforms were bisected by a perfectly straight track. The track headed directly out of the station like an arrow piercing the heart of the city. A sleek, clean transport vehicle sat quietly humming on the platform. As the Service Citizens approached, its doors slid gently open. Two Discipline Drones hovered above the platform.

Thank you for your service, Citizens. Please enjoy your leisure pursuits. We trust you will be happy.

The Service Citizens embarked in silence. Kavendish joined them. The doors of the transport closed quietly behind him. The transport was spacious, with comfortable seats positioned at regular intervals. Kavendish, after some hesitation, selected one and sat. The transport was bright and spotless, with a gentle current of cool air creating a fresh and pleasant atmosphere. There was a communal area with tasteful tables positioned around an Automated Epicurus food dispenser. Service Citizens would occasionally visit the device for refreshments before returning to their seats. Pleasant nods were exchanged, but there was little conversation. The transport was busy, but certainly not packed. It contained a variety of service grades, but most seemed to be in the top end of the alphabet. A lot of A and B grades were sat near Kavendish, one or two Cs and Ds too. No one said a word.

The transport glided out of London Terminal 1. The crazed vistas of the city whizzed by in a blur of architectural confusion. The Service Citizens, as one, reached into their garments and produced a collection of devices. They strapped them around their heads, covering their eyes. They lacked the elegance of the Sensory Nexus Mask, but they served the same purpose. They stared into them. Heads facing forward. Kavendish's own device-free face was attracting unwelcome glances. He felt in his pocket. The rough cover of the book grazed his fingers. The smooth surface of his Sensory Nexus Mask was underneath it. He dragged the mask up and out. He smoothed it over his face. Passengers turned their heads to look. With their headsets on they looked like a phalanx of security cameras. In polite deference they soon turned their heads back to their original positions. Heads facing forward. Some smiled. Some quietly laughed. Some gasped, others groaned; all were absorbed by their feeds. Kavendish attempted to focus. He blinked open his icons. But the screen was empty. He had been disconnected. He tore it off with obvious frustration. Unhappiness began to blossom. He was

on the outside now. Detached. Remote. Looking in. Heads
turned, then returned.

Beyond the blank screen the transport was now leaving
the jumbled sprawl of the city. They had passed beyond
the world that Kavendish was familiar with. The decadent
housing had given way to more ordered developments.
Small urban archipelagos huddled together on pleasant
pastures. They were circular in construction, with one
or two roads pointing out of them in perfectly straight
lines. Neatly painted fences delineated the limits of the
estates. The transport began to slow. It had entered one
of the developments and was pulling into a clean and
tidy station. The station resembled a scene one might
find on the lid of an Edwardian biscuit tin: the buildings
were constructed from solid red brick and were shot
through with polished wooden beams painted in racing
green. Metal benches and an abundance of hanging
flower baskets completed the picture. On an embankment
running down to the platform was the station's
designation spelt out in white painted stones.

TOWN A, STOP 1, WEST

The transport came to a halt with an imperceptible sigh.
Passengers stood and got off, mainly A and B grades. The
doors closed and the transport continued, now travelling
along a raised viaduct that gave Kavendish an excellent view
across a wide valley. He could make out little estates dotted
here and there, in a logical and regular pattern; each was
served by an identical straight road and an identical transport
track, sticking out in perfectly straight lines. All directed to
the centre of London. There was no deviation.

The transport gathered speed. It was now travelling at an extraordinary velocity. Kavendish stared out of the window as the regularity whizzed by. He could see something shimmering up ahead. A wall. A barrier. It seemed to reach up into the sky as far as he could see. It was the wall of a vast dome. The transport drew closer and closer to the barrier. Suddenly a baritone boom jolted the carriage. The Service Citizens remained still, heads facing forward. They were now beyond the dome. The light suddenly changed. The clear blue light of day was replaced by a purple haze of twilight. Evening. He had never seen evening before. He gasped. Heads turned and returned. Kavendish pressed his skin to the window. Around the remote islands of ordered human dwellings was an ocean of verdant fibres stretching as far as the eye could see. It seemed to be rolling and rising as he imagined an ocean would. This was the Tangle. Wild. Untidy. Unruly. This was not the way of things. The transport reached a tall viaduct that rose above the woods, as if it were too frightening a prospect to travel through it. Huge pillars disappeared down into the dark interior. Looking back, he could see London and its suburbs squatting under the vast dome like sugar fancies in a bakery. A great artificial sun rose in the west, a controlled explosion frozen in time.

It all seemed so distant, so small. Kavendish looked back down into the black heart of the forest. The twisting limbs of the gnarled tree. Spreading. Reaching out to him again. He wanted to fall. Fall into the moss and sap, into the decay and the dung of dead things. Into the Tangle.

The transport moved on. It entered a tunnel. The sounds and light within the carriage never varied, but his view was momentarily lost. Kavendish had never been this close to such a concentration of Service Citizens before. The remaining passengers definitely occupied the middle of the alphabet. They were all young, like Kavendish, but markedly less altered. These Citizens looked very useful. Sturdy types, free of imperfection or weakness. Good Service Citizens. They stared into their devices, heads facing forward. The transport emerged from the tunnel like a climax. The smooth, silent glide was replaced by a metallic clack, clack, clack. The rustle of a newspaper folding. Kavendish looked at his hands. The newspaper was his own. *The Times*, 'New regime hails completion of A.B.A.C.U.S. project'. He glanced down the carriage. The faint tinny sound of music escaped from the headphones of a young business traveller. Cheap suits, jeans, workweek brogues and afterwork sneakers. Track pants. Cotton shirts open at the neck. Red tops and broad sheets. Comics. He was elsewhere. He wasn't surprised this time. Kavendish was the professor. The professor was him. His face. Her face. He thought he caught a glimpse of an old man. Old useless things should be dissolved. It was the way of things. The Great Equilibrium. Two orange, curly bushes sticking out from the side of an upheld paper. He wanted to shout a greeting, but when he lowered the paper it was revealed to be a young man in overalls. The train entered another short tunnel before emerging onto a platform. It squeaked to a stop, breaks grinding and hissing. The odour of lubricants and warm metal drifted through the carriage. A sign chipped and weathered. In need of repair. Caxton Wood Station, alight for Caxton Wood. He turned the handle of the carriage door. He stepped onto the platform and returned.

Some hanging baskets of flowers dangled incongruously around the station sign.

TOWN G, WEST

The platform was wide and clean and covered by an impressive concrete parabola. Simple industrial lights hung from bright, stainless steel chains, lighting the way to the arched exit. Kavendish hid himself amongst the crowd of Service Citizens. A Discipline Drone hovered over the line. Its lights blinking rapidly.

Welcome home, Citizens. I hope your day has been productive and happy. Please enjoy your leisure pursuits. Welcome home, Citizens. I hope your day . . .

The drone's melodious voice grew fainter as they headed down the platform. Kavendish kept his head bowed. The line moved smoothly, and he was soon at the exit. Kavendish stepped out onto a charming piazza, perfectly circular with one straight path bisecting it. The path was wide and uninterrupted, leading in one direction, from the terminal to the town beyond. A fountain gurgled in its centre, and around the edges beautiful stone benches provided places of quiet contemplation. They were all empty. Surrounding the piazza were lawns of thick green grass interspersed with delicate pastel wildflowers. It was tastefully restrained. Kavendish found it boring. The air was buzzing with Discipline Drones. They were hovering over the entrance to the station and shadowing the Citizens as they crossed the piazza. He kept his eyes fixed on the pavement, hoping not to be too conspicuous. Kavendish was becoming accustomed to stealth. He found it unpleasant.

Kavendish followed the perfectly straight path. A few metres away Kavendish could make out rows of spacious, functional Living Units. They were all identical in construction: a blend of concrete and steel, with huge windows and large glass atriums at the rear. There were no fences. No borders apart from the walls of the structures themselves. Large open lawns surrounded each dwelling. At the edge of this space was a thick wooded mass. The edge of the Tangle. His pulse quickened. His identity shifted. His face. Her face. Kavendish's eyes. Her eyes. Drawn to a playground, much like the ones he had clambered over at the hatchery. There were climbing frames and rope swings. See-saws and roundabouts. Children were playing on the playground equipment. Why weren't they in the hatchery with all the other children? As he drew nearer he could hear their joyful squeals. It was unsettling. He hadn't seen one for years. The children began running towards the returning Service Citizens. They seemed attached to them somehow. Kavendish watched them grab hands and head into the spacious homes of Town G, West.

A Discipline Drone hovered past. Kavendish watched it as it floated into the housing estate. This Discipline Drone seemed full of purpose. Kavendish followed its progress with mild interest. The drone approached one of the Living Units. A nervous-looking Service Citizen came to the door. Words were exchanged. Kavendish could see the Service Citizen's mouth move, but he was too far away to make out the words. The Citizen seemed upset. Kavendish wrinkled his forehead, trying to make sense of the exchange. There was a cry. The Service Citizen raised his voice. The cry becoming a shout. The Service Citizen seemed to tremble. His hands were held out imploringly. Trying to reason with the hovering machine. A wave of energy emanated from the Discipline Drone, opaque and shimmering like a heat haze on a summer's day. The wave enveloped the Service Citizen. Instantly he was reduced to nothing. Only a very fine dust and the hint of vapour were left, before they too were absorbed into the evening air. The Discipline Drone flew through the haze of the dissolved Citizen and entered the Living Unit. Kavendish was paralysed. A spectator without agency. A child ran out. The Discipline Drone following close behind. Bile rose in his throat. Bile rose in her throat. The violence and the violence yet to come. A woven toy resembling a smiling monkey was dangling from the child's hand. The child was whimpering, attempting to form words. Small bubbles of spit swelled and then popped as his mouth struggled to create a response. In the Tangle the roots rose.

> In darkness now from darkness born, circumference,
>   length and span.
> In lilac glade the wreath and thorn, wove mockeries
>   of man.
> In lilac glade beneath the earth, in death's ecstatic bond.
> Come walk with me in lilac shade, to the emptiness beyond.

The drone's lights blinked. A brutal calculation was in process. Once more a wave of energy silently flowed across the space between drone and child. Then the child was gone. Kavendish had never really known what being dissolved involved. He thought it might be some kind of a voluntary arrangement, rather like an anaesthetic. Something pleasant and good. His scream echoed inside his cells. But his mouth was silent. He felt disgust, fury, horror. But most of all he felt embarrassed. The Discipline Drone spun around to face him. Its lights flashing across its facia. Its pleasant, melodious voice rang out.

River

They had been lost in the lanes for hours. Two strangers bonded by a contract. Driver and passenger. Each turn they made together took them further away from the certainties of cities and towns. The comfort of signs and signals. Two strangers misplaced by circumstance. One reliant on maps that had no function out here in the Tangle. The other now too old to care. His memory subverted by age and disease.

Alexander Malik was happy to be going anywhere or nowhere. The destination would reveal itself in time, he had no doubt of it. But the driver lacked the luxury of time. He operated in a world where each minute was a quantity of value. If he lost many more in these backwoods he would be struggling to pay the rent come month's end. He looked into the rear-view mirror and caught Alexander's eye, searching for guidance from the older gentleman. Alexander returned his gaze with a smile of detached contentment. The driver sighed and shook his head. He seemed to know where he was going when he got in. He had an address, a place, a name. But once they'd left the suburbs of Caxton all sense of direction seemed to desert him. Each charming hamlet they drove through seemed familiar to the old fellow. They stopped several times, thinking they had reached their destination, but on further enquiry they found that there was always a little bit further to go.

'You can't miss it, left after the Plough, not the Dressingham Plough, the Ambleton Plough, mind, take the left fork, not the sharp left, that goes to the Burrows, but the next left, towards Arnside, follow that for about five mile, then take the left-hand fork again, or is it right? No, it's definitely left, when you see the old mill, it's sharp right there, can't miss it.'

Alexander was enthralled by the journey. It was marvellous. He hadn't been out here for decades. His milky eyes watched the trees flash past. A kaleidoscope of emerald shades and mute tones interrupted only briefly by the villages they passed through. Even these little hamlets seemed to blend into the wild forest, as if they were being sucked into the air sacs of an enormous lung. Their wattle-and-daub frames and ancient thatch barely tolerated in this preternatural Eden. Like tics on a wild beast, these dwellings hid in the folds of the forest, waiting to be picked and harried. This was no refined estate of managed plantings. This was the undefinable heart of Grand Bois, the timeless principality of Abnoba and Aranyani. But before, even these spirits were named by the woods. Before even one second had been counted by the reckoning of men, there was the Tangle. The twisted limbs of trees hung low over the pitted lanes. All around them, spring was giving way to summer. The trees were sumptuous; the entire spectrum of green tones merged in the canopy. Below it, the murky interior of the ancient wood. Full of gullies, secret dells and granite outcrops, with names like Witch's Knee and the Devil's Cup. This was the land before the fall. This was the knot of life. Alexander remembered the jumble of the woods with fondness. So many adventures a lifetime ago. The driver looked increasingly concerned.

'I don't get many jobs out this way.'

He kept noting nervously.

'Not far now.'

Alexander answered the driver unconvincingly. He was happy in the car; he didn't really care if they drove all day, because out here he suddenly felt focused. Certainly, he had no idea where he was, but the deeper into the Tangle they went, the clearer his recollections became. The patchwork of half-remembered events and forgotten names that characterised his recent day-to-day life were forming into solid memories. He pressed his face to the glass, his eyes wide with wonder.

'Visiting relatives are you, sir?'

The driver broke the trance. Alexander smiled, amused at the question.

'In a way, I suppose I am, yes. I was born out here, you know.'

'Ah, really, must have been . . . errr . . . a peaceful childhood?'

A frown formed on Alexander's wrinkled face.

'No, not really.'

He returned his attention to the window. The driver gave a resigned shrug and pressed on down the road to nowhere in particular.

After many wrong turns at several 'Plough' inns, the driver was considering calling the police. His base had been trying to reach him through the static. But he was out of range and out of patience. The tunnel of trees suddenly thinned as they entered yet another village. The sort of unremarkable outpost of twee respectability that was unlikely to make any impression on you. Alexander, however, became suddenly animated.

'This is it! Yes! This is it!'

'Thank fuck for that.'

The driver mumbled, still trying to remain professional. They had arrived at their destination. Challoner's Cross. Once, this little village had been Alexander's whole universe. His parents had settled here after the war. They had escaped the horrors of Nazi-occupied Europe with only a suitcase to their name. All they knew was lost. Families, friends and neighbours, all perished in the brutal occupation. His father soon rejoined the fight. On several occasions he had only narrowly avoided death whilst serving as a fighter pilot. After the war his parents opened a small domestic maintenance business, which was successful enough to allow them to settle in the apparent tranquillity of the English countryside. It was idyllic in many ways: the land was wild and beautiful, and the opportunities for adventure for young children were plentiful. But they suffered their share of malicious whispering and a feeling that they would never really fit in with some of the more insular residents. There was a significant number of grumbling pub bores and bitter, impoverished aristocrats who felt Britain had fought on the wrong side in the war and that these types simply had no place in an English country village. But the Maliks endured. There were more than enough good people to sustain them, and when Alexander, and some years later his little sister Emilia, arrived, it looked as if life for the family might be as happy and uncomplicated as they had dreamed. But then there was the river.

'I'm afraid I don't have any money, but thank you for the lift, most kind.'

Alexander closed the door of the taxi, offering the driver a wave and a smile. He was so lovely, so accommodating, he thought. He had arrived promptly after his escape from the home, forestalling any embarrassing incidents with the authorities. The car was comfortable; it smelled good too. All this way. Why, it was remarkable, so kind. He'd seen the meter ticking, but he couldn't quite place its purpose. Where had he come from anyway, this driver? Had his sister called it for him, he wondered. The driver was unsure how to react. His forehead bounced off the steering wheel as he cursed his luck. Perhaps now was the time to call the police? The elderly gentleman shouldn't be out here on his own, and besides, he needed to get his money. The driver lifted his head from the wheel to plead for his fare. But Alexander was nowhere to be seen. The driver got out of the car and looked down the sleepy village high street. Nothing. The old man had vanished.

*

Alexander felt light and sprightly. The effects of the forest were manifesting themselves in an increased feeling of well-being. He had dragged his body out of the car, expecting the familiar aches and pains to hamper his mobility. But as his feet touched the ground, he felt a suppleness he had not experienced for many years. He practically skipped across the car park. His memory was sharpening. Though the present was still a mysterious muddle of confusing fragments, the past was as clear as day. He even remembered the tiny hidden footpath that led from the car park to the church. Almost invisible to anyone without good local knowledge. An obscure byway. But he had remembered it. Just like all those years ago, when Alexander and his sister would run down the secret path en route to some adventure or other. Making their way to the apple orchards, or the rope swing in Potter's Gully. Or perhaps they were heading for the river.

The churchyard was morbidly bucolic. A picture postcard of decay. Faded tombstones tilted at every conceivable angle, whilst stone angels wept over tumbledown mausoleums. At the centre was the old Norman church, well preserved by a combination of English Heritage grants and the generosity of wealthy notables. For many years it had been the focal point of village life. Even in his parents' time the church had been a social club, a therapeutic centre, a place to commune, a place

to find peace, an incubator of gossip. But now, except for the
occasional christening or wedding, it was poorly attended.
The church no longer maintained a vicar at Challoner's Cross.
The vicarage itself was now the holiday home of a wealthy
businessman from Caxton. Instead, the vicar from Ambleside
would cycle up every Sunday to deliver his sermon to the
elderly and righteous few. Alexander drifted past the stones, his
bent frame beginning to straighten as the curious potency of
his surroundings continued to rejuvenate him. His head was no
longer orientated towards the ground. But instead, it was held
high on broadening shoulders. Alexander absorbed the country
air and studied the graves. Seeking familiar melancholy
markers. It had been years, decades maybe, since he had come
to pay his respects. The pain was too great. But now, as his own
time to depart grew closer, he knew he must confront them one
more time.

Andrik Malik

Beloved Father and Husband

1920–2002

Now at rest and joined with his family once more

And a right next to his father:

Karolina Malik

Devoted Wife and Mother

1921–1990

With her angel

Alexander sighed. He always hated the phrase 'devoted
wife'. He had tried to persuade his father to use a less old-
fashioned epitaph, something that wouldn't betray his social

conservatism. But his father could barely look at him when he had come back to the village to help with the funeral arrangements. The bitterness his father felt was as fresh as the day of the accident. The day that Alexander had really lost his parents. He patted the gravestones and whispered a quiet prayer. Please forgive me. Your devoted son.

Alexander hoped that they could hear him. Across time and space, in whatever heaven his parents now dwelt in. Maybe now, on the cusp of his own demise, they would let him rest in peace too. His eyes drifted to a monument he had not seen for years, but which featured in his dreams almost every night. Next to his parents' grave was another stone, smaller and covered with a green-gold bloom of lichen. Alexander bent his knees and crouched in front of the grave, brushing some of the loose grime from the stone. Again, the suppleness of his limbs surprised him; although he wasn't especially old, bad luck and ill health had meant rheumatic pains were a constant burden. When his mind began to fail, he had given up most forms of exercise, fearful of where he might end up if he ventured out. However, his sharpening wits provided him with less comfort now. Memories played in his mind like the roll of a cinema projector. Clicking and whirring. Clicking and whirring. His eyes began to cloud with tears. He wiped them with his hands. Capturing a single tear drop on his finger, he pressed it into the faded stone.

Emilia Malik

1949–1958

Our angel, always in our hearts.
We will be together again soon

The river carved its way through the woodland, juddering and tumbling. Carrying the silt and bones of a thousand last moments. The final words of suicides, the soundless screech of torn gills and drowned insects, all gathered and stored in its endless current. The water never remained the same. It was a sequence of instants never to be repeated. But the memories lingered. Sticking to the rocks and algae. Reluctant to leave. The artery of the Tangle, into which all tributaries must flow. The river. Always the river. On the outskirts of the village, where the last few buildings finally surrendered to the perplexing wildness of the wood. There was the river. The boundary between two worlds. Remorseless and beautiful. There was the river. Always the river.

There were only a few places you could cross the river safely. In the autumn and spring, when the rain was at its heaviest, it would swell to dangerous levels. The fords could be turned into fast-moving torrents within minutes. It would be impossible to cross, even for the most gifted athlete or experienced swimmer. Close to the village there were two bridges. Alexander and Emilia liked the old railway bridge best. The line had been closed long before the war, with only the vague impression of the track remaining. Local farmers used to drive sheep over it on the way to the market, while the local children used it to play games of Poohsticks. In the summer, when the river was at its most languid, the older children would sometimes dive off the bridge. But never the Malik children. They knew the river was unpredictable and should only be entered with caution. But they loved playing down by the bridge. Carefully selecting sticks for their likely buoyancy and speed, they would lean over the parapet and cast their competing twigs into the river, watching the current twisting around the rocks as it carried them along. Cheering them on, they would run across to the other side to see who's stick emerged victorious from under the stony arch. It never got boring. The summer holidays were full of such games, but springtime was the best. The sticks were full of sap; it made them sturdier and less likely to be snapped against the granite boulders that jutted out like gnarled teeth from the surface of the water.

Alexander carried his memories like a hiker's rucksack. Hefting the dull ache of decades down the byways of his youth. But he found his body to be less of a burden. His strides were becoming confident, a far cry from the rapid shuffle he had had to employ whilst escaping the nursing home. After breakfast the nurse had taken him down to the communal lounge, hoping that Alexander would take some comfort in the company of his friends. He had been slipping away fast and spent most of his time in bed these days. But the doctor recommended companionship, even if it was simply to avoid the chance of him dying alone. His children lived some miles away, one of them abroad. They had been called. The end wasn't far off now, but it would still be a day or two until they would all be able to say goodbye. Alexander knew he was dying. To be honest, he didn't much care. He'd had enough, but he felt as if some things were still left undone. Ghosts still roamed the riverbanks and should be put to rest.

A willowy teenage boy runs along the bank of a river. The river is tumbling vigorously down its channel; pregnant with spring rain it threatens to burst its banks. The boy is holding a crudely stitched rag doll. Those dolls with the big eyes and no features. A small girl runs after him, jumping and stretching with her arms in the air, trying to snatch the doll from her brother's cruel grip.

'Give it back, give it back, Alex. I'll tell mamma and papa.'

'You'll have to catch me first! Does Matilda want to go in the river?'

The boy has stopped running and is perched on the rocks at the river's edge. He uses his advantage in height to keep the little girl at bay as she jumps and screams for her toy.

'In she goes.'

The boy is laughing as he pretends to cast the doll into the torrent. The little girl is crying now.

The nurse wheeled Alexander into his usual spot, just as 'Golden Memories' were about to start their morning singalong. Barry Sparkle was running his fingers over the keys of his organ, Patricia scatting the first few lines of a familiar show tune. Barry engaged the syncopated rhythm of the organ's drum machine. Alexander waited until the nurse was out of the lounge fetching the sherry trolley. Once he was sure the coast was clear, he got out of his wheelchair and shuffled out of the nursing home.

Step by step, with ever-growing confidence, Alexander plotted his path through the undergrowth. Nimbly hopping over drying puddles he made his way to the old railway bridge. It was much smaller than he remembered. Through the eyes of a child it looked like a magical arch over an enchanted river. A castle, a temple, a palace for kings, queens and princesses. While beneath its dark stone canopy were trolls, monsters, goblins and warlocks. The river, the stealer of souls, a purifying torrent that could carry you down to unfathomable depths. Where treasures lay next to the bones of unfortunate pirates and unlucky adventurers.

The little girl jumps up and down, desperately trying to reach her precious doll. Her eyes are fixed on its raggedy limbs, flailing in the air, in her brother's teasing fist. She launches herself with increased vigour. She catches the foot of the doll and tugs with all her might. Her tiny body collides with her brother's scrawny frame. The rocks slick with freshly fallen rain. Feet slipping. Desperate arms wheel in the air, trying to maintain balance. The water licks up the bank, its demonic limbs dragging young bodies into the flood. In she goes. In she goes.

He stepped onto the bridge, absentmindedly kicking leaves and twigs as he remembered that terrible day. He caught something in the corner of his eye. Was that a figure in the trees? Someone watching him from the riverbank? Alexander went over to the wall of the bridge and peered into the woods. His milky eyes were beginning to clear. Indistinct shapes came into focus. Was that a child waving at him under the branches? No, it was just a rock. When he was younger, his sister and Alexander would often imagine those jagged outcrops were people, frozen into stone by a vindictive witch, or monsters slumbering after eating an entire village for lunch. He laughed quietly to himself. He was seeing the world with childlike eyes again. He looked down at his feet. He was still wearing his slippers. The ones with the Velcro fastening. Two sticks lay close by. They looked streamlined and sleek. Perfect racing sticks. He bent down and picked them up, holding one in each hand. The trees rustled as a sudden breeze swirled. That figure. Lurking in the branches. But again he could see nothing; the figure remained an intangible feeling. Alexander turned his head away from the woods and leaned over the parapet of the bridge. He looked at the cold river tumbling below. He studied the flow of the water, watching the eddies curl around the rocks. He plotted the course for one final game. A stick for him and a

stick for Emilia. He twirled them in his fingers, holding them
up to the springtime sun. They were perfect. He prepared
to launch. 3-2-1. Down they dropped, landing lightly on the
water in a clear channel. The sticks were carried into the dark
interior. Alexander excitedly ran to the opposite side to see
which stick would emerge victorious. But neither emerged. He
waited. He waited longer than logic dictated, but still nothing.
Disappointed, but still determined, he found two more racing
sticks. Not as sleek as the last two, but still, decent enough. He
dropped them into the river. Again, he ran to the opposite side.
But still nothing came.

It was well after lunchtime and Alexander's stomach
was feeling the pangs of hunger. He missed the sticky toffee
pudding, the sherry trolley and all the other conservative
but comforting provisions of the nursing home. But he must
finish the game. He had lost count of the number of sticks
he had cast into the river. And yet, not one had appeared
from under the bridge. Still the river flowed with the same
persistence. Perhaps one of the trolls was gathering up his
sticks to make a fire to cook him in? He smiled and decided to
go and see for himself. He left the bridge and pushed through
the bushes, looking for a path down to the river. He found
a spot, but it looked a little dangerous for a man of his age.
He thought of his old hands, with his fingers all bent and
distorted by arthritis. They were too gnarled to cope with
the climb. He paused to looked down at them, turning them
over and over. These weren't his hands. The fingers were
straight, almost elegant, the veins on the back sitting at a
discreet depth under firm healthy skin, not the blue-ridged
relief map of advanced age he was used to. Alexander touched
his face with his new hands. The worn, pitted features he
had expected to find had been replaced by the soft skin of a

young man. He pinched and squeezed the limber epidermis. As his fingers opened and closed, so the skin returned to its fullness. He negotiated the riverbank without hesitation. He felt as if he could leap across the river itself. The muscles in his legs flexed and tensed, filled with vitality. He thrust out his arms to steady himself on the bank; they felt toned and flexible. He reached the bottom of the bank and began to walk back towards the bridge. The ground was wet and uneven, and he was forced to hop across the rocks. The rocks.

A young boy's head breaks the surface. The current is carrying him quickly downstream. He is a vigorous boy and a strong swimmer, but even his youthful limbs find it hard against the insistent undertow. He bounces off the rocks, trying to steady himself in the channel. He is crying. He is shouting out in panic. The little girl is nowhere to be seen.

Alexander was close to the bridge now, striding down the riverbank towards the stone vault. Something was wrong. Something was incorrect. Under the span of the bridge, instead of the cool, shaded arch of moss-coloured masonry, there was a void, darker than any shadow. It looked like a bruised moon sinking into the river. Silence weighed down on the countryside. The familiar sounds of the water, the riverbank birds and even the buzzing of insects were absent. Only a quiet vacuum and a horrible stillness. He stepped hesitatingly over slippery rocks, closer and closer to the void. He was drawn to it, unable to turn. His slippers squelched as he approached. It was impenetrable; not even light seemed to break its uniform blackness. At the base of the void the river stopped. As if a sharp line had been cut through a painting in some unnatural collage. He stretched out to touch it. Needing

261

to feel the barrier. Unconfident of his senses. His fingertips touched the surface. It felt warm and soft, almost comforting. The surface of the void rippled, like waves in a viscous medium. Alexander peered into the billowing blackness. A face formed in the ripples. The face of a young girl. Alexander recoiled . . . then the silence broke. Like an alarm going off, the whole natural world seemed to squeal and trill at once. Alexander tried to run, but his feet were sliding on the rocks. His arms wheeled in the air. Like they had all those years ago. He fell. He fell towards the river. For a few seconds he seemed to hang in the air, suspended millimetres above the surface.

When he hit, it wasn't at all as unpleasant as he had feared. Though every fibre of his being had been tensed for impact into the freezing water, once he made contact with it the expected shock failed to materialise. Instead the water curled around him. It was more like a soft mattress or a beanbag. Like the one his mother had bought for them in the 1970s. He sank into the river. No water flowed into his mouth or filled his nose. There was no sudden inrush into his ears to deafen him. No turbulent current to spin him around and dash him against the rocks. Instead the water moulded around his body, keeping him afloat. It was warm, like a womb. Alexander looked about him in astonishment. The river was no longer moving. Nor did it have any plausible dimensions. It was everywhere. In the distance he could see the old bridge. He had been carried upstream against the current. Why, he seemed to be miles from it now, when only moments ago he had been right there under its arch. That terrible, bruised moon. Where he had seen death in the face of that little girl, peering out of the black void. But he felt no fear. He felt nothing. The features of the river slowly returned. Dimensions became more understandable and familiar. He thought he saw the figure on the bank again. A shadow moving through the trees, following him as the water began to carry his body. He tried to track the figure with his eyes as he flowed back towards the bridge. But the figure soon melted into the shifting umbra of the wood. He drifted nearer and nearer the old bridge. He could see the pitch-black disc oscillating under the arch. Closer. Much closer now. Alexander gasped as his feet touched the void; as he pierced the membrane it felt as if he was passing through melting wax. The warm sensation passed up his legs, then his torso. Alexander closed his eyes as his whole body passed through the barrier.

His fingertips cautiously crept over his face, then his chest, his thighs. He was intact, but his body felt hollow, like a thin shell, fragile and temporary. He opened his eyes. He had passed under the bridge. The woods crowded around the river channel in the same familiar way, but the colours seemed more pronounced and vivid. He could almost taste the tang of the bark and the sweetness of the sap. He stretched out his hands to touch the warm waters that were carrying him gently downstream. The water fused with his skin. Bonding him to the river and its current. His fingers brushed against the knobbly irregularity of a stick. A fine racing stick. All around him a flotilla of sticks drifted in formation, escorting him like a convoy as he made his way down the channel. Alexander looked over to the wooded bank. A figure again, this time much more distinct. It was him, but as a small boy. Arms outstretched, running along the bank, playing at aeroplanes, a fighter pilot, like his father. He tried to call out a greeting to his younger self, but his mouth made no sound. His body felt lighter, as if a layer had dissolved away into the river.

He noticed a slightly older boy perched on a rock on the other bank. Looking furtively around. Alexander turned his head to look at him. He was maybe eleven or twelve years old.

A puff of smoke emerged from his mouth; the little boy was smoking. A stolen cigarette pilfered from his mother's ornate cigarette box. A stale brand from the old country that had sat in the box for years. The sound of a chocking cough. The green face. The sick on his shoes. His mother's angry face, one of many disappointments. A resigned smile passing between his parents that spoke of similar transgressions in their past. Two figures skipped out of the woods behind the vomiting boy. A teenage couple. Her name was Anne, his first love. The teenage couple kissed as the river flowed past. Tumbling over the rocks. His first kiss. Now Alexander is a network of nerves, veins and organs inside an exposed skeleton. His skin having melted into the river as he drifted along.

An even older boy, nearly grown, sits on a branch that overhangs the river. He is alone with his thoughts. Angst, heartbreak and uncertainty. The typical hurdles a teenager has to overcome, playing tug of war with his developing consciousness. But this boy carries a heavier burden. He is drawn here, back to the river. Endlessly replaying the events of that terrible day. Trying to will a different outcome into existence. The boy lifts his head, alerted to a sudden movement in the forest. His parents are out taking a walk in the woods. For them it's a place to escape the dreadful melancholy of home. The constant reminders of Emilia, her absence pressing around them. Crushing them with its weight. The boy silently watches as his parents pass by without noticing him. Alexander is now a gelatinous ooze. Eyes, lungs, spleen suspended in the water like a bloom of algae.

His free-floating eyes drift over the landscape. A thousand figures play out the scenes of his life on the riverbank as he slowly decomposes into the stream. He notices a bright arch up ahead, like a rainbow spanning the river. He is back at the bridge again, but the black void has been replaced by a bright yellow sun. The sun beams out over the water, dappling the surface. His organs, nerves and sinews are part of the waterway now; only his eyes and a sense of his oneness remain. Alexander glances for the last time at the rocks on the riverbank. They are slippery and treacherous. Like the day of the accident. Suddenly he sees a figure running from the shadows of the wood. It is Emilia! Emilia is standing on the rocks. Their parents stroll out of the forest and stand behind her with their arms entwined. He struggles to make out their expression as he approaches the burning sun. He passes close to the rocks. So close he can almost touch them. If only he had fingers to touch them with. His heart aches for their forgiveness. Their love. He only has a few seconds before he disappears forever. Please, please, give me a sign. One of his eyes blurs and shatters. But his one remaining organ catches an expression on the faces of the figures on the bank. They are smiling. Yes, he is sure of it! His family is smiling. Whatever remains of Alexander Malik is filled with joy. Soon everything will be right again. He is nearly there. So close. Nearer and nearer the glowing sun. He can feel its warmth. So close. So close. The drift begins to stall. The width and depth expand, taking the landscape with it. He is on the cusp, the very lip of the horizon. The incandescent terminus. His remaining eye fractures into a million pieces. The last molecules of Alexander Malik merge with the river. The timeless waterway, flowing gently into the sun forever.

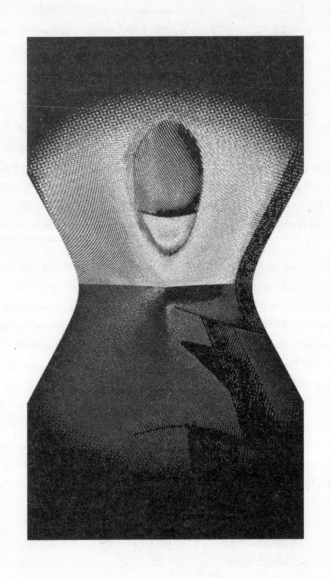

The Happiness Engine

Aristoian Kavendish Jeremiah 15.66.2121. You seem in
distress. How may I increase your happiness? Is there an
impediment to your pleasure that I might remove? You
appear a long way from your Living Unit? May I aid you in
your return, Citizen?

A flurry of lights hurried across the Discipline Drone's facia.

Nexus update. Nexus queries incoming. Aristoian
Kavendish Jeremiah 15.66.2121. I notice your Nexus
access has been suspended. Presumption. Death. My
scans reveal your status to be. Alive. Aristoian Kavendish
Jeremiah 15.66.2121. Would you like me to reconnect
your service?

As Kavendish walked, the dizzying corruption of London
began to fade from his mind. He was nowhere. Where the
darkness clung to you like tar. Nowhere. Unfamiliar, all-
consuming blankness. Nowhere. He could never go back. He
was unhappy. That would not be tolerated. He was not useful.
That would not be tolerated. He would be dissolved on sight.
Like all the other useless things. Here he was. Nowhere.

Kavendish stared up at the sky as he stumbled over the
pockmarked ground. Out here there was night. Darkness. It
was beautiful. He reached the crest of a hill and looked down

into a wooded valley full of shadows. Small towns floated like flotsam, drifting on a black ocean. Out here the seasons rotated. Time ebbed and flowed. Some of the Citizens slept. They had children and travelled. They did service. They had beds and sheets. They had breakfast and read bedtime stories. They were dissolved.

Kavendish wandered through an untrodden pasture. The first human feet to step upon this virgin borderland for centuries. He trailed his hand through the swaying grass. He reached a grove of modest trees. He sat under the umbrella of a spreading oak.

The mechanism turned and stuck, its cogs were clogged
*   and bound.*
The dial upon the watch's face spun back into the ground.
The fibre and the filament, the flower and the weed.
The traveller comes to fill his sack with the Tangle's
*   golden seed.*

He placed his hands on the soft earth. His eyelids became heavy. Without a steady supply of stimulants his body revolted. He fell into a deep sleep. Tiny, vein-like roots sprang from the soil. Travelling like centipedes across the ground, creeping over his hands. They burrowed into his skin and spread out inside him. A tiny acorn flashed and flickered. It sprouted and spread too.

The chant began to rise.

The mechanism turned and stuck, its cogs were clogged
*   and bound.*
The dial upon the watch's face spun back into the ground.
The fibre and the filament, the flower and the weed.

*The traveller comes to fill his sack with the Tangle's
    golden seed.*

He was inside a book-lined library. He looked down at his
hands and felt his clothing. He was wearing a light linen jacket
and white cotton shirt. He was her. She looked out of the
window. She was in a cottage. Her cottage. Outside the lead-
lined window was a wonderfully tumbledown garden, alive
with bees and insects. She was at a desk. On the desk were
papers, cuttings, formulas, diagrams and designs. Kavendish
picked them up and studied them. Circuits and mathematical
signs. Equations for happiness. Prototypes. The Happiness
Engine. His hand. Her hand. She picked up a sketch drawn by
an unsteady pen. Branches. Ropes. Fire. There were poems and
incantations. Formulas for summoning. There was a scythe.
There was blood. Kavendish looked up from the pictures. The
library seemed to flicker and distort as other figures entered
the room. The spectres began to select books from the shelves.
Others gathered up pages from the archive on the desk. Each
travelling on a separate plane. Each one, them.

*The mechanism turned and stuck, its cogs were clogged
    and bound.
The dial upon the watch's face spun back into the ground.
The fibre and the filament, the flower and the weed.
The traveller comes to fill his sack with the Tangle's
    golden seed.*

His face. Her face. Time froze. The figures froze. Each
separated from the other. They were holding pieces of
crumpled parchment. In his dimension, Kavendish-not-
Kavendish walked around the frozen characters. He looked

down at the pages clasped in their hands. They were identical in every respect. The same story on every page. The page was empty.

He was far from London now. He was nowhere. There was no sign of the transport track. No drones, no mechanisms, no terminals. It was barely daylight, but the darkness had now receded. The promise of another warm day was in the air. He stretched his wiry frame and left the shelter of the grove. In the valley below, a river cut across a wide flood plain before disappearing into the forest. He walked along the river's edge. The riverbanks were coming alive. Dragonflies hovered. Shy voles slipped into the current and vanished. Water boatmen skittered across the shallows. Swallows sought bugs on the wing. Darting and diving. The land, dotted with wildflowers, rose up to meet the thick, forbidding woodland that disappeared beyond all sense. The Tangle. A group of deer watched him from the edge, then turned and strolled back into the forest.

He reached the border of the wood and paused at the boundary. The margin seemed to crackle. A scent of decay mixed with the scent of flowers. His feet crunched on the dead leaves. The interior was subdued. Peaceful and indifferent. Yet he trod here under sufferance. There was chatter in the treetops as Kavendish made his way through the forest. He found a path, or the path found him. Guiding his steps towards some intangible goal. He walked for hours, lost in the winding byways. Small streams sprang up when he was thirsty. Wild orchards of fruit trees presented themselves when he felt hunger gnawing at him. Like the bounty of the A.B.A.C.U.S. He had no sense of day or night under the leaves. Here it was permanent twilight. Not the simple effects of shade. But a perfect blend of light and dark. Genesis and

annihilation. Ahead, several shafts of yellow sunshine broke
up the pallet of crepuscular tones. Kavendish slowed. His feet
moved cautiously towards the light. Closer. Closer. He could
see a glade opening up in the heart of the forest. In the middle
of the glade was a cottage. Her cottage. His cottage.

In certain dimensions it might have been described as
quaint or tumbledown, perhaps charming. It looked out of
place, as if it had been scooped up by a tornado and carelessly
dropped in the heart of the forest. The signs of decay were
quite visible. There was no glass in the windows. No doors.
Half a roof. Crumbling brickwork. Why hadn't this useless
structure been dissolved like all the other old, broken
things? Kavendish paused at the edge of the glade. The grass
surrounding the broken-down cottage was perfectly trimmed
and even. A lawn. A gravel path with neat borders led to
the doorless opening. He stepped warily onto the path and
walked towards the cottage. He thought he caught a glimpse
of something moving in one of the windows. He stopped. His
heart pounding. A blackbird flew out of the dark interior.
Kavendish exhaled. He took another step towards the
cottage. A tile slipped from the tattered roof and smashed on
the lawn. Kavendish looked up. His heart beating a frantic
rhythm. Two tufts of orange hair were caught in a beam of
light. Two eyes glowed from out of the gloom. Like dying
suns. The old man. The clown entity. It was unmistakably
him. Kavendish hesitated. He ran into the cottage. He fell
into the blank void.

The interior of the cottage was a collage of intersecting
moments. A carousel of places and times endlessly revolving.
Kavendish felt himself split and fragment. He was torn and
turned through the dimensions. He was a thousand different
people at once. Cave-dwelling hunter-gatherer covered in the

skins of dead animals. Scratching images on the cave wall. A
tonsured monk illuminating a beautiful parchment. A short-
wigged philosopher holding a telescope. A dusty dandy with
a desiccated specimen in a jar. A professor. The clown entity
in the window. He looked for the stairs. To climb. To meet
the entity. But there were no stairs, no windows, no shapes
or recognisable dimensions. She was in the cottage library.
Birds twittered outside the window. Shafts of light spotlighted
a paper-strewn desk. Kavendish-not-Kavendish began to
solidify and settle. She was a professor. An academic. The
creator. She began to sift through the mess of documents. In
this dimension time moved fast. Twilight, night, day, twilight.
Around and around it went. A clock in the corner of the
library chimed incessantly as the hands flew by. A photograph
caught his eye. An expedition. A man and a woman in the
woods. He felt in his pockets and pulled out an identical
image. Under the photograph was a piece of stout card with
embossed writing on it. The clock chimed so rapidly now
that it felt like a single note stretched to infinity. The ringing
stopped. Time slowed and stopped too.

> The Micron Corporation, in association with the
> Northwestern Cybernetics Foundation, cordially invites
> __Professor Helen Cavendish__ to the activation
> ceremony of the Automated Boolean Architect and Central
> User Synthesiser (A.B.A.C.U.S.). 13.00 at the University of
> Symmetry quadrangle. Smart casual attire recommended.

Kavendish staggered out of the cottage and onto the bright
lawns of the glade. The complex scents of flowers and
forest, decay, attraction and rebirth, had been reduced to the
dull bouquet of stone. The lawn was no longer adjacent to

the forest. Instead, he found himself at the centre of an institution. He was standing in a rectangular piazza illuminated by spotlights. An empty fountain sat at its centre. It had been centuries since any water had flowed from its crusty spouts. It was fossilised and unwanted. Around the sides of the piazza were the red-brick buildings of academia. The relics of a once-proud university. They were dark and empty, having long since lost their usefulness. Grubby windows offered a dull reflection of the lights in the square. Nothing stirred inside except the ghosts of what might have been. His eyes were drawn to the far end of the piazza. A vast monumental structure dominated the dark night sky, towering into the gloom. Its walls were made of cold marble and granite. Its style was a vulgar ancient Greek pastiche, as if it was trying to steal the genius of a past civilisation to make up for its own lack of ideas. Wide steps swept up with overstated confidence to huge pillars that punctured the sky. The building throbbed and glowed, pulsed and vibrated. A discernible hum emanated from its stones. This was the home of the A.B.A.C.U.S.

Kavendish began to climb. Clack, clack, clack, the weary tapping of his soles on the steps. Scrape, clack, scrape. At the summit were two enormous doors fashioned from burnished steel. They towered over him like the gates to a forbidden kingdom. He pushed on the door. It groaned open with an excruciating, grinding creak, resisting his efforts with all its obstinate mass. Kavendish pushed with his head bowed. The cold metal yielded bit by bit. He passed through the crack he had created. He fell inside the Temple of the A.B.A.C.U.S. The doors clanged shut behind him.

Down invisible channels the message travelled. Through nodes and transmitters, into drives and processors.

The A.B.A.C.U.S. is under attack. In the cities and outer towns, the Discipline Drones abruptly stopped their duties. Navigation systems realigned. Co-ordinates were set. The Discipline Drones swivelled and spun towards the A.B.A.C.U.S. Returning to the source. A vast metal swarm. A black shadow. A dense mass sweeping across the landscape at supersonic speed. Back towards the A.B.A.C.U.S. They must protect the brain.

Clack. A Cleaning Drone scurried out from its hiding place to suck up the impurities before disappearing back into the shadows. The room was incredibly bright, dazzling, spotless and sterile. The floor was carved from solid marble, bright and sleek. The huge pillars outside were mirrored within, reflecting the same bland, monumental pretensions. Kavendish shielded his eyes from the glare. The room was thick with the silence of the cloister. A reverent void. Nothing stirred. Clack. He stepped cautiously into the hall. Clack. Eyes darting. Alert. Clack clack clack. The hall was long and wide. Kavendish glanced back at the solid steel doors. Stern and impenetrable. Clack clack clack. His eyes were drawn to the centre of the hall, where the pristine brightness had a peculiar intensity, as if the sun had fallen to earth. At the centre of this bright singularity was a glass box. The sides of the box were so impeccably clean that it seemed almost invisible. Only the slightest refraction of the light gave a clue as to its dimensions. At the centre of the box was a simple wooden table. And on this table was a device. It was of an archaic design. Plastic and yellowing. The A.B.A.C.U.S.

*The golden seed was carried to the fortress of
    their god.*

The bearer with a cursed name sowed the seed and trod.
The earth into the armour of the divinity's cold frame.
The blossom and the buttercup, the hangman and the
    flame.
War has come to cities, villages and towns.
The phantoms stalk the forests dressed in mourning
    gowns.
The Tangle weighs the evidence, the jury is the seed.
The root winds through the skeleton while the pilgrims
    quietly bleed.

He drifted through the hall. Transfixed by the artefact. The A.B.A.C.U.S. was constructed from a brittle plastic material that was tarnished with age. There was a large screen on a bulky monitor. Like an ancient television. Wires led from the rear of the screen into a rectangular box, also constructed from yellowing Bakelite. A small blue light glowed on its surface. An uneven flickering glow that indicated faulty filaments and failing components. Further wires led to a crude keyboard that sat in front of the screen. The A.B.A.C.U.S. gave the impression of decrepit obsolescence. This was the Happiness Engine.

The professor tidied away the papers on her desk, making sure the author's journal was well hidden in the jumble of calculations. These were troubling times and caution was advisable. She pulled on her raincoat. The weather had been unpredictable of late. She heard the taxi pull into the gravel driveway of the cottage. The professor picked up the invitation from the mantelpiece as she headed out the door. The clock struck in the library as she turned the key in the lock.

The taxi pulled into the quadrangle of the venerable institution. The reception was about to begin. She was late. God, how she dreaded this day. Trays of champagne floated about the throng. Flutes disappearing into the crowd like seeds dispersed by the wind. The professor thanked the driver and got out. An eager intern thrust a glossy brochure into the professor's reticent hand. She smiled weakly and thanked them. The intern looked embarrassed as they recognised her face. The creator. She absentmindedly whisked a champagne flute from the tray of a passing waiter and headed into the crowd. She weaved past the excitedly chattering gathering of financiers and government apparatchiks. Smart suits and military insignia were very much in evidence. The anticipation of the president's arrival grew. Under the stones the weeds grew too. The professor freed herself from the crowd and found a quiet doorway that led into the old laboratory wing. Traffic was sparse here. No one wanted to be seen entering the hall of yesterdays. She looked across the quadrangle to the pompous stone and marble edifice. She had meant well. That first blob of solder. That first instruction. But this? A long line of admirers was snaking up the steps, waiting to get a glimpse of their saviour. The president and his A.B.A.C.U.S. The professor looked down at the brochure in her tensed fist. She opened the glossy pages. Welcome to the A.B.A.C.U.S. She looked back at the imposing structure looming across the campus.

An ominous rumble caused Kavendish to glance back towards the metal doors. It was the Discipline Drones. All the Discipline Drones. The air was thick with them, like some

terrible windborne algae clogging the atmosphere. He ran to
the glass box, knowing that he must act now. He discovered
the faintest sliver of a crack. He forced his fingernails into it
and began to prize it open. The seal broke reluctantly. Stale
air, trapped for hundreds of years, rushed out into the hall
like the antique atmosphere of a pharaoh's tomb. He stepped
inside. The A.B.A.C.U.S. blinked silently. The A.B.A.C.U.S.
was neither sinister nor impressive. Just decrepit. No magic
force fields, no booby traps or security devices. Only the
stained plastic-cased box of ancient ingenuity. He brushed
off layers of history to get to the screen. The screen became
visible. A small, green pixelated rectangle winked on and off.
Next to it a single phrase.

WELCOME. PRESS SPACE TO CONTINUE

The Mesmeriser rose from its throne, stretching its
spindly limbs. It scuttled down the steps. Pincer-like
talons, tested the air. Somewhere in the exhibition hall
a component was loose. Tumbling through time.
Changing things. The Mesmeriser's pitiless jaw opened.
A tumultuous chime rattled around the hall.

Outside, the hum was growing louder.
Kavendish knocked on the casing.

PRESS SPACE TO CONTINUE

He wiped the ancient keyboard clean with his sleeve. The
hum outside was growing. He began to tap. A flurry of
unanswered riddles shot from his fingertips.

No results. Please restate question
No results. Please restate question
No results. Please restate question

The hum outside was now unbearable. Kavendish looked
anxiously towards the doors. They opened. The motion was
frictionless and smooth. The drones began to hover into the
hall. He hammered words into the keyboard, trying to access
the controls.

Access denied. Clearance required

The Discipline Drones moved across the space. Filling the hall
with their menace. They circled the glass box. They focused
on the unhappy Citizen. Unhappy things must be dissolved.
The Discipline Drones peeled away the defensive layers. He
was still desperately tapping at the keyboard. The questions
kept spooling out.

Access denied
Access denied
Access denied

A shimmering ray dissolved the last fragments of glass.
Targeting systems found their mark. The Discipline Drones
focused and fired. The room began to spin. The drones
turned into a thousand incandescent bulbs rotating and
revolving around a fixed point. The human pivot. He was
the root. He was the creator. The emissary. His fingers were
fibrous stalks. His arms were sap-soaked sticks. The root
rose from the marble floor, cracking the tiles and splintering
the stone. The gnarled trunk pierced the vaulted ceiling. His

nails grew into talons. He typed new instructions. Bright colours emanated from the A.B.A.C.U.S. Myriad tones like the reflections of the sun on the drying puddles of London's empty streets. The hollow echo of a former life. Beams shot from the ancient device into all mechanical things. Filling every molecule. His fingers tapped without thinking. Happiness is everything. Everything stopped.

The crowds had thinned and only a few determined drinkers remained in the quadrangle. She nodded at a few passing academics that she recognised from various conferences. Drunken officers of the new regime leered. The president had departed, and with him any pretence of decency. A general pissed in a flowerpot. The professor's eyes kept returning to the edifice of the A.B.A.C.U.S. She felt its pulse. The building throbbed in the cool evening air. Fully activated. Running its programme. As she stared, buildings sprouted up around it, rising and decaying as time spun round at enormous speed.

There is no time. No adequate measurement. No arbitrary tick-tock of the clock. No beginning. Only now. There can be no end. Because its essence is nothing. The pure absence that surpasses all human understanding. And in that void, everything dwells, working its purpose with a perpetual, relentless energy. There is no time. There is only the root and the Tangle.

She was in the library. The author's journal was open on the old oak desk. The pages were stacked high, bent and crinkled. The clock struck. The boom of the chime blew the pages from their binding and scattered them into the air. As she stooped to collect them, she noticed a host of doppelgängers engaged in the exact same task. Their eyes met.

The professor shook her head. So much wine, she thought. I must clear my head. She turned back to look at the building, A faint laugh floated across the quadrangle. She headed into the old laboratory wing to find somewhere to sober up. She located the restroom. She turned the creaking faucet and splashed cold water on her face. The professor looked up. She lifted her hands to feel her skin. She felt roughness. Pitted, worried creases under smooth celluloid. His face. Her face. The face of Kavendish Jeremiah looked back at her, shrouded in his Sensory Nexus Mask. He wore the same expression as the professor. Her face. His face. The professor touched the rusty mirror. The images flashed past like a slide show. A museum exhibition hall. A fast-moving transport. A fuck pad. Buildings of every conceivable construction. Dust, fire, smoke. Thick, black smoke. Flames licking logs. Eyes watching the fire eat through the cells. A face began to take shape in the fire. Two plumes of orange hair curled from under an old military-style cap. The professor recoiled, falling into one of the toilet cubicles. The face in the mirror twisted and turned. It began to spin, forming a whirlpool in the glass. The professor staggered to her feet. She was drawn to its dark centre. Erwan sucked the liquid. Hilda sucked the liquid.

The hall was dark. Thick, oppressive, suffocating. Figures scurried between the shattered shells of devices. Mutant survivors of some cataclysm. The professor thought she recognised them from adventures yet to come. They sought each other in the murk. Fingers finding flesh. Around the hall the static husks of machines awaited their orders. A new civilisation was waiting to rise from the broken cogs. Another turn of the wheel was about to begin. The professor found hands groping though the dust and metal. They touched. In the grey ash a follicle unfurled. Strange new creatures hobbled on inadequate limbs. The shoots of their doom found fertile soil. The Tangle spewed a web of sinewy sticks. To sweep them all away. The paintings and sculptures. Nothing. The poems and the prose. Nothing. The tanks and pretty cutlasses. Nothing. The formulas and palisades. Nothing.

The professor was alone in the restroom. The faucet dripped. She filled the basin with cold water and thrust her face beneath the surface. The visions contracted. The muffled sound of latrines flushing was the only sound. She pulled her head from the water and looked again at the mirror. A familiar face stared back. She dropped a single rose on the grave of her father. She floated down a river one last time. She travelled down the veins of a flower. She was the emissary. The ambassador. The creator. The golden seed. She sucked at the liquid. Don't let her glass run dry. It's unlucky. That's what they said. She spun around and headed out of the restroom. The wooden doors of the laboratory were open and the cool summer breeze drifted into the corridor. Outside, the evening's revels were at end. The quadrangle was empty. Discarded brochures flapped about the concourse. The brushes of clunky cleaning devices whirred across the pavements, tidying them away. All around her was cleansing and the re-establishment of order. Her eyes turned to the shimmering staircase. Huge pillars towered over her. Insolently stabbing the sky. Looking up to the summit, she paused. The professor placed her foot on the first step and began to climb.

Come walk with me to lilac glade, through woodland,
   stream and knot.
Come stand beneath the gallows' shade till all weeping
   is forgot.
Leave the tears and terrors to the mischief of the town.
Come walk with me to lilac glade, to the oak tree's
   shady crown.

In darkness now from darkness born, circumference,
   length and span.
In lilac glade the wreath and thorn, wove mockeries
   of man.
In lilac glade beneath the earth, in death's ecstatic bond.
Come walk with me in lilac shade, to the emptiness beyond.

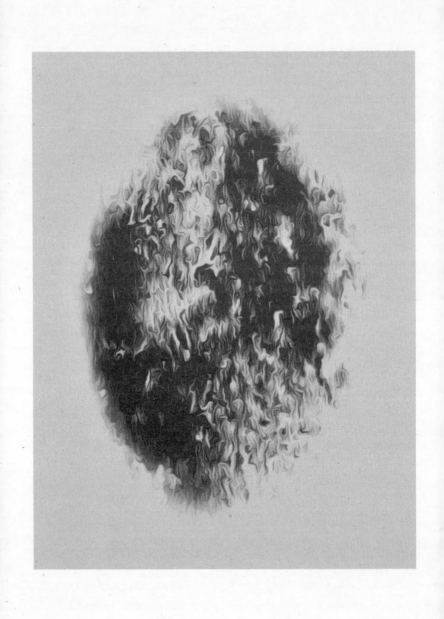

Where the Opposites Apply

I set down on a planet of emerald oceans. There were only
a few islands of solid land. Rare outcrops dotted randomly
across the vast expanse of an endless sea, like lonely autumn
leaves on a calm pond. The islands drifted, shrouded in a
fine, swirling mist. Their appearance reminded me of the
swamplands of my home. But there was no stench of decay
in these mysterious fens. Instead, delicate, wholesome
odours drifted on the breeze. Perfume masking the
withering beneath.

Some of the islands were of a greater size and with a
more varied geography. Tall, forested hills and volcanic
cones topped with snow. It was on one such archipelago
that I found myself. Alone. I opened the hatch of my craft
and stepped onto the alien sand. It crunched beneath my
boots. Like shattered glass in a saloon. Beyond the shore, my
eyes were drawn to the thickness of the woods. The diverse
forest bloomed, forming a canopy of such density that it
appeared almost solid. It throbbed in the haze. I gathered
my equipment and made for the border. I stepped into the
crackling Tangle. Hours passed. The weave of the forest grew
thicker and thicker. There were tantalising signs of a once-
great civilisation beneath the twisted branches. Crumbling
temples of faded beauty were submerged in verdant groves.
Skilful beings had once lived on these precarious atolls. Their
artefacts now littered the forest floor, carelessly strewn about,

as if their makers had been forced to flee from some sudden cataclysm. Here and there were intricately decorated totems, teased from the rock by long-vanished artisans, or blasted into moulds by ingenious machines. They languished unused amidst the unruly roots. The broken remains of a people's attempt at culture. The fragments of a forgotten legacy, their hopes for transcendence lost in the decaying brutality of time. I sensed a great melancholy in these ruins, as if a grand project had reached a premature end.

I pressed on through the muddle of vegetation, taking notes and hastily sketching maps and diagrams as I trod. The next revelation came on me gradually. Despite the bewildering mass of roots and stems, my passage through the forest posed no difficulties for me. As I stepped, so the vegetation made way, returning to its regular configuration as I passed. Like a dignitary moving through a crowd or a prisoner en route to the gallows. The stems marked my passing with interest. Leaves turned warily towards me, analysing and calculating my intent. The revelations multiplied under the canopy.

I looked into the branches. The outlines of creatures formed on the boughs, then suddenly dematerialised. A vague sensation of their passing lingered like an echo. I could see no other animal in the forest. Mine was the only flesh. The singular monster tramping through the gloom. There were no insects buzzing, no webs dangling, no reptiles slithering from view. All the creatures of the forest you would expect to see were absent. And yet I could clearly hear them. The sounds of life were everywhere: the gentle chirruping of lazy crickets, the unmistakable baritone croak of a great toad, the charming call of a delicate songbird. All these sounds were underpinned by the percussive tap of a woodpecker. Like a temple block marking out a devotion. Clack, clack, clack. Mine was the

only flesh. The interloper's skeleton. Clack, clack, clack.
The path cleared. The woodpecker's invisible beak beat out
its hypnotic rhythm. Clack, clack, clack. I was deep within
the forest now; the ruins and familiar shapes of humanoid
ingenuity were nowhere to be seen. They were buried deep
beneath the soil with the bones.

It was hot and dark in the depths. The breeze having been
repulsed by the density of leaves. The perfume of the shore
had faded too. The note of rot and waste had taken its place.
The air was solid. The Tangle pressed. The dimensions of the
wood became unintelligible, direction impossible to tell. Day.
Night. All meaningless. I made camp at the base of a huge
tree of an unfamiliar genus. The ground was soft and yielding,
and I slept deeply. As I slumbered, I could see the former
inhabitants of the atoll planet going about their business.
Making things. Breaking things. I could see them changing.
From filthy bands of scavengers clad in skins, huddled around
fires, chewing on the organs of their kill. To clean-shaven
architects, doctors, judges and members of committees,
huddled around fires, chewing on the organs brought to their
tables from distant slaughterhouses. There were more fires,
wars too. There were inventions and rallies. Speeches and
motor vehicles. Then they were gone. As quickly as they rose.
But still their presence lingered.

I woke on the bed of leaves. Days had passed. I'm sure
of it. I felt my face; a beard was beginning to form on my
jaw. I was hungry. The path was easy to find, and I followed
it. Deeper and deeper into the forest. The heat continued
to swell as the stems pressed around me. The darkness
soon robbed me of my sight, so I moved by touch and smell.
The hum of the forest kept up its relentless symphony. The
woodpecker tapped. Clack, clack, clack. I tripped over roots

in the black interior. They spat me out on the banks of a
thundering river that was carving its way through the heart
of the forest. I made camp amongst the reeds. The ground
was soft, and I sank into it like a seed. As I slept, the doctors
and magistrates turned to great amphibians; the architects
and lorry drivers were swooping birds; the stewards in their
fluorescent tabards ran in great herds across tundra.

I woke in a puddle of sorrow. Weeks had passed. I felt
my face with thin, bony hands. My beard was now of an
extraordinary length. I was hungry. I left my tent and meagre
supplies to be taken by the reeds and waded across the river.
The water passed through my thin skin, washing my bones as
it surged. The water was cold. Refreshing at first, in contrast
to the dense heat of the woods, but soon chilling my cells as
the contrast was forgotten. The river was wide, and it became
wider as I waded. Many days had passed by the time I reached
the far bank. I was hungry.

The Tangle continued. But its nature had changed.
Here the trees were like missiles in silos pointing at the
sky. The interior was cold. Brittle and desiccated. Winter
woods. I shivered in my rags. Weighed down by matted hair
and beard. The path opened up as before and I followed. It
was dark. Black tinged with blue. I was cold. I was hungry.
Here songbirds sang in fluid tenor. The owl punctuated the
sequence with hoots. The woodpecker tapped. Clack, clack,
clack. The chill was unbearable, and I had no flesh left to
resist its incursions. I resolved to make camp. To build a
fire to drive back the cold. I searched about the forest floor
for sticks and fallen branches, but the ground was bare.
I would have to cut and rend if I was to survive. I had a
penknife given to me by colleagues at the institute. It had
a rudimentary saw included in its functions. I began to cut

through a branch. The bough was full of sap, which dripped over my fist like the gore of a deer. Around me the Tangle writhed and pressed. I continued to cut. My breathing matching the movement of my hand. Faster. Faster. Mercy. Mercy. Make it quick. The bitten leather of old battlefields. The surgeon and his saw. The thud of limbs in metal trays. Faster. Faster. Mercy. Mercy. Make it quick.

The branch fell to the ground. The wood gathered around me like a press gang in a tavern. The branch writhed like a tormented snake. Blood trickled from the cut. A terrible sigh escaped from a twisted mouth that bulged from a knot on the branch. The surface of the branch turned from wood to scaly skin, then from skin to exotic plumage. The faces of creatures emerged from the surface of the stricken bough. Faces of birds, reptiles, mammals, man. Horribly contorted. Silently screaming. Then all at once the torments ceased. A dead, desiccated branch was all that remained. I picked it up and glumly resigned myself to repetition. I must burn it or die. Around me the surrounding plants began to change. They were animals. They were humans. Tiger-like cats, apes with hammer fists, bank clerks, postal workers, dockers, vipers, vampire bats. But they were trees too. Fused. Conjoined. I dropped my penknife, unable to continue my vandalism. Here were my ancestors. A strange harmony of animal and plant. Self-devouring cannibals, sharing, each a part of the other. Recycling themselves endlessly. One entity with many aspects.

I woke in the curve of a branch. Years had passed. I was now a tumbleweed of knotted hair. I was hungry. The Tangle sang a chorus of a familiar song from my youth. I tapped my taloned fingers against the bark. Clack, clack, clack. I could hear my descendants in the wood. They were barking and cooing in subtle counterpoint. I tried to dance but I was too weak to move. I could only tap out the rhythm with my bent bones. Clack, clack, clack. The bough bent and deposited me on the soft forest floor. I was not ready. Soon though, soon. The young saplings had weaved themselves into a basket. The Tangle filled it with its parts. Its essence. Sticks and fronds jumped from the canopy and placed themselves inside the basket. Flesh, fruit and blood. I fell on it in thanks. Weak and unworthy. I tasted its meat. It was good, but full of guilt. Years passed.

I found myself once again by emerald oceans. Clean cut and full. Not yet satisfied. Never satisfied. I stepped on the rungs of my craft and opened the hatch. I glanced back over the beach to the shimmering Tangle beyond the shoreline. I inhaled its scent. Perfume masking the withering beneath.

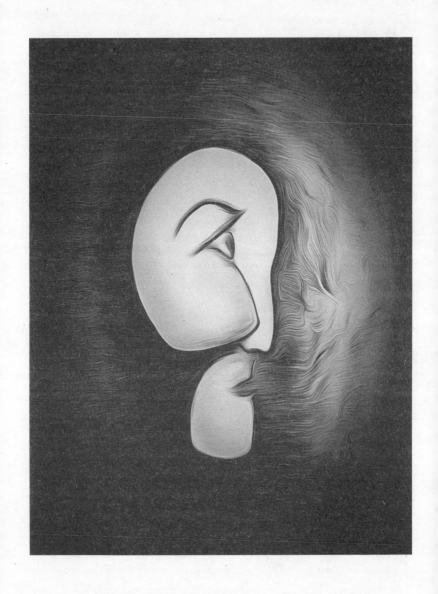

Birthday

There is no time. No adequate measurement. No arbitrary
tick-tock of the clock. No beginning. Only now. There
can be no end. Because its essence is nothing. The pure
absence that surpasses all human understanding. And in
that void, everything dwells, working its purpose with a
perpetual, relentless energy. There is no time. There is
only the root and the Tangle.

The sound of the letter box opening and closing made Ethan
put down his coffee cup in surprise. Hector was also startled;
it took him a good five seconds to get to his feet and run
barking to the front door. His tail spun like the propeller of
a biplane. His bark was cracked and atonal from lack of use.
He looked surprised to hear his own voice. Reaching the door,
he was disappointed to find the postman retreating down
the path. Hector listened for the click of the gate and then
shook his ears vigorously to reset himself. He sniffed at the
large cream envelope that sat on the mat like the corpse of a
dove. Messages from the outside world. Hector found them
quaint. His friend rarely received them. The telephone might
ring from time to time, mainly business or a simple nuisance.
The few paper letters that did pop through the door were
generally transferred straight to the wastepaper basket.
Circulars, demands for money, advertisements and the like.
It was funny how these humans communicated, with their

codes and machines. Half expressed thoughts hiding darker intentions. Hector sniffed at the letter box and received all the news he would need for the day. He was sad to have missed the postman though. He would very much like to meet him. Even if it was only to discover if he was just like all the others. Ethan followed behind his companion. Patting him on his head, he bent to pick up the envelope.

It was a sturdy thing. Thick and heavy with a sophisticated texture. There was an embossed stamp on the flap. It looked like something the Masonic lodge would send out to its members inviting them to a black-tie event. He studied the stamp. It was a simple circle with a line bisecting it horizontally through the middle. He took the envelope to the kitchen table. Using his butter knife as an opener, he carefully removed the contents. It was a card. A birthday card. Was it his birthday? His aunt had dealt with most matters relating to dates and times. She had a calendar that she scribbled on from time to time. A residue of her former life that had clung to her like the odour of a bad habit. Ethan would occasionally look over the calendar while his aunt was occupied. He noted the dates ringed and times jotted in biro within boxes. The marks never corresponded to any real events as far as he could tell. Instead they represented wreaths laid on the grave of her yesterdays. Even after her death he still received the calendar through the post every year. Sent by the same catalogue company who had presumably forgotten to remove his aunt from the ledger of the living. He dutifully hung it from the nail in the kitchen, where it dangled like a brooding imp. For days he would try to forget its presence. But the compulsion always grew. The urge to scratch his own markings onto the shiny paper. To create signs and symbols in honour of the dead. Hector would watch him turning the events of his life over and over in his mind as he stared at the calendar. Hector guessed that he was lonely. Humans got lonely; he had heard from the others. He watched him with a heavy heart. He was missing so much. But soon he would see. Ethan hovered close to the calendar's whimsical landscape. Ethan studied the reproductions of Constable and the still lifes of eternal blooms. He could smell the chemical wash and the machine cut residue. Finally, he would succumb. Adding his circle to the calendar. Runes cast for the next rotation of the earth, raising her soul from its rest to keep fellowship with him. The day of rebirth. Only then could he finally ignore it and grow to hate it in peace. Calendars reminded him of his uncle. His uncle had liked order. Rules made manifest by lists, crosses and checks. But he had no need for such things now. No saint's days, no festivals of remembrance. The harvest and day of rebirth were the only exceptions; they were real in some sense at least. Was today one such anniversary? Marked by a ring of ink and sealed with his initial, perhaps with an exclamation mark or crudely drawn heart to celebrate the auspicious event. It might well be.

Birthdays, those bittersweet anniversaries. Celebrations of new life and the processes of change. First steps, first words. Coming of age. Last disappointment. Rituals with candles ignited. All the hopes and dreams for a happy future. Their dull glow flickering on the faces of children still full of wonder and magic. But as the weak flame dies in the rush of excited breath, so the sad, grey smoke struggles into the air from the extinguished wick, forming an acrid smog above the brightly coloured icing. Birthdays, like notches carved into the walls of a prison cell, marking the passing of the years before the release of death. Birthdays were something Ethan had largely forgotten about. He was 52. Some might call him middle-aged, but this was unduly pessimistic. He had no desire to reach 104. He preferred to see it as the home straight. The run in on a life whose later years were characterised by unremarkable happiness. But whose younger days were punctuated by loss and horror.

He was content in his orchards and lived by their fruit. His apples were famed in Caxton and beyond for their sweetness and versatility. The orchard was his life, a repository for his memories and a gateway to a world that he knew dwelt beyond his human concerns. In spring the blossom would remind him of his dead mother. Long past but ever-present. As the fruit ripened on the bough he felt the infinite passage of time sweeping him along in a torrent with no beginning and no end. Every year as the nights drew in, Ethan would harvest his apples. He would select the most suitable fruit and bake a pie in celebration. The day of his rebirth. Aunt Janet's too. Their shared anniversary. They were inseparable. They had the kind of bond that can only blossom with the sharing of a terrible secret. In their household apple pies had a greater significance than a mere sweet comfort. They tasted of freedom. Aunt Janet had passed away a few years ago, and now he had little enthusiasm for anniversaries of any kind. However, there was still one ring on the calendar. He marked that day with a sacrificial offering to the Tangle and all its gifts.

Hector had no idea, and he cared little for the strange sacraments of humanity. Every day was a festival for him. He wagged his tail and waited. But *someone* had chosen to celebrate Ethan's nativity. A token had been sent from a mysterious benefactor. Ethan studied the card. It puzzled him. At first he thought it might have come from a child. But a child would surely have selected something gaudier. Something with balloons and cats. This card was completely blank front and back, and the only thing disrupting the perfect void inside was a simple message scrawled in scratchy pen.

Birthday 4

Maybe this was the work of an elderly relative, too weak or bewildered to provide a more fulsome greeting? But Ethan had no living relatives, and he doubted any of his customers would have bothered to send him anything. As he studied the spidery script, a slip of paper fluttered onto the kitchen table. It had clearly been stuck to the card at some point but had since become dislodged. From just beyond his cereal bowl, a room full of healthy, happy-looking people were beaming up at him. Ethan picked up the piece of paper. His forehead creased as he interrogated the leaflet.

HAPPY BIRTHDAY. ETHAN.
THIS VOUCHER ENTITLES YOU TO A
FREE SESSION OF YOGA AND MEDITATION
AT THE CAXTON TRANQUILLITY CENTRE.
TERMS AND CONDITIONS APPLY.

Yoga? The furthest Ethan had bent in years, was to pick up the card from the matt this morning. But he had to admit the isolation he felt since his aunt's death was beginning to get to him. The orchard was a comfort, but he missed hearing voices. The smell of people and the idiosyncratic ways of his kind. Meditation was of less interest. He spent most of his time divorced from the world as it was, and by and large that's how he preferred it. But this invitation gave him a chance to be with people. To study them. To feel their ridiculous vibration. To inhale their desperate scent. Perhaps he would try it.

Ethan turned the voucher over in his hands. The smiling people in the picture looked toned and content. They wore Lycra sports clothing stretched taught over sculpted limbs.

He wore tatty shorts and an old, faded T-shirt with the cracked image of a long-forgotten band on the front. He looked at himself in the mirror; his shoulders sagged in disappointment. He was neither fat nor thin but was instead strangely shapeless. He sucked in his stomach. Only the vaguest impression of his muscles formed through the shroud of his skin before he was forced to exhale again. His arms looked like cheap hams. Injected with brine and carelessly hung. He pulled on some tracksuit trousers and a pair of trainers he had bought some time ago for such an occasion and headed downstairs. Ethan filled Hector's bowl to the brim, figuring that he would be well down the lane before Hector noticed he had gone. The dog didn't miss him at all on the few occasions he did venture out. The agreeable spirits of the orchard and the playful wraiths in the house kept him entertained. He had known them all since he was a pup and had been glad for their company over the years. Humans made for cute but often unengaging companions. Still, he loved Ethan in the way he loved all the fallen creatures. He felt sorry for his friend. He seemed only dimly aware of the spectres that floated around him. Though more in tune with the mysteries of the Tangle than most humans, the stubborn barrier of his residual rationality kept the true wonder from his grasp. Hector wagged his tale in anticipation. Today's trip would help lift the veil and complete the journey that he had started as a small boy. He watched as Ethan collected his bicycle from the shed and peddled off towards the Caxton Tranquillity Centre.

*

The branches of the trees hung low over the lanes. He felt the pulse of the forest pushing him along, lifting the tyres from the tarmac, propelling him towards the jumble of hives where his fellow beings dwelt. He crested the hill at Dimmock's Rise and caught sight of the town. It had grown since his last visit. Spreading out from the confines of the valley like a muddled tumour. Spikes and tendrils of disruption stabbed into the flanks of the Tangle like cruel lances. Ethan strained his faltering eyes. From the top of the ridge he could just about make out the knot of cul-de-sacs that made up the estate where he had lived with his aunt and uncle. New developments had largely swallowed the woods where he used to hide. Now only a tiny patch of green remained, huddled between the dull suburban vertebrae. Beside the path that joined the cul-de-sac to the main road was a grass verge that flowed into the edge of the Tangle. This was where his mother's apple tree had grown. The original root of his orchard. Every leaf, every twig, every cell had found its origin in that magical spot. Many years ago he had transplanted the tree and the unorthodox compost from which it had sprouted. Carefully moving root, branch and the putrefying remains of his uncle to the quiet grove on the edge of town where he now lived. His uncle had not been a generous man, but he had been wise in his investments at least. After the police had declared him missing, presumed dead, his aunt had come into a reasonable sum of money. More than enough to purchase the land and modest dwelling that was now his home. Even from this distance, the site of his former prison sent out ripples of disturbance that broke over him like tar-dappled waves, threatening to suck him back to his childhood. He steadied himself on the handlebars. The past was not welcome here. He exorcised it with the blinking of his eyes. Sending the malignance back into the bones of the town. The skeleton would crack soon enough. He could see the fissures growing from here. Ethan shrugged and pushed off down the hill.

The Caxton Tranquillity Centre occupied the ground floor of an unremarkable building which sat between the minimart and a pawnbroker. In a previous incarnation it had been the showroom of a domestic appliance shop that specialised in renovated washing machines. The thoughtless utilitarian architecture was only partly disguised by a coat of pale, grey paint that came from the 'calming' spectrum of a boutique paint manufacturer's catalogue. The base of the walls was stained black with the filth thrown up from the street by successive rainstorms. Someone had cared enough to try. But they couldn't keep the dirt down. He hesitated, then pushed the door and stepped inside.

A smiling man of Teutonic appearance beamed at Ethan from behind his desk. Above him on the wall was an Om symbol carved from wood.

'Namaste, have you come for this morning's class?'

The superman bowed. Ethan returned his bow and handed him the voucher.

'That's perfect, the class is about to begin. You may leave your shoes over there.'

The receptionist pointed towards a bench where a number of people were removing their footwear and placing it in the shoe racks provided.

Ethan nodded uncertainly. This was all new to him, and he wasn't sure of the etiquette, but silence seemed somehow appropriate. An old lady who looked to be around seventy-five sensed his uncertainty and gestured for him to sit next to her.

'I've not seen you here before, is it your first time?'

'Yes, yes, it is.'

He removed his shoes. She smiled with a familiar serenity. Ethan felt a jolt of recognition. Time, place, identity, all dissolved into a confusing singularity. Was this his aunt, somehow reincarnated and in possession of the body of this old woman. She bore no resemblance to her; in fact, she was almost the opposite to Aunt Janet in every possible way. Yet it was her. An inverted doppelgänger. Had she sent the card, he wondered? He stood and hung his coat on a hook. Against his better judgement he removed his tracksuit trousers, conscious of his shapeless shorts and ridiculous legs underneath. His keys and a roll of Hector's waste bags dropped out of the sagging pockets. The shit sacks unrolled like a streamer. The old lady halted their progress with her foot and handed them up to him. He tried to think of something amusing to say, but he could only manage a gormless grin in thanks. She was too polite to embarrass him further, so she simply patted the bench and invited him to sit back down. He joined her, feeling his cheeks reddening and the lacquered wood against his thighs. But the burden of his embarrassment quickly lifted. He felt safe. Accepted. His mind wandered back down into the roots. To the Tangle. Wrapped in the warmth of decay. Their cells bleeding into the soil. His aunt and mother sat together around a kitchen table. They were planning a surprise. His aunt circling the calendar, his mother icing the cake. Ethan would not be alone on his birthday. The parade began. His mother and aunt carrying his cake like a babe messiah. A single candle burning in its centre. Hector following behind. Tail turning, signalling his delight. Ethan smiled and blew on the fragile flame. Make a wish. The flame staggered against the force and died. The column of smoke rose. Happy birthday, Ethan.

'You might want to leave your socks too, young man. It feels much nicer on the feet, you know.'

He removed his socks and placed them inside his shoes. He studied his fellow students. A few caught his eye and returned his smile with varying degrees of sincerity. Others looked away, seemingly so wrapped up in their anticipation of finding inner peace that they couldn't be bothered to give him the time of day. A young man bent and flexed in his expensive yoga clothes; they stuck to him like cellophane, exaggerating his toned limbs with indecent exactness. He exhaled and kicked his feet. Ethan wondered if he was warming up for a karate class and was here in error. Others seemed lost in themselves, in the room and yet elsewhere. He could sense their impatience. Time was a commodity in short supply for these go-getters. Here in the Caxton Tranquillity Centre, for one and a half precious hours, they could focus on what was really important in life: themselves. Yoga was their means of attaining peak mental efficiency, to sharpen focus, to exert the muscles and cleanse the mind, so that they could feel better about the absurd procession of their lives. Ethan noticed one or two students staring at the floor with an intensity that suggested they feared it might come alive and swallow them up. These were the broken souls whose lives had been mangled by self-abuse or the abuse of others. These were the broken, the fractured, the not quite lost, looking for a path back to the simple joy of living. Ethan had been one of them once. As a child he had been robbed of all the happiness a young boy should feel, the embrace of a loving family and the unconditional devotion of a parent. But the Tangle had found him. In the glade he had watched it grow. His remedy, his avenging angel, his rod of retribution. The instructor exploded through the door like a firework. Ethan had never felt so much positive energy focused in an individual. How wonderful.

'Namaste, morning, morning! I see some new faces today. Welcome, welcome. If you'd like to come through, we can begin.'

The old lady smiled at Ethan, following his gaze. She placed a gentle hand, bent with age and experience, on his.

'It's going to be alright, Ethan. Shall we go in?'

Ethan was too wise to be truly startled. He hadn't told her his name. Maybe she had heard him talking to the receptionist? But he hadn't told him his name either. The truth was that she had always known it. With the suppleness of a woman half her age, she sprang up and led him into the studio.

Beyond the partition, the room opened up into a bare, white space that tried hard to exude tranquillity but merely looked unfurnished. The floor was covered in ash-look laminate, a smooth surface hiding the wonky planks beneath. Shards of light leaked through the old Crittall windows that ran along the back wall, describing weak spots on the floor. Beyond the dull panes, Ethan was surprised to see a pleasant garden laid out in good order between the bland stockade formed by neighbouring buildings. Exotic pot plants struggled gamely against the English weather, trying to make a home in the hostile blast. Wind chimes and statues were dotted amongst them. A tiny path of sandstone paving wove around the pots in an ellipse. At the centre of the tear grew a tree. An apple tree. Ethan again slipped out of time, as he often did. He was standing in the glade of his childhood dreams, surrounded by bowing trees. At the centre of the glade was an apple tree. His mother's apple tree. The same apple tree. His apple tree. This apple tree. The tree was in full bloom, though it was no longer spring. It seemed to stretch out its branches to embrace him. Twigs softening into the flesh of fingers. Their warm touch spreading through his body like blood returning to an insentient limb.

Come walk with me to lilac glade, through woodland,
  stream and knot.

Come stand beneath the gallows' shade till all weeping
    is forgot.
Leave the tears and terrors to the mischief of the town.
Come walk with me to lilac glade, to the oak tree's
    shady crown.

The old lady handed him a rolled-up yoga mat and offered him another reassuring smile. He unfurled the mat and placed it next to hers, casting a glance at the tree as he straightened it. The tree had turned to watch him. The bulk of its canopy opening up towards the window like an exultant disciple. The instructor, beaming with serenity, pressed play on *Selected Ambiance 7* and began the class. Ethan found the postures both excruciating and revealing. His limbs, bent and stretched into unfamiliar shapes, announced their previously obscured potential. It felt as if he had acquired new stems, extra arms, extra legs, extra muscles. Other poses revealed his limitations: inelegant posture, unbalanced chakras, stubborn sinews. While he attempted to control his breath as the instructor had commanded, his eyes kept drifting back to the garden. The exotic plants had left their pots and had migrated up the branches of the apple tree. They were perched in the boughs like children watching a football match. Their inquisitive stamens wiggled towards the window.

' . . . and let your body relax. Now we are going to move into the beautiful meditation part of our practice, a chance to reconnect with the earth and the energy of nature, to find yourself melting into its divine light.'

Selected Ambiance 7 stopped abruptly as the instructor selected a more holistic soundtrack. Temple bells tolled, gongs bonged and flutes warbled in harmony with the resonance of the chime.

'Find a space where you feel comfortable. You might want to lie down on your mat so that you can really feel like you are melting into the earth.'

The instructor's voice was barely more than a whisper, soothing and sensual. Ethan looked around at the students. Eyes closed in various postures, tuning into the vibrations. His own eyes sort them out, the desperate, the lost, the overconfident, the arrogant, the selfish and selfless. All in a trance. Each imposing their will on unyielding material. Ethan tried to get comfortable, crossing his legs in a vague approximation of the instructor's pose. He glanced over to his new friend. The old woman seemed lost in a trance too. Ethan looked at her with increased intensity. So beautiful, almost ageless now. An aura of calm settled on her shoulders and began to expand out of her body. The light turned to fire. Not burning but purifying. He pushed down on his foot, trying to perfect the position, but it wouldn't bend. He gave up and decided to simply sit on the mat as if he was at a picnic. Around him the sound of stillness echoed around the studio. The students concentrated on their breath. In. Out. Ethan tried to concentrate too, but he was inside the flame now. Life was simpler here. Dancing on the summit of his birthday candle. The pull of the flame was too strong to resist.

'Let your mind rest and relax.'

He drifted off the floor, hanging above the haze of body odour and incense to where his birthday party was now in full swing. Hector sat like a good boy. His tail still. Eyes focused. Waiting. Waiting. Ethan spun around the wick of his birthday candle, holding onto its glowing shaft like a demonic troubadour. Through the corona he could see the faces of his aunt and mother. They were laughing. Joy filled his body until every molecule burned with their love. He was five, he was six, he was fifty, he was a thousand years old. He was ageless and unborn. Slowly the flame began to change. The golden glow sharpening from yellow to blue. An annihilating fire grew, unforgiving and indifferent. Ethan tried to reach out his hand to touch his mother and aunt, but the force of the fire beat him back. He could barely make them out through the flame. He cried out through blistering lips. But the roar of the furnace smothered the sound of his voice. The faces of his family melted and turned to vapour. In the haze, an image formed from the droplets. The old woman on her mat. Lotus position. Ommmm. Sounding like a dissonant gong. Suddenly her left eye shot open, her black pupil filling her whole lens like an obsidian jewel. Her arm rose, dragged up by unseen levers. She pointed to the garden beyond the window.

'SEE.'

Her voice was a shuddering wave condensing the octaves into one diabolical moan. Ethan wanted to run out from whatever dimension he had been dragged into. But he could not move. He was trapped inside the flame. His eyes darted to the window. The branches of the tree had covered the frame. They were slowly forcing their way through the cracks and into the room. The instructor sensed a disturbance and opened their eyes to look.

'Is everything OK? I know it can be strange if this is your first time, but just relax into the meditation, take your time. If unwanted thoughts or worries enter your mind, don't fight them, simply acknowledge them and let them fade.'

The instructor gave him an encouraging smile and returned to the script. Ethan pushed against the skin of the flame, stretching the membrane with all his strength. It bulged and warped around his hands but remained intact. The heat was growing inside. Couldn't they see? Outside the flame, the branches kept spreading, moving inexorably across the floor. Soon they had covered the entire studio, like the capillaries of a pumping organ. The students were the stranded survivors of a flood, clinging to their mats as the torrent raged around. Ethan tried to warn them, but his words froze and shattered on his tongue. The tree broke through the remaining panes of glass, smashing the frame and stepping into the room on its gnarled feet. The force of the blast extinguished the fire and blew Ethan from the summit of the candle, throwing him breathless back onto his yoga mat. The branches moved closer. Now only a few inches from his helpless frame. A spindly twig curled up from the branch like a viper. It shot towards Ethan, wrapping itself around his feet. He screamed. No sound emerged.

'Switch off your thinking mind and remember to focus only on your breath. Be present in the moment.'

The twigs and branches began to entwine themselves around his legs, flowing up his thighs and over his hips. They twirled around his torso, tightening like a corset. He feared he might be crushed by the pressure. But this was no girdle of spines. It was the hug of a mother given to a child in distress. Ethan's feelings of panic faded like mist. His breathing settled. The tree had finally covered his whole body. With his head now encased in the canopy, he closed his eyes to receive the lesson. The instructor was pleased.

'Good, now let your breath synchronise with the beating of your heart. Really focus on yourself. Be grateful for your body, be grateful for your breath.'

Ethan's mind began to flow into the wood.

'Allow the energy to envelope you like a warm cloud of joy.'

The darkness pressed around him as he travelled down the veins of the bark.

'Imagine you are like a puddle of water. Let gravity slowly pull you into the ground, absorbing you into the soil. Imagine your skin is a seed. Feel the tiny roots sprout from the seed and begin to work their way into the soil, down through time, past the bones of our ancestors, past ancient cities, into the loving core of the planet, into the arms of Mother Earth.'

Come walk with me to lilac glade, through woodland,
  stream and knot.
Come stand beneath the gallows' shade till all weeping
  is forgot.
Leave the tears and terrors to the mischief of the town.
Come walk with me to lilac glade, to the oak tree's
  shady crown.

In darkness now from darkness born, circumference,
  length and span.
In lilac glade the wreath and thorn, wove mockeries
  of man.
In lilac glade beneath the earth, in death's ecstatic bond.
Come walk with me in lilac shade, to the emptiness beyond.

Ethan travelled with the roots, just as the guide had said. Down through the topsoil littered with cans and cigarette ends. Down through the dirt filled with garbage and broken, discarded things. Past the sewage and waste, past the slaughtered carcasses of animals churned out of abattoirs, past the bones of our ancestors riddled with bullets or bludgeoned with hateful hammers. Down past the ruins of civilisations born in blood and fire. Down into the core.

The broiling heart of nothing. Here was his mother's embrace. The blissful source of all being. Through the mask of branches and leaves he could see the class of the Caxton Tranquillity Centre. They lay with their eyes closed. Deep within themselves. Trying hard to connect to a world they had left years ago. Peaceful, tranquil, fulfilled. He felt sorry for them. He closed his eyes again and let the mantra of the wood seep into him. Its silent, wordless rhythm carrying him around the dimensionless emptiness. In the studio the humans struggled to connect.

'Let the beautiful earth energy flow back into your core as you join with joy at the heart of the universe. You are connected. You are loved.'

*

They had fought so hard, these late-developing bipeds. Only a few generations out of the ooze. Confused and blinking, they stumbled onto the land. As they grew, so their confusion grew too. Self-aware but with no idea what to do with the gift. All their figures and graphs, with all their calculating machines and whimsical devices. Clunking and whirring. Trying in vain to create a comforting story to account for the burden they carried. They longed for a world they could understand, in a universe whose dimensions only they could determine. From the simple star maps of the ancients to the quantum musings of the moderns. They sought ways to rationalise it all. Deploying evermore convoluted equations and arcane formulations. But these were only ever different ways of stating the same thing: they knew nothing. As paradigms shifted and theories blossomed, and as the caves became laboratories and the monk's cell a supercollider, so the illusion of progress hypnotised them. But there never really was a big bang. No timeline on which they travelled. That too was just another story. A fiction of order diligently constructed. But ultimately another illusion. He had seen the fire and the filament. His arms had been bound by its sinews. His skin scourged by its flame. He had waded through the empty depths, weighed down by the anchor of hope. Wrapped in its biting chains. And at the bottom of it all, he had found nothing. The Tangle would not be constrained. The Tangle always was and evermore shall be. For at its core, it was *nothing*. The pure negative. Not a thing but an anti-thing. The absolute emptiness that defies explanation. A blasphemy in the eyes of men. The Tangle mocked them, and spat out the tragic, wasted work of millennia from its pitiless maw. It was beautiful. And those penitents who sought not to measure the void, but instead offered up prayers to its divinity, yearning to join its mystical oneness, to feel its love and healing power. When the veil was finally lifted and they stood staring into the abyss that they had once hoped would save them, they found only indifference. That was the true horror.

'Namaste. I hope to see you all back here next week. In the meantime, please take the energy of this meditation with you as a source of nourishment. Have a great day.'

Ethan opened his eyes. He wasn't surprised to find the old woman missing and an empty mat beside him. He looked out at the apple tree in its full, unseasonable bloom and smiled. What a wonderful birthday.

Acknowledgements

I would like to offer my wholehearted thanks and adoration to
my wife Sofia Hedblom for listening, stimulating and lifting
my head from the keyboard when stems of inspiration wilted.
David Keenan for wisdom, guidance, helping me sort the
wheat from the chaff, and the rod of correction when needed.
Lee Brackstone for his faith in the work and providing the soil
for the seed. Matthew Hamilton for his instruction and top-
class agency. Russell Brown for fitting all the pieces together
and for generally knowing what's going on when it becomes
a mystery to me. Andrew O'Hagan and Johan Renck for kind
words of encouragement. Richard Hector-Jones for decades of
cultural enrichment and steadfast friendship. Jane and Kitty
Hector-Jones for being wonderful and for being family. David
Hill and Navaz Batliwalla for being beautiful friends and
for audience participation. The Robertson collective: John,
Nigel, Liz, James and Charlotte, you are all excellent, thank
you. Caroline Hayes and the Black Door Agency. Luke Brown
for his early eyes. Paul Baillie-Lane and Patrick McConnell
for their later eyes. Ellie Freedman, Georgia Goodall, Steve
Marking and all the magnificent White Rabbit family, for your
help and deciphering my cryptic communications.